MAGGIE SHAYNE
EILEEN WILKS
ANNE MARIE WINSTON

BROKEN
SILENCE

 *Silhouette Books*

Published by Silhouette Books

America's Publisher of Contemporary Romance

Special thanks and acknowledgment are given to Maggie Shayne, Eileen Wilks and Anne Marie Winston for their contribution to the FAMILY SECRETS series.

SILHOUETTE BOOKS

BROKEN SILENCE

Copyright © 2003 by Harlequin Books S.A.

ISBN 0-373-21811-7

The publisher acknowledges the copyright holders of the individual works as follows:

THE INVISIBLE VIRGIN
Copyright © 2003 by Harlequin Books S.A.

A MATTER OF DUTY
Copyright © 2003 by Harlequin Books S.A

INVITING TROUBLE
Copyright © 2003 by Harlequin Books S.A

Visit Silhouette at www.eHarlequin.com

Printed in U.S.A.

DANCING AWAY DANGER?

Bluebonnet Ball intended to quiet concerns about genetically engineered individuals

Greenlaurel, TX

The nation is still spinning from the news of covert scientific experiments that resulted in genetically altered children who were allegedly adopted by unsuspecting families. Questions have been raised as to what special powers each of these extraordinary individuals might possess, and allegations have been made linking the World Bank Heist to such a person.

Here in Greenlaurel, Texas, a city steeped in wealth and tradition, with the highest adoption rate in the nation, townspeople are giving in to speculation. A group of society matrons hopes to alleviate the town's fears with this year's Bluebonnet Ball. "We just want to show everyone that nothing has changed," says May Ellen Ingram, president of the Belles of Texas Historic Society, whose own grandson, Jake Ingram, currently heading the investigation into the World Bank Heist, is adopted. "We're still the same people we were before. The ball will go on this Saturday, and the world will see that our community is above this sort of petty nonsense."

But will the Bluebonnet Ball be enough to extinguish the flames of fear currently consuming the country? Or will Greenlaurel, like the rest of the world, have to face the fact that their former days of innocence are long gone?

MAGGIE SHAYNE,
a *USA TODAY* bestselling author, has written more than
twenty-five novels for Silhouette. She has won numerous
awards, including two *Romantic Times* Career Achievement
Awards. A five-time finalist for the Romance Writers of
America's prestigious RITA® Award, Maggie also writes
mainstream contemporary fantasy and romantic suspense,
and has contributed story lines to network daytime soap
operas. Maggie lives in rural Otselic, New York, with
her husband, Rick, with whom she shares five beautiful
daughters, two English bulldogs and two grandchildren.

EILEEN WILKS
is a fifth-generation Texan. Her great-great-grandmother
came to Texas in a covered wagon shortly after the end
of the Civil War—excuse us, the War Between the States.
She's tried everything from drafting to a brief stint as a
ranch hand—raising two children and any number of
cats and dogs along the way. Not until she started writing
did she "stay put," because that's when she knew she'd
come home. Readers can write to her at P.O. Box 4612,
Midland, TX 79704-4612.

ANNE MARIE WINSTON,
a RITA® Award finalist and bestselling author, loves babies
she can give back when they cry, animals in all shapes and
sizes, and just about anything that blooms. When she's not
writing, she's chauffeuring children to various activities,
trying *not* to eat chocolate or reading anything she can find.
You can learn more about Anne Marie's novels by visiting
her Web site at www.annemariewinston.com.

CONTENTS

THE INVISIBLE VIRGIN

Maggie Shayne

Chapter 1

Rosie pushed her glasses up higher on her nose and watched her grandmother's approach. She was glad of the long, winding path from the mansion to her own beloved little cottage, which had been built to house the Linden estate's gardener. The entire family had been scandalized when Rosie had returned home from college and claimed it as her own, two years ago.

Grandma Marjorie walked the path, wearing a floral print designer dress and a string of marble-sized pearls, looped around her neck three times and still hanging low. She wore matching earrings and bracelet and a wide-brimmed straw hat with roses embroidered all over it. Her horn-rimmed prescription sunglasses had diamond chips at the outer corners and her shoes cost three hundred bucks if they cost a nickel.

Not for the first time, Rosie wondered if she might have been adopted, or found on the doorstep one day. She strengthened her resolve, and continued pulling tiny weeds from the rich, dark soil of her flower bed, pretending not to notice Grandma Marjorie's approach.

The older woman stopped at the edge of the flower bed, planted her hands on her hips, and said, "My goodness, child, don't you get enough of digging in the dirt at the botanical gardens all day? I can't bear to think what your nails must look like!"

Rosie sat back on her heels, brushed the soil from her hands, and then glanced down at her nails. Specks of soil on her glasses made it hard to see very clearly, but she knew well enough what her nails looked like. "Good thing I don't model rings and bracelets or star in dish soap commercials for a living, I guess. I'd be out of a job."

"I suppose you think you're amusing. We both know you don't *need* to do anything at all for a living. Much less wallow in weed patches and exist on the pittance they pay you for it."

Smiling, Rosie got to her feet. "I like my job. And I like being independent. And by normal peoples' standards, they actually pay me pretty well." Her grandmother looked mildly annoyed, so Rosie gave up. She would never change the woman's mind about her own lifestyle choices. "Come on inside. You can rest a minute and I'll get you a cold drink. But don't waste your time trying to talk me into that Bluebonnet Ball again, Grams. You'd just be wasting your breath."

"Hmmph. Just because you live on your own earnings, doesn't mean you don't have to do as I say, young lady."

Rosie held the door for her. "Actually, Grams, that's pretty much exactly what it means."

Grandma Marjorie walked into the cottage, looking around and trying to hide her approval. Rosie had made the place into a personal paradise. Plants were everywhere, along with fountains and figurines. It was like an indoor garden, and she loved it. The old woman sighed and took a seat in a wicker rocking chair with a thick cushion. "Regardless of all your arguments to the contrary, my dear Rosemary, you *are* going to attend that ball."

"I buy my clothes retail, Grams. I don't own anything suitable and I don't have any interest in spending a week's salary on a dress." As she spoke, she walked into the tiny kitchen area, filled a glass with ice, then poured lemonade over it. "Besides, I'm not the least bit interested in this sort of thing. You know that. Society bores me."

"Maybe so, dear, but do lunar orchids bore you?"

Rosie stopped halfway back to her grandmother, the glass in her hand shaking, cubes clinking against the glass. "What?"

"I have managed to procure an extremely rare African lunar orchid. You probably already know this, but this particular orchid blooms only three nights each year, during the full moon phase. This one is due to open on the night of the ball."

"You…you…who's taking care of it?"

"A competent gardener, dear."

"Gardener? A gardener? It should be under the care of a botanist. Do you have any idea how delicate—?"

"Oh, pish-tosh, child, it's only for a week, just until the ball. After that, I plan to give it away."

"Give it away?" She didn't mean to shout the question.

Grandma Marjorie smiled. "Yes. Why, would you like it?"

Rosie narrowed her eyes on the scheming, conniving, dear old woman. "Is this some kind of attempt to blackmail me into going to that stupid ball?"

"It's not blackmail, it's a bribe." She rose, taking the lemonade from Rosie's hands, drinking long and slow from the glass, then setting it on the wicker end table beside her chair. "The orchid will be at the center of the garden maze. Attend the ball, and it's yours."

Grandma Marjorie stood there, waiting, staring Rosie down, knowing she had won. She had made an offer that neither Rosie, nor any other botanist in her right mind, would refuse.

Sighing, Rosie nodded. "Fine," she said. "You win. I'll go to the ball."

"That's better," Grandma Marjorie said as she sauntered to the door, looking supremely triumphant. "See you Saturday night. Eight sharp."

Rosie sank into the chair her grandmother had vacated, feeling as if she'd just lost a major battle. She took her glasses off and used the end of her shirt to wipe the smudges from the lenses. "She's up to something," she muttered. "And like an idiot, I walked right into it."

All hell broke loose at work the next day. An unfamiliar fungus was attacking an entire section of the botanical gardens, and tropical plants were dropping like victims of the plague.

To Rosie, it was almost as bad. When she examined the wilting plants, she could feel their pain. It hit her the way seeing children or puppies suffer hit most other people. She knew it was odd, but she thought of plants as living beings, with feelings and moods and even emotions. The gardens were in turmoil, and she had to find a way to ease it.

She worked nonstop, spent hours in libraries, on the phone and the Internet, consulting with the top botanists in the country. She was the only botanist on staff. The other members of her team were master gardeners and apprentices, along with a handful of botany majors. It was up to her to find the solution. She spent hours in the lab at the local university, studying samples of the fungus under a microscope until she had identified it, and then testing treatments. The only fungicides that were effective, were so powerful they would also kill the plants.

The grueling efforts went on all week. She worked at the gardens, at the lab, at the office and at home. By Saturday night, she was exhausted, but still no closer. She was at home in her cottage, poring over the few books she still hadn't skimmed when she stumbled on the answer buried deep in the pages of an out-of-print book. It was the least likely source of information, she had thought, which was why she hadn't read it earlier. It was a collection of folk wisdom about plants, gathered from indigenous peoples. No science, just tidbits handed down from generation to generation.

The solution: ants. A certain, tiny ant secreted a substance known to kill the fungus, while not harming the plants themselves.

She made two phone calls to entomologists who helped her identify the ant as one found only in South America, and led her to a supplier. Finally, she ordered an express shipment of ants, and hung up the telephone. She sighed in utter relief. Problem solved. It would work, she knew it would work, she felt it right to her bones. Everything would be fine. Her precious plants were saved.

She sent off an e-mail to the rest of the team, letting them know the crisis was over. The ants would arrive in the morning and she would release them into the affected flower beds the moment they did. All would be well.

Rosie leaned back in her chair, feeling extremely pleased with herself and completely exhausted. She'd barely slept since the onset of the crisis, but it was worth the sacrifice. She had only lost a few plants. Most could be saved. The staff and her employers would be pleased, but hardly thrilled. This was her job after all. It's what they paid her to do. She so wanted to share this achievement with someone who would appreciate it. Someone who would get it.

Her family would not get it. Her older sister, Tara, was more concerned with social standing and money than much else, and preoccupied at the moment with her fiancé, Jake Ingram and plans for a dream wedding. And her younger sister, Phoebe, was only interested in clothes, parties and men. Rosie was the black sheep of the family. Only she would be as thrilled by having used insects to conquer a fungus and save some plants, as she would have been had she destroyed an asteroid and saved the world.

The telephone shrilled, and she sat up to grab it, hoping it wasn't some problem with the ant shipment. That was the worst thing that could happen now, she thought.

It wasn't. It was the second worst thing that could happen.

"Child, where are you?" Grandma Marjorie demanded. "Everyone has already left for the ball, and I really can't wait any longer. Are you almost ready?"

The ball? Oh, hell, the ball! Rosie glanced down at her T-shirt, jeans and bare feet. Her glasses slid right off her nose into her lap. "I'm running a teeny bit late, Gram. Why don't you go on ahead, and I'll meet you there."

"You're not trying to back out on your promise, now are you?"

"No. No of course not, Gram. I said I'd be there and I will."

"I'm counting on it, dear. You have one hour. Then the deal's off." Grandma Marjorie disconnected.

Rosie put the receiver back into its cradle, and wondered just how in the world she was going to find a dress, get into it and get to the ball within the next hour. Oh, but that orchid—it would be magnificent. She bit her lip, put her glasses back on and ran to her bedroom closet, knowing even before she looked that she would find nothing suitable there.

She was just going to have to exercise a little sisterly prerogative. She may not be a clotheshorse or a fashion plate, but both her sisters were, and their closets were overflowing with ball gowns worn once and racked for life. There had to be something.

She grabbed her keys off the shelf, and drove her VW Bug—another source of unending embarrassment to her family—down the winding path to the mansion. Then she let herself in and went directly to Tara's bedroom.

Dresses and gowns, designer suits, rows and rows of shoes and purses, scarves and belts hung there as if daring her to make an appropriate choice.

She would, inevitably, make the wrong ones if she tried. She didn't give two hoots what the upper echelons of Texas society might think about her, but her family did, and she didn't want to embarrass her ultra-image-conscious sisters. There, on the bed, like a sign from the heavens, was a green taffeta gown with short, puffy sleeves and a sweetheart neckline. It was not anything Rosie would have chosen for herself, but then again, neither was anything else in Tara's closet. Rosie had no sense of fashion, her sisters and her mother had told her so often enough that she believed it. So just because she hated the dress on sight, didn't mean it was unsuitable. And the fact that it was laid out on her sister's bed certainly suggested that Tara had at least considered it as an option for tonight's affair. That must mean it was a viable choice.

She snatched the gown off the bed, and raced into her sister's private bathroom. Fifteen minutes gone, she thought, glancing at her watch. She had a twenty minute drive, which left her twenty-five to get ready.

She stripped off her clothes and dove into the shower, telling herself that the orchid her grandma had promised her would be a prize more than worthy of all the trouble she was going through.

At least, it had better be.

Chapter 2

Nothing worked out the way she had expected. In fact, though she seldom attended society functions, Rosie had assumed this one would be nothing she couldn't handle. She was educated, intelligent, capable. Certainly she could hold her own with a group of socialites.

And she probably could have, had she accumulated more than a few hours sleep over the past week. Or perhaps with more than an hour's lead time.

As it was, she was a wreck. She'd decided her hair in its usual ponytail would be insufficient, and like an idiot she'd applied some of her sister's "volumizer" mousse and attempted to style it with the help of a blow-dryer. The result was that the normally tame dark blond length of it had swelled up as if teased, and several strands insisted on sticking up at odd angles, no matter how she tried to smooth them down. Her solution had been to pin it into a bun and hope for the best. The dress was a little too big. She hadn't thought so at first, but apparently the thing was designed to fit tightly. Her initial relief at its surprising comfort wore off by the time she got halfway to her destination. The puffy little sleeves kept sliding off her shoulders and she realized belatedly that if she bent over in front of anyone, they would have a pretty good view of her bra. Too late to turn back though. She would just avoid bending over.

Hell, she wouldn't have to be there long. At least she'd remembered to rinse the ever present smudges from her glasses. She'd be able to see, if nothing else.

She pulled her VW into the elegant, curving drive of the Silverwood Estate, a place so palatial it made her stomach ache, and stopped near the front entrance, where a uniformed attendant waited to park her car for her. When she handed him the keys he looked at the Bug as if it were a dead fish, but tried to cover it with a welcoming smile.

She faced the palace, squared her shoulders and walked to the huge, open doors. Light and music spilled from the place, accompanied by the voices of the beautiful people of Greenlaurel and vicinity. Another uniformed fellow stood in the doorway, smiling even while looking her up and down in surprise. She supposed she should have borrowed some jewelry, she thought self-consciously. She wasn't wearing a scrap of it, besides her precious locket.

"Your name, madam?" the doorman asked. He had a list in his hand.

"Rosemary! You're finally here! You've already missed the opening dance." Grandma Marjorie, draped in glamour, hurried in between them before Rosie could get a word out. She had her by the arm, hustling her into the crush within a second. Rosie sent the doorman an apologetic shrug, and went along peacefully. Her grandmother was eyeing her as she walked at a pace that should be reserved for far younger women, tugging Rosie at her side. "My goodness, that's an…interesting dress you picked out."

"It's Tara's. I borrowed it." She pushed an errant sleeve up while nearly tripping on the hemline. It was a bit too long, as well.

"And whatever have you done to your hair?"

"Look, Grams, I did my best. Let's just make the rounds and get this over with so I can slip out to the gardens."

"Nonsense, child. You're here, and it's a party. Try to enjoy yourself for once."

It would do no good to argue that if her grandmother really wanted her to enjoy herself, she'd have let her stay at home. She'd have far rather been wrist-deep in topsoil than drowning in perfumed bodies. But that was something Gram would never understand.

She looked around the room, as her grandmother dragged her along, introducing her to people whose names she forgot the moment they were uttered. Her parents were sitting at a small table with some of the Texas elite, sipping champagne, smiling, laughing. Phoebe was harder to spot, but her crowd of admirers wasn't. She was in her element, dressed to kill and batting her eyes at a dozen young men, all eager to be her next flavor of the month.

"This is Rodney Monroe, dear," Grams was saying, having waylaid a handsome man who had been unfortunate enough to be caught alone. "Rodney, my granddaughter, Rosemary."

He looked at her, and it was obvious he had to force his smile to remain in place. "Charmed," he said, taking her hand. "Marjorie, she's every bit as lovely as you said."

Oh, hell, this was a setup. If Grams had spoken to this starched and polished pretty boy ahead of time, it could be nothing less.

"Would you dance with me, Rosemary?" he asked.

"Of course she will!" Grandma Marjorie answered for her, giving her a nudge and a glare that told her she'd damn well better.

"Of course I will," Rosie muttered.

Rodney swept her into his arms for a whirl around the dance floor. It was not pretty. The dress kept tripping her feet, and the sleeves fell down her shoulders, and her hands were not free to push them back up. There she was, in the middle of snob-central with her bra straps showing, and her glasses slowly inching lower on her nose.

"What do you do, Rosemary?" he asked, as if he really cared.

"Look, there's no need to make small talk. Just dance me toward those French doors in the back, and you're off the hook."

"Off the hook? Rosemary, you wound me."

"Oh, please. I promise I'll tell Grams you were Prince Charming incarnate. Just get me out of her sight."

"If that's what you want." He eased up on the fancy footwork, and danced her through the crowd, edging ever nearer the back of the huge ballroom. She glanced back at her grandmother, saw her watching, forced a smile, until finally the woman's attention was pulled away by her dear friend Ida Conrad. Ida spotted them, gave Rosie a wave.

So they were in on this together, Rosie thought. God, they needed a life.

The crowd closed in, breaking the line of sight,

and Rosie planted her feet. "That's fine. Perfect. Thanks for the dance."

He frowned down at her. He was pretty, too pretty, a blue-eyed blonde. His hands were as smooth as a baby's bottom, and she suspected he'd had a professional manicure. Probably hadn't had dirt under his fingernails since he was six, if then.

"Can I get you a drink or anything?" he asked.

"No, thanks. You're off the clock."

"Pardon?"

"Go."

Looking puzzled, he gave a helpless sigh, shrugged and turned to wander away through the crowd in search of more willing females. Relieved, Rosie glanced toward the French doors. Smack between her and escape, she spotted Tara and Jake. Jake spotted her at the same moment, and with a look of concern etched on his face, started toward her.

Tara clasped his arm, and he said something, nodding toward Rosie. Then Tara saw her, and her face just froze. She blinked as if stunned, said something to Jake, then left him standing there as she headed for Rosie like a missile.

Rosie thought about leaving, but Tara was on her in moments, clasping her arm and tugging her into an alcove beside the baby grand, where potted palms sorely in need of more exposure to sunlight, provided a semblance of cover.

"What the hell are you *wearing?*"

Rosie glanced down at the green dress. "Look, I'm sorry I borrowed it without asking first, but I didn't have a choice."

Tara rolled her eyes. "Good grief, Rosemary, I could care less if you want to borrow a ball gown, but why this one?"

"It was on the bed," Rosie said, frowning. "I thought it was something you were thinking about wearing, so I figured it was a safe choice."

Her older sister closed her eyes as if in anguish. "It was on the bed because I was going to give it to charity. It's five years out of date, and too big for you to boot. No one at this ball would be caught dead in that thing. It's hideous, Rosemary. My God, surely even you could see that? Do you need even thicker lenses on those glasses or what?"

Tara, when angry, could cut right to the quick.

"And your hair looks as if something's nesting in it," she went on.

Rosie was angry. "Will you get over yourself already? No one gives a damn what I'm wearing. I didn't want to come, Grams gave me no choice. I won't be here long, I promise. The minute I can make my way to the back doors, I'm out of here, and you won't see me again."

Tara scowled. "You may not care about the impression you make on people, Rosemary, but you consistently refuse to consider how that impression reflects on the rest of us.''

Rosie lifted her brows. ''Lucky for you, almost no one here knows who I am.''

She'd meant it as sarcasm, but Tara's frown eased. ''That's true. I suppose we should thank our stars that, due to your hermitlike tendencies, almost no one realizes you're a Linden.'' She looked around the room, studying faces. ''And if you get out of here fast enough, maybe most of them never will.''

''Gee, thanks for that, sis. It just warms my heart to know how you really feel.''

Tara's face softened. ''It's not that I'm ashamed of you. God, Rosie, how many times have I offered to take you for a makeover, help you shop for clothes and bring you with me to one of these parties. I'd love to show off my little sister—but, not like this.''

''Message received. I promise, I'll get out of here as soon as possible, and I won't tell a soul my last name on the way.'' She pulled free of her sister, and reentered the crowd, more self-conscious than ever thanks to Tara's pep talk, but determined to make her way to the French doors at the back, and escape this mess into the gardens.

''Rosemary,'' her sister called.

She ignored her, kept on shouldering through the crowd. Then she collided with a stranger, an older man with thick gray hair, pale blue eyes and a pinched face.

"Pardon me," he said. "I'm so sorry."

"My fault," she muttered, eager to just skirt past the man and continue on her way.

"Oliver Grimble," he said, extending a hand.

"Nice to meet you." She tried again, but he sidestepped, blocking her.

"And you are?"

"I'm Rosie, and I'm leaving."

"Oh, dear, I hope our little collision isn't the cause."

"No, of course not. If you'll excuse me—"

"I take it you're a friend of Zachary Ingram."

She frowned up at him. "Now, why would you assume that?"

"He's watching you, and he looks concerned." He nodded in the direction from which she had come, and she turned to see Jake staring in her direction, still looking worried, speaking to Tara and from the look on his face, none too happy with her.

He was going to make a great brother-in-law, she thought. Already he acted more like a big brother than a relative by marriage. He really cared, and she didn't think he was pleased about the way Tara had treated her just now. Maybe he'd overheard part of their conversation.

She sent Jake a smile that told him she was fine,

then turned back to the stranger. "That's not Zachary Ingram. It's his brother, Jake."

The man gave a sheepish grin. "My mistake. My goodness, perhaps I should borrow your glasses."

"Oh, a lot of people confuse them. They look quite a lot alike."

"Are they twins then?"

"No. Just have an uncanny resemblance."

"Fascinating."

She didn't really think so, but whatever. She started to edge around the man again, but he stopped her with a hand on her arm. His grip was a little too firm, and his insistence a little too forceful.

"Now, which one is the genius?" he asked.

"I'm sorry, who did you say you were again?"

He glanced down at her, and his grip on her arm eased instantly. "I'm sorry. Being new in town, I'm naturally curious to get to know the people in my social circle. I work for David Castleman. Honestly, you've been more than gracious. Perhaps we can talk again later?"

"Yeah. Perhaps. Now if you'll excuse me…"

"Of course." He sketched a bow, letting her move past him.

Rosie made a mental note to tell Jake about this stranger and all his questions. And then she filed it away in the back of her mind as a clear path opened between her and the doors. She hurried to it, only to be waylaid again.

In fact, she was stopped by the handful of people who *did* know who she was—last name and all, unfortunately for Tara. They were only being polite, so she tried to be polite back, even while wishing they would talk to someone else so she could make her escape. The only current hot topic she knew enough to discuss was the gossip about David Castlemane selling the land he'd inherited—land that bordered Greenlaurel State Park—to a developer. And her only opinion on that was that the billionaire businessman should be taken out and horsewhipped. Hardly a suitable comment to make at a social function, but political correctness had never been her strong suit. Besides, it seemed there was even juicer gossip tonight. Everyone was whispering about some supposed ''genetically altered'' children who'd been adopted, maybe by local families, years ago. They'd be adults by now. Mutants. They could be anyone. Sounded like typical tabloid trash to Rosie.

It took nearly an hour to make her way to those French doors and escape. Finally, to her relief, she got through the doors, closed them behind her and took a deep, cleansing breath of the night air, fragrant with the scents of flowers wafting from the nearby garden.

Thank goodness, she'd made it out of there.

She'd done her duty, arrived within the prescribed time, danced in full view of her grandmother, even did some mingling, though she did it poorly. Now she was free, and she wouldn't go back into that room for all the orchids in the world.

She walked down the concrete steps, heeled off her shoes, sat on the top step and peeled off the knee-high nylons. She'd seen no need for pantyhose with a floor-length gown, though her sisters would probably disagree. Finally, she sank her bare feet into the cool, green grass, and let it soothe her.

The maze was just a few yards ahead of her, and it looked deserted. Thank goodness, she thought, moving slowly forward to enter it. There would be no one there. No one but her and the plants.

Chapter 3

Mitch Conrad had escaped the party, with its "eligible" young women and their pushy mothers, and, worse yet, his matchmaking grandmother, Ida, at the first opportunity.

It wasn't as if he minded having women foisted on him from every angle. It was just that he'd been at this long enough to know exactly how it played out—time and time again. Some pretty, well-bred, fine-mannered society filly would flit her lashes and tease him a little, and then, just when he started to think maybe this time she would stick around, it would all change. The second she set foot on his ranch.

There would be the inevitable, "B-but I thought you were a Conrad?"

And he would explain that he *was* a Conrad, but that he'd decided to leave Conrad Oil and its billions to his father and brothers. The business came, he knew, with side effects. Ulcers, high blood pressure, heart palpitations. Moreover, it required hours and hours spent indoors, in an office. He would sooner jump from the towering steel-and-glass building than be held captive inside it. It would kill him.

And once the appeal of the money was gone, most of the women stopped seeing much appeal of a more personal nature in him. Some stuck around, but only until they caught him with manure on his boots, dirt and sweat streaking his face and blisters rising on his hands. He hated society and all its trappings. He was only here tonight because his grandmother had begged him, and then resorted to tears—actual tears!—when her begging had failed.

What the hell could he do? Say no and let the precious old meddler cry? It wasn't in him. So he was here. He'd danced a few dances with hopeful young women, and he'd had a few beers, and then a few more, smuggled in with the help of a conspiracy-loving waiter, since Mitch detested champagne, and wine made him pucker up as much as biting into a lemon would. And then he'd sneaked out the back and taken refuge behind the giant wall of green hedges, so no one from the house would spot him and come to fetch him back inside, and because somewhere in the middle of this big flat-topped greenery, his co-conspirator was supposed to have stashed a six-pack.

It turned out that the greenery wasn't a wall of hedges. It was a maze, its sides taller than his head. He liked it. Miguel, the waiter, had chosen well. No one would ever find him in here.

He wandered the maze for a long time, finding little open spots every now and then, with benches and flowers. Still he kept wandering. Miguel had said something about a fountain, and he hadn't come to that yet. When he finally did, he was glad he'd kept going.

The spot was a huge circle, private and pretty, bathed in moonlight. A stone fountain held court in the center, with a Greek goddess in its middle, draped in concrete leaves and vines, pouring water from a wine pitcher. Situated around the fountain were benches and plots of flowers. Every now and then a plant was contained in a concrete urn instead of in the ground. White gravel lined the path. Mitch walked forward to the first bench, peered underneath it and spotted the six-pack there, waiting.

Perfect. He shrugged out of his black jacket, tugged loose the bow tie—God how he hated them—freed the top two buttons of his starched white shirt and pulled out a long-necked brown bottle. He tugged one of the urns—which was heavier than it looked—closer to the bench, then used it to prop his feet on when he sat down, twisted the cap off the bottle and took a long pull of beer.

He could almost imagine he was at home, sitting on the ground, back against a tree, sipping a well-earned cold one after a hard day wrangling cattle.

Bit by bit, he let the tension ease from his body. He'd done his duty, he told himself. He'd made Grandma Ida happy. Put in an appearance and even danced with a few hopefuls. His family had been pressuring him big-time to pick a wife, settle down, start a family. The problem was, none of the women they kept foisting on him were the kind of women he wanted. He didn't want polish and shine. He wanted someone who would feel as ill at ease at this ball as he did.

His beer was gone. He opened another.

And then he heard a voice.

A woman's voice.

His first instinct was to pick up his six-pack and slip away before she could catch sight of him, but then he caught her words, and relaxed back on the bench, curious to hear more.

"Look at you," she was saying. "Nobody tries to dress you up, drape you in some stupid fabric, dangle jewelry from your petals or paint them with eye shadow or lipstick."

Frowning, Mitch leaned forward, craning his neck to see around the corner. There he saw a woman, leaning over, speaking to a rosebush. As she did, the strap of her garish green dress slid down, baring her shoulder, and she mindlessly pushed it back up again.

"No one wants you to be anything more than what you are," she told the rose. "And that's enough. You're so lucky."

She heaved a heavy sigh as she straightened, then turned and started coming toward him. She was, he realized, the furthest thing from one of those society females inside the house. Her dress was ugly as sin, and too big, to boot. She kept tripping over the hemline but didn't seem to care. She wore round, gold-rimmed glasses and her hair was fighting hard to escape the unimaginative bun it was pinned into, with pieces falling loose and hanging every which way.

She was, he thought, the anti-deb.

So he stayed where he was, intrigued, and wanting to know more.

She came a few more steps, then paused and reached out a hand to cup a flower blossom before she leaned in close and smelled it. She closed her eyes in ecstasy, and he noticed that she was pretty behind those glasses, standing there in her too-big dress, moonlight flowing over her.

"You're perfect just the way you are," she told the flower. He didn't know what kind of flower it was. Not a rose, something else. "People could learn a lot from plants."

"You can say that again," he muttered, not quite meaning to vocalize the thought.

She spun toward him, looking startled out of a year's growth, he thought, and tried to take a step backward at the same time. She caught her foot on the dress, tripped and over she went, even as he shot off the bench to try to catch her in time.

He knelt beside her where she'd landed on her backside, slid a hand to cup her head and curled another around her shoulder, which was bare because the dress strap had fallen again. "Are you okay?"

She blinked at him, her eyes unfocussed and uncovered. "Yeah, um, do you see my glasses?"

He helped her to sit up, then looked around. "Uh, unfortunately, yes." He picked up the glasses, held them up to her. Both lenses were shattered.

She took them from him, peered closely at them. "Oh, hell. I'm blind as a bat without them. Especially at night. Oh, and the orchid!"

He frowned, looking around them. "You landed on an orchid?"

"No. I came out here looking for one. Actually, that's the only reason I came to this party in the first place—to see the orchid bloom tonight. It's supposed to be here somewhere." She peered around, squinting.

"If you describe it to me, maybe I can help," he offered.

"Gram said it was in a concrete pot with fairies on the outside."

"Oh." He glanced back at the urn he'd been using as a footstool. "Then this must be it here." Taking her hand in his—an act that sent a little tingle of awareness sizzling through him when her fingers laced with his and held on—he led her closer to the bench. "This one here?" he asked.

She leaned close to the plant. "Oh, yes. This is it. It hasn't opened yet, has it?"

"Not since I've been here." He sat down on the bench, guiding her to sit beside him. She did, leaning back, sighing.

"I, uh, have a contraband six-pack of beer under the bench here. Would you like one?"

"Oh, God, you have no idea."

"I'm taking that as a yes." Smiling, he reached down, pulled out a beer, twisted off the top and handed it to her.

The woman took a long, slow pull on the beer, and then, to his surprise, leaned back on the bench and put her feet up on the edge of the flowerpot. They were bare, her feet. Bare, and cute as hell.

"So who are you?" she asked. "You working the party tonight?"

He blinked. So she thought he was staff. One of the employees. Well, that stood to reason. He couldn't think of another guest who would rather be in the garden drinking beer when he could be inside hitting on rich, eligible women. "Not by choice," he said, because it was the best noncommittal answer he could come up with. "You can call me Mitch."

"You can call me Rosie," she said. "And should anyone ask, I have no living relatives, so the last name is unimportant."

"I like the way you think." He clinked the top of his bottle against hers. "So, Rosie, how come you're out here in the garden, barefoot, instead of in there dancing with some rich bachelor, hmm?"

"Don't tell me you broke your glasses, too," she said.

He frowned at her. "I see twenty-twenty. And I think you're adorable."

She held up her beer. "How many of these have you had?"

"Not that many."

"No? Well, thanks for that, Mitch. That's a sweet thing to say."

"Hell, I meant it, Rosie. I've always figured you can't really be sure what any of those primped and polished ladies actually look like unless you manage to take 'em down and scrub their faces clean, then wash all the goop outta their hair."

She laughed at that. "I tried to put some goop in my hair, and you can see the results." She drained the beer. He took the bottle from her and stuck a fresh one in its place. Then he reached behind her head and pulled a few pins from her hair. It fell around her shoulders, long and dark blond in the moonlight. A little stiff in places.

"I usually just wear it in a ponytail."

"So why did you change it tonight?"

"Hell, Mitch, I couldn't show up here in a ponytail any more than I could arrive in my blue jeans. They'd never have let me in."

"They'd have called the police."

"And maybe the press," she put in. "As if I haven't already embarrassed my poor sisters enough tonight."

Then she did have family. Here. At the ball. Who the hell was she?

She sipped the beer, sighed and let her head fall back against the bench. "God, I haven't been this relaxed in a week. I figured this party was going to be one tense encounter after another."

"No tension here," he told her. "I came out here to get away from it."

"Me, too." She frowned then, sitting up and looking skyward. "What happened to the moon?"

He looked up. "Dark clouds just slid over it."

"You think they'll pass? The orchid won't blossom without moonlight."

"You know, I don't think so. The clouds look to be pretty thick, and—"

The slow roll of thunder cut off his words, and

then what had been a mild breeze grew stiffer. "I think we'd better seek cover," he said.

"Not back to the mansion. Can we slip around to the parking lot from here?"

Taking her hand, he drew her to her feet. "No, it's all fenced in. Gates are all closed until after the ball for security reasons. We can't leave without going back through the damn mansion."

"Then I'm here for the night," she said. "Rain or otherwise."

"There's something over that way. Come on."

The thunder boomed again; then the clouds burst all at once, and they were soaked to the skin in moments. Mitch was running, pulling her along beside him, and she was going full throttle even though she could barely see—and then he realized that she was laughing. Soaked by rain, running blind and barefoot over the wet paths and laughing so hard it was making her gasp.

He stopped running, turned to face her, caught her face between his palms. "Have you lost it, Rosie?"

"I haven't had this much fun in years," she confessed. She blinked at him, water streaming over her cheeks and dripping from her hair.

And for some reason he couldn't have identified if he'd wanted to, he leaned down and kissed her.

She didn't object. Didn't act all offended and shocked that he'd behaved like a normal, red-blooded male, the way any other woman in attendance at this event would have done.

Nope. She kissed him back. Sort of went all soft in his arms, then parted her lips and let him taste the beer she'd been drinking to his heart's content.

Damn, he liked this woman. Even though he knew it would only lead to disaster.

Chapter 4

She didn't believe in pretenses, though if there had ever been a time one might be called for, it was probably right now. She should probably pretend she wasn't enjoying this kiss as much as he was. She might have even attempted to, if she hadn't just downed two beers in the space of fifteen minutes, and on an empty stomach. She'd never been much of a drinker. One drink could put her in a mellow, happy state. Two made her tipsy. She'd had two.

And this cowboy was holding her pressed to the length of his body, and kissing her as if he really meant it, in the pouring rain. And she liked it. She liked that he didn't care about her hair, or manners or makeup. She liked that he thought she was pretty in spite of those things. She liked that he had no clue who the hell she was, and that it was so dark he probably wouldn't know her if he saw her again. The darkness, the beer, the week of tension, the lack of sleep and the anonymity made her giddy.

He stopped kissing her, took her hand, and pulled her along. In a few moments they were inside, out of the rain. And it was even darker than before. She couldn't see anything. Nothing at all.

"What's this?"

"A shed of some kind," he told her. "We can hole up here until the rain stops."

"Oh."

Out of the darkness, his hands pressed to her arms, rubbing up and down. "You're cold."

"I'm all right."

There was a moment of quiet. "Are you suddenly shy, Rosie? Cause you don't have to be, you know."

"It's just…odd. Me being out here, like this, with you."

"Seducing society debs in garden sheds isn't my usual routine either."

She smiled to herself in the darkness. "I'm no society deb."

"No. You're a woman. Not one of those *ladies* in the ballroom. A real woman." His hands slid underneath her arms, and around her waist, pulling her close to his body again. She was out of her element. She'd only had one boyfriend in her life, Dan, back in college.

But this was different. This wasn't Dan with his clumsy, hurried gropings. This was a stranger.

He kissed her again, using his tongue this time, and she liked it and saw no reason to pretend she didn't. She even used hers a little. He moaned and drew his mouth away from hers, trailing a hot path over her jaw and down to her neck, where he suckled and nipped. She liked that, too. This guy was turning her on way more than Dan ever had.

His hands found the zipper at the back of the dress, inching it lower as his mouth went to work on her shoulder, pushing the errant sleeve aside with no effort at all. The dress fell to her waist, the sleeves to her elbows. He bent her backward, and kept exploring, mouthing her breast until he found its center. She thought she would cry out loud when he flicked his tongue over her distended nipple, then closed his mouth around it and suckled her. She loved it, and yet his words kept echoing in her ears. *She was no lady.* She certainly was proving that right now, wasn't she?

There was a loud boom of thunder, a crash at the rear of the shed, and she jerked away from him so suddenly she nearly stumbled. Would have, if he hadn't been holding her.

"Wh—what was that?"

"It's just the storm. It's all right." He pulled her close again, but by then she had already shrugged the stupid dress back up over her shoulders. "You're so skittish."

''I think something fell on the shed,'' she whispered, evading him when he tried to kiss her again.

He sighed, easing off, his hands soothing on her shoulders. ''I'll go out and check, if you want me to.''

She nodded, realized he couldn't see her in the darkness and spoke aloud. ''Yes. Please. I think that would be a good idea.''

''All right.'' His hands fell away from her, and a slash of gray appeared when he opened the door. ''I'll be right back.''

She heard him walking away, beyond the howl of the wind and the crashing thunder. As soon as his footsteps took him beyond her range of hearing, she dashed out of the shed, back through the maze. She knew perfectly well what would happen if she stayed. She would make love to a stranger in a dirty garden shed. God, she didn't even know his last name.

She made her way through the maze, and that was no small task without her glasses in the pouring rain. But eventually, by following the noise from the ball and her path by memory, she arrived back at the entrance, and there she paused, wondering just what she was supposed to do next.

''Rosemary? Is that you?''

Jake's voice came to her through the rain, and then he was trotting toward her, across the lawn. When he got to her, he slid his coat from his shoulders and draped it over her head. ''What happened?

I saw you slip out, and got worried when the storm hit. Are you all right?''

"I'm fine, I just…found it all a little overwhelming." He was leading her back toward the French doors, where light from the party spilled out. "I can't go back in there, Jake. I look like a drowned rat."

He paused, glancing down at her. "We can go in through the kitchens. There's a side door from there to the parking lot. Okay?"

She nodded hard, and he led the way, skirting the party, taking her in through a small door. She let him lead her, barely peering out from beneath his coat, mortified at the thought that someone might see her—equally worried that if Jake so much as looked at her face, he would know what she'd been doing out in the gardens.

He hustled her outside again, and they never encountered a soul along the way. They were striding across pavement a moment later. "Here's your car," he told her. "The valet has the keys. I can go get them from him—"

"No, that's fine. I keep an extra set in the ashtray." An extra pair of eyeglasses, too, she thought with a sigh of relief. Rosie Linden was nothing if not prepared. She tried the door. It wasn't locked, thank goodness. There would be no need to lock it, not here in a private area where only guests and trusted employees could get at it. She slipped out from beneath the coat, handed it to Jake. "Thank you," she told him. "You're one in a million, you know that?"

As she got in the car, he stood there with his hand on the open door. "Are you sure you're okay? Nothing…happened out there tonight, did it?"

"Just got caught in the rain. I'm fine. Really. Thanks again, Jake."

"Good night, Rosie."

"Night." He closed the door for her, and she fetched her extra keys, started the car and turned on its headlights.

When she drove away, Jake was still standing there, watching her.

Mitch returned to the shed, having found that a rather large limb had fallen onto the roof from a nearby tree. There didn't appear to be much damage, but it was hard to tell in the darkness. He stepped inside, closed the door, brushed the rain from his shoulders. "It was just a limb," he said. "I don't think it's serious."

There was no reply.

"Rosie?"

Only silence, and a blanket of emptiness answered his call. She was gone. And he didn't even know who she was. His heart sank. He realized he hadn't exactly been behaving like a gentleman with her, and he could have kicked himself for that. He'd had an inkling that she was the kind of woman he'd been looking for—the kind without pretense or artifice. And now she was gone, and he was clueless as to how to find her again.

He stepped out of the shed, and stood in the rain, looking around as if for an answer. Lightning flashed, and something on the ground gleamed its reflection. Frowning, Mitch bent and felt around until he found the item. Tiny, metallic and heart-shaped, it was suspended from a chain. He felt hinges on one side, and realized it must be a locket. Rosie's locket. Surely there would be a clue hidden inside.

Closing his hand around the precious find, he put it into his pocket, and then he made his way back to the party, stopping along the way to retrieve his coat and tie from the bench where he'd first met her, along with the last couple of beers from the six-pack.

He didn't hesitate reentering the ballroom, though he drew a fair share of curious glances, and probably embarrassed Grandmother Ida to the roots of her hair. He ignored them all, and kept on going, across the ballroom, through the crowd, and out the front entrance, where he told the valet his name, and asked him to bring his car around.

While he waited in the light spilling from the entryway, he took the locket out again, and gently pried it open. He expected to see a photograph inside, maybe one of Rosie. Instead, there were only three tiny rose petals, their pink color faded with time, and a tiny, faded photo of a little girl sitting

in a patch of dirt, her face and blond hair streaked
with soil, and alight with a killer smile.

It had to be Rosie. But it told him nothing. He
closed his eyes against the rush of longing, and disappointment. He wanted to know who she was and
whether she really was as different as she seemed.
There had been something so special about her—
something that touched him on a level that hadn't
been touched by other women. And when he kissed
her...when he kissed her he felt it right to his toes.
More than sexual attraction. More than desire.

Was it real, he wondered? Or was it just the effect of too much beer, too much stress and the intimacy of a like-minded stranger in the dark. He
might have had the chance to find out, if he hadn't
frightened her off by coming on like a bull in the
presence of his first in-season heifer.

He had to know, he decided. He couldn't be sure
of anything until he saw her again, and so that was
what he had to do. Besides, he rationalized, he had
to return her locket to her.

"I'll find you, Rosie," he told the little, dirty-
faced girl in the photo, closing her safely inside the
locket once more. "I'll find you."

Chapter 5

First thing in the morning, Grandma Marjorie and Ida Conrad sat sipping tea at their favorite breakfast café in downtown Greenlaurel. "Hardly the smashing success I was hoping for," Ida commented. "My Mitch made a complete spectacle of himself, dashing through the ballroom, dripping muddy water all along the way, and carrying beer of all things! I swear if I ever find a woman who can tolerate him it will be a miracle."

"My Rosemary didn't do much better," Marjorie said. "I think she forgot about the ball entirely and then threw on the first dress she could find at the very last minute. She looked like a child playing dress-up. And vanished shortly after she arrived."

Ida sighed. "It's difficult to do what's best for these young people when they refuse to cooperate."

"I should say so."

Ida sipped her tea. "Though, I have a feeling Mitch might have met *someone* before his public spectacle."

"Really?" Marjorie set her cup down. "What makes you think so?"

"Well, he's been asking for a copy of the guest list." She steepled her fingers in thought. "He also asked if I knew the identity of a girl in a green dress who went by the name of Rosie."

Marjorie's head snapped up and her eyes shot to Ida's. "Do you think…?"

"Well, it could be. I just wonder how you would feel about the two of them. Mitch is hardly the catch of the season."

"That might just be his strongest selling point where Rosemary is concerned." She sighed. "But when could they possibly have met? She was barely there an hour. And I never saw them cross paths on the dance floor."

"I don't know. I suppose the only way to find out is to put them together somehow. See if any sparks fly. It's obvious he has no clue who she is."

"Hmm. Well, let's keep our ears open. At the first opportunity, we'll set them up to meet again."

"Good. I'm all for it."

"Poor Rosemary," Marjorie said with a sigh.

"I'm afraid her mother is quite put out with her over her performance last night. And her sisters are livid."

"Oh, surely they'll get over it."

"I'm not so sure. They're planning a lunch meeting with her today. Oh, they're calling it an intervention, of all things. It looks more like an ambush to me."

"That won't be pleasant."

Marjorie shrugged. "No, it won't. I'll go along, just to see to it they don't go too far."

"What do they have in mind?"

Marjorie rolled her eyes. "They're determined to make a lady of her. I'm afraid they'll make Henry Higgins seem an amateur."

"Oh, dear." Ida sipped some more, then considered. "Although I can't say I blame them. I've had much the same sort of program in mind for my Mitch. And if he's going to court a Linden..."

"And if she's set her cap for a Conrad..."

The two women exchanged knowing glances and smiled. Then they finished their tea in companionable silence.

By morning, Rosie told herself that she had put the night completely behind her. Oh, just because she'd dreamed about her encounter with the stranger all night, that didn't mean anything. Of course she'd dreamed of it. It was a once-in-alifetime experience, and one she hoped never to repeat.

Her locket was missing. That troubled her, but she expected she would find it easily enough by visiting the grounds of Silverwood again by daylight, on the excuse of retrieving her other set of car keys. She'd just retrieve the locket then, along with any other clues she might have left behind that could scandalize her entire family. She thought of her broken glasses. Where had they ended up? Today she was wearing the spare set she kept in her car for emergencies. Their rims were black, but they were narrow and round and serviceable.

She'd washed the goop from her hair, buried the ruined dress in the bottom of her garbage bin and was once again comfortable in her ponytail and blue jeans.

The ants were delivered to the botanical gardens shortly after she arrived that morning, and she released them into the affected flower beds, feeling a thrill of achievement. The staff members gave an impromptu round of applause, and she knew everything was going to be fine.

Until her lunch hour, that was. Because she received a telephone call from her mother at five minutes to twelve, telling her to be at the country club within fifteen minutes for lunch, and her tone brooked no argument. Rosie didn't offer any, but she knew something was up.

God, could her mother have found out about Mitch, and the shed and... Please, not that, she thought as forcefully as she could.

Her feelings of trepidation grew steadily worse when she walked into the country club and saw, not just her mother, but the entire female contingent of the Linden family waiting for her at a private table. Tara and Phoebe flanked their mother, Sherry. Grandma Marjorie sat across from them. The only empty chair was between Gram and Phoebe.

A waiter pulled it out for Rosie, and she sank into it, mentally cringing. They were all dressed perfectly, as always. Hair coifed, makeup flawless, nails done to perfection. Tara and Sherry both wore chic designer skirts, blouses and blazers, Sherry's in shell-pink, Tara's in blue. Phoebe wore a pretty maroon silk pantsuit with wide legs that swished when she walked, and Gram was in another of her endless supply of floral dresses.

Rosie eyed them all, licked her lips. "So what is this about? Someone call a family meeting?"

"I did," Tara said. "And the others were in agreement. Rosemary, this is an intervention."

Rosie frowned from one face to the other. "Are you all insane? I'm not using drugs and I hardly ever drink alcohol."

"Not that kind of intervention," Phoebe said.

"There's another kind?"

They all nodded. All except Gram, who just

watched her with a sympathetic look on her face. "Rosemary," her mother said. "You are a Linden. I know you don't particularly care about what that entails, but the rest of us do. You have a responsibility to uphold the image this family has worked so hard to establish and to sustain. Now we've let you slide for a long while. And while the cottage and the car and the career you've chosen are all things we're willing to tolerate—"

"Tolerate?"

"—there are other things that we simply cannot overlook any longer. You're twenty-four years old dear. It's time you started acting like it."

"Besides," Tara said. "You're never going to find a suitable husband like this. My God, hon, the things you do. Getting caught in that storm last night in the gardens…"

Gram spoke at last. "You…you were in the gardens when the storm hit?" She eyed Rosie as if she knew something.

"Jake told you about that?" Rosie asked, ignoring her grandmother's knowing expression.

"I had to drag it out of him," Tara said. "Honey, men don't respect you if you don't put forth a certain image. The way you looked last night…well, anything could have happened."

She blinked in shock.

"Things are going to change, Rosemary. From here on in, things are going to be different," her mother said. "Now, your days are your own. Wear what you want, do what you want. But your nights belong to us."

"We're going to take you shopping," Phoebe said. "Get you some decent clothes so you don't embarrass us at social functions."

"I don't *attend* social functions," she argued.

"You do now," Tara told her. "You're going to go to the right places, meet the right people, behave the right way and look good doing it."

Rosie pushed her chair away from the table. "And what if I refuse?"

"Oh, please," her mother said. "The first thing we'll be dispensing with is your tendency toward melodrama. Honestly, Rosemary, sit down."

Rosie stood there.

"Perhaps," Gram said, "if you put a time limit on it."

Tara frowned. "A time limit?"

"Yes. Say, Rosie agrees to go along with this scheme of yours for, oh, say, six months—"

"One month," Rosie said.

Gram shrugged. "One month, then. If she's not happier, more confident and more sure of herself at the end of that time, then the experiment was a failure and you all give up gracefully."

Rosie licked her lips. Tara scowled, but her mother seemed to consider. Finally she sighed, nodded hard. "One month," her mother said. "But we get to dress you for work as well as for evening, since we'll have so little time. I promise you, you'll love the new you as much as we will. There is no way you'll want to backslide after a month of seeing your true potential." She looked up at Rosie. "Agreed?"

Closing her eyes and sighing, Rosie didn't think she was actually being given much of a choice in the matter. She sat back down. "Agreed," she muttered.

"Good."

Marjorie excused herself at the first opportunity, and found a private spot to phone Ida. "We were right," she told her friend. "It *was* my Rosie. She was in the garden in the rainstorm, too."

"I thought so," Ida said. "Mitch is having some sort of cattle related crisis at the ranch. But I think I can turn it to our advantage. I'll call you later."

Chapter 6

The veterinarian shook his head slowly, his hand on the neck of an ailing longhorn. "I'm just not sure. They've definitely been into something that's making them sick."

"I sent the grain to that lab you suggested," Mitch said. "So far it's clean."

He looked into the big brown eyes of the cow, one he called Daisy, who was a prize winner, and produced the best calves in Texas. He knew the poor thing was in absolute misery, and there wasn't a damn thing he could do about it.

"I doubt it's the grain, or they'd all be sick," Dr. Wallace said. "Ditto with the water. Besides, the tests we ran just in case all came back clean.

As it is, this thing is very spotty, a few cows here and there sick as hell, the rest showing no symptoms at all.'' He licked his lips. ''You know, your grandmother called me this morning.''

''My grandmother? Ida?'' Mitch was surprised. Why the hell would his grandmother be contacting his vet? He had mentioned the sick cattle when he'd phoned her this morning to ask for the guest list from the party. And he supposed he'd mentioned that the vet was working with him to find an answer.

''She said she had a feeling there was some kind of vegetation involved. She was very insistent about it.''

Mitch frowned even harder. ''Grandma C is not the type to get *feelings* about things.'' He wondered what the old busybody could possibly be up to now. Dragging him to balls was bad enough, but if she planned to start meddling in his ranch...

''To tell you the truth, Mitch, her call got me to thinking. It's actually a possibility. In fact, the more I examine these animals, the more I think she could be on to something. They're eating something that's making them sick, and if it's not in the grain or the water....''

''Then it has to be in the pastures,'' Mitch finished. Giving the ailing cow another pat on the shoulder, he walked out of the barn, stepping into the blinding sunlight and scanning the horizon. He owned the land for as far as the eye could see in any direction. There were woodlots and meadows, wildflowers and weeds. "How the hell can I begin to figure out what?"

Dr. Wallace drew a breath, sighed. "Your grandma had a suggestion about that, too."

"Why am I not surprised?"

Wallace shrugged, dipped into his pocket, pulled out a folded slip of paper and handed it to Mitch. "It's the number of an excellent botanist, she said. A Dr. Linden."

Mitch took it, looked at the number, and felt even more suspicious. One of Grandma C's fondest dreams had been that of matching up one of her Conrad grandchildren with a member of the Linden family. Though he doubted any of them were botanists. This must be a distant cousin or something. Or the name might be coincidence. Though with his grandmother, there was usually no such thing. Still, he couldn't put his finger on a clear reason why he shouldn't give this botanist a call if there was the smallest possible chance he or she could help his cattle. "Hell, I suppose it can't hurt," he said at last.

"Nope, it can't."

Sighing, still suspicious of his grandmother's motives, Mitch returned to the house, washed up and placed the call.

A woman answered, with the words, "Greenlaurel Botanical Gardens, Dr. Linden's office."

Botanical Gardens, huh? Well, he supposed that made sense. "I need to speak with Dr. Linden, please."

"Who's calling?"

"My name is Conrad, I own the Double C Ranch."

"One moment, please Mr. Conrad."

There was a pause, and a moment later, another voice came on the line, another woman. "Hello? Mr. Conrad?"

He wondered how many secretaries he was going to have to work through before he got to the good doctor, sighed, and started over. "Yes," he said. "I'm calling for Dr. Linden."

"This is Dr. Linden. How can I help you?"

Mitch nodded. First suspicion confirmed, he thought. Dr. Linden was a woman. No doubt a woman his dear grandma Ida had in mind for him. Shaking his head slowly, he decided he might as well go through with the call. Hell, he didn't have to marry her, just get her out here to take a look at the pastures. It was for the good of the longhorns.

"I'm having a problem with my cattle," he said. "My vet seems to think it might be plant-related, and he suggested I contact you."

"I see."

"We've tested the grain and water. It all seems

okay, so he suspects there might be something growing in the pastures that's making them sick."

"Sounds like a logical guess." He heard static on the line. "I'm assuming you'd like me to come out and—" She said more, but there was too much static to hear her.

"Sorry, can you repeat that? We don't seem to have a very good connection."

"I apologize—my office forwarded your call to my cell phone. I said, would you like me to come out to your ranch and take a look around?"

"Yeah, and the sooner the better."

"I'll have to charge you a small fee."

"One of my best breeders is sick, lady, and she's worth twenty grand. You can charge me anything up to and including that. Give me some results, and I'll pay you without a complaint."

He could almost hear her smile coming through the phone lines, and suddenly there was something hauntingly familiar about her voice. "I was going to suggest a donation to the Botanical Gardens," she said. "And it needn't be anywhere near that amount."

"Whatever." The woman didn't care about money. Or she was pretending she didn't. How odd was that? "Can you come tomorrow morning?"

"I'm booked in the morning. How about early afternoon, right after lunch?"

He frowned, thinking about the cattle auction

he'd planned to attend. There was a prize bull he'd been wanting to acquire for two years, finally coming up for sale.

"All I need," she said, "is for someone to be on hand who can show me around the place."

That worked. Sam could handle that job. "Fine. Tomorrow at noon. I'll have my foreman, Sam, waiting to take you around." And wouldn't it just put Grandma's knickers in a twist to learn that her latest matchmaking attempt hadn't even resulted in a face-to-face meeting?

"I did say *after* lunch," she reminded him.

"Twelve-thirty?"

He heard her sigh, and knew damn well that didn't leave her time to eat, unless she munched a sandwich on the drive over from the Gardens—but dammit, his cattle were suffering.

"Fine. Twelve-thirty." She hung up, and he did, too.

When she got home that night, Rosie went directly to her cottage, hoping to avoid her mother and her sisters with their big plans. It didn't help. They were waiting at the cottage for her to arrive.

She got out of the VW, closed the door, and walked up to the front door of the cottage, only to open it and find them all sitting inside, sipping iced tea in her sunny, plant lined living room.

"Surprise!" Phoebe said.

Rosie closed her eyes, prayed for patience. "Not now, you guys. It's been a long day, and I'm completely exhausted."

"Nonsense. Now go on, go take a shower and change your clothes," her mother instructed. "We've landed you an appointment with Luigi Viscante, and we only have an hour."

She frowned, wondering at their excited expressions. "*Who* is Luigi...whatever you just said?"

They each blinked at her as if she were stupid, then exchanged exasperated looks. "Only the most exclusive stylist in Greenlaurel," Tara told her. "I swear, Rosemary, sometimes I think you live in a cave."

"We can't be late," Phoebe said. "If you're late, you lose your appointment, and you'll never be given another."

"Go, shower, dress. Hurry up," Sherry said, her hands gentle on Rosie's shoulders, but brooking no resistance, as she pushed her toward the little bathroom. She gave a little shove, then pulled the door closed on Rosie, leaving her alone in the bathroom.

Sighing, Rosie reminded herself that she only had to put up with their nonsense for a month. After that, they would leave her alone.

Wouldn't they?

She stripped off her clothes, dropped them into the hamper, and stepped into a cool, soothing shower, rinsing away the day's grime, if not its stress. And when she finished, she stepped out again, toweling down. She pulled on her favorite worn-out terry robe, and with a towel wrapped around her head, walked directly from the bathroom into her bedroom.

She pulled open a dresser drawer.

It was empty. What the…?

She opened another, and another. All the same. Empty.

"Mother!" Mad as hell she bellowed at the bedroom door. "Where are my clothes?"

"Check the closet, dear," Sherry called back.

Bracing herself, Rosie opened the bifold doors of her small closet.

It was full. Chic designer skirts, silk blouses, blazers and tailored jackets, slacks with creased and tailored waistlines. Shoes lined the floor, and an entire stack of silky underthings, most with their tags still attached, sat on the shelf.

"Oh. My. God."

She whirled at the sound of happy laughter from the doorway, to see the three conspirators standing there, looking pleased with themselves. "Surprised?" Phoebe asked.

"Stunned," Rosie replied.

"We've labeled them for you dear," Sherry put in. "The green tags mark the daywear, you know, casual but professional, and just a touch elegant. Those are what you wear to work. The pink tags are for informal gatherings, and the red are evening wear.''

''Mom,'' Rosie began.

''We tagged the shoes, too. And each one also has a letter on its tag, to match the outfits. *A's* go with *a's*, *b's* with *b's* and so on. Even you can't mess up.''

Phoebe rushed past her, yanking a pretty sundress from the rack. ''Wear this for the appointment.'' She shoved the dress into Rosie's arms. ''There are silk stockings in with the lingerie. Hurry up now.''

Then she and Tara left the room. Sherry, however, remained. ''Don't you have something to say, Rosie?'' she asked.

''Yeah,'' Rosie said sadly, knowing full well her mother was expecting a thank you. ''Where are my jeans?''

Chapter 7

Rosie was absolutely miserable. The sleek, figure-hugging suit was the best she could do for work the next morning. She'd rushed to her hamper first, expecting to find the jeans she'd taken off before diving into the shower the night before—but the conspirators had apparently thought of that. They'd covered all their bases. So she'd been forced to sort through the rack of impractical clothes and settle on the least impractical of the bunch. The pants were sleek and shimmery, in a deep shade of green. They hugged her hips and her legs, and ended in tiny slits above the ankle. The blouse was such a pale green you had to look twice to realize it wasn't white, with lacy eyelets in the shapes of flower petals. There was a loose, flowing jacket that went with the outfit, and she put it on only because she was afraid someone might check the closet to see that she'd dressed "properly."

She found a pair of flat shoes, slippery on the bottom, too shiny on the top, and black. Their mix-and-match tag did not identify them as "going" with the outfit, but they were the only pair without heels, and therefore the only pair she was likely to wear.

She tucked the blouse into the pants, pulled on the jacket, and went to stand in front of the mirror.

Her hair still showed the effects of last night's attack. It had been a perfectly acceptable dark blond. Now it had been "kicked up a notch" as the stylist had put it. It was lighter than it had been before, the way it used to be when, as a teen, she would spend the entire summer in the hot Texas sunshine and chlorinated swimming pools. It was curlier, too. Of course it wasn't a real perm, she'd argued too loudly to allow that, but the temporary curls had her hair looking as if she were heading out to a party instead of a flower bed.

The biggest change, of course, was her eyes. Not only had the team who'd worked on her plucked and shaped her eyebrows, but her mother had "surprised" her by stealing her glasses while she'd been distracted by the painful process. She'd left a tiny case, containing a set of contact lenses in their place on the small salon table, beside her purse.

At least they weren't color-tinted. Then again, with the clothes, the new eyebrows and the lighter hair, the green color of her eyes seemed greener anyway.

She barely recognized herself.

Sighing, she vowed that she would shop in secret, purchase some jeans, hide them at the office, and somehow, reclaim her former self. Though it wouldn't be today, she realized slowly. Today she had to grab lunch on the run and meet that rancher to discuss his ailing cattle, return to work in the afternoon, and then attend a dinner party with her mom and sisters. Suddenly, it seemed as if her life had been taken over.

"It's only for a month," she muttered, and started out of the bedroom.

"Hey, sis," Phoebe said, rising from her favorite chair to greet her, startling the living daylights out of her. "Wow, that looks great!"

"Yeah. It'll look even better after I've finished crawling around in various flower beds today. You guys really should have left me some work clothes."

Phoebe shook her head. "Mom says as the head honcha at the gardens, you have a staff of grad students and master gardeners under you, and that they are supposed to be the ones getting their hands dirty. You are supposed to be the one handing out orders, and overseeing things.''

"Mom knows my job better than I do, I suppose.''

"Then she's wrong?''

Rosie held her sister's gaze for a moment, then sighed. "Not exactly. I don't *have* to get my hands dirty. The problem is, that's the part of my job I like best.''

Phoebe rolled her eyes. Rosie reached for her ever present denim backpack, only to find that it had been replaced by a brand-new leather attaché case with her initials embossed on the front. She sighed, shook her head. "Stay as long as you like, Phoebe, but I have to go.''

"Not yet.'' Phoebe grabbed her arm, tugging her back through the cottage. "You're not ready.''

"I'm perfectly ready. Phoebe, what—?''

Her kid sister shoved her into a chair in the bedroom. "Oh, this will only take a minute. Come on, I have my orders. Close your eyes.''

Oh, God, she had a makeup case with her. Rosie closed her eyes. "And just what are you getting out of this?'' she asked as her sister expertly painted her face.

"The satisfaction of seeing my ugly duckling sister become a pretty swan,'' she said. "And a Ferrari.''

"A Ferrari?''

"Hey, I drive a hard bargain. You're no picnic to work with. Now stop scrunching up your eyes, I'm only giving you a light touch."

Phoebe's light touch consisted of a liquid base, blush, pressed powder "to finish," eyeliner, eye shadow that matched the color of the suit, mascara and three layers of color to her lips.

"This stuff will last all day," Phoebe informed her. "You won't have to reapply and it won't smear. We shouldn't have to touch you again until dinner at the Jackmans'."

"Oh joy." She pulled free of her sister's primping and got to her feet. "Can I go now?"

"Would it kill you to put on some earrings?"

"Yes. As a matter of fact, it would. I would keel over on the floor and go into convulsive death throes, which would probably ruin this *darling* suit and smear this *adorable* makeup."

Phoebe puckered her lips and shook her head. "Not the makeup. Nothing's gonna touch that makeup."

Rosie closed her eyes in exasperation. "Get out of my house, Phoebe."

"That's gratitude for you. Fine, go, have a nice day. See you at dinner."

"Not if I go with my gut instinct to run away and join the circus."

Phoebe left, and Rosie clutched her new briefcase and went to work.

The response she got there made her even angrier. Everyone she passed did a double take, and then started spewing praise. Her secretary brought her coffee. She never brought Rosie coffee. And her staff hopped to do every hands-on job that came up throughout the day, treating her as if she had been elevated to princess status, and was too delicate to do the down and dirty work. She'd have overruled them, but her superiors suddenly found tons of work for her to do that kept her in the office. Phone calls she needed to return, research on exotic trees, ordering plants and planning new sections and displays.

If she didn't know better, she might think her influential and obscenely wealthy family had bribed them with a donation. The problem was—she *didn't* know better.

They couldn't have bribed everyone in town though. Everyone was treating her differently, it seemed, from the traffic cop who pulled her over to tell her she had a brake light that wasn't working, and then fell over himself being polite and friendly to her, to the kid behind the counter of the fast-food joint where she grabbed a meal to go, who smiled more than she'd ever seen him smile and threw a free apple pie into her bag.

She'd been coming to this place for lunch a couple of times a week for years. The kid had *never* given her a free apple pie. No wonder so many women took so many pains to look good. It made men stupid.

She ate her lunch as she drove the VW out to the Double C Ranch. It was easy to find, only a half hour's drive, and when she pulled in, she realized that this was going to be the best part of her day. The place was beautiful. She saw lush rolling acres of healthy green grass, herds of contented looking, fat longhorns grazing happily, outbuildings in perfect repair, all freshly painted, and the house was the jewel of the crown. A one-story adobe structure, sprawling but understated, with windows and doors that were all arched at the top.

She got out of the car, and took a breath of fresh, clean air. God, this place was something.

A tall man came up to her, smiling, and said, "Dr. Linden, I presume?"

Mitch was in the house, packing for the overnight trip to the auction he had no intention of missing. He had his bedroom window open, because he preferred the fresh air to the air-conditioning, except on the hottest days, and so he heard the car pull in, and he heard his foreman's familiar voice as he greeted the good doctor.

But then he heard *her* voice, and everything ground to a halt. He stood there with a pair of jeans in one hand and a shaving kit in the other, staring down at the open suitcase on his bed, as she said,

"Gee, that's the first time I've heard that," her tone teasing.

And she sounded so much like his mystery woman from the other night, that Mitch's skin prickled.

"I'm Sam McKenzie, the foreman here at the Double C. Boss is heading out of town today, but I can show you around the place."

"That will be just fine, Mr. McKenzie."

"Heck, ma'am, you can just call me Sam."

"Well, you can call me Rosie," she said.

The shaving kit and jeans fell from his hands. Mitch spun around and ran to the window, but by now Sam was walking toward the barn with "Rosie" at his side, his hand on her elbow.

He took a good long look at the woman. She couldn't be his Rosie. She couldn't be. She was too "done." And her hair was lighter, and different somehow. As they went out of his sight, he slid his gaze toward the driveway to see what she'd been driving. A VW Bug was parked next to his own pickup truck.

The woman was a walking contradiction.

And yet, he had to know. He had to know. He picked up the phone, dialed the barn extension and waited for Sam to pick up. When he did, he tried not let his frazzled, hopeful state come through in his voice, though he doubted a man who'd known him as long as Sam had, would miss it anyway.

"I want you to have the woman wait there, and come to the house."

"Why's that, boss?"

"Because I've decided to show her around the ranch myself."

In a quieter voice, Sam said, "Caught a glimpse of her, did you? Well, hell, I can't say as I blame you. But I don't think she's your type."

"No, I didn't catch a glimpse of her," he lied. "I changed my mind because I'm worried about my cattle." He licked his lips. "Why, is she pretty?"

"Only enough to knock your socks off. So what are you gonna do about the auction? Riley's Pride is gonna go fast."

"That's why I'm going to send you in my place. So get back here, pronto. Let her cool her heels for five minutes while I give you the skinny on what we're willing to pay for that bull, and then I'll take over. All right?"

"Sure thing, boss. I'll be right there."

Chapter 8

Rosie waited for a long while, just near the front of the barn where Sam the foreman had told her to wait. She glanced at her watch, and wondered if she would ever have time to do some top secret, surreptitious shopping on the way home and still make her early dinner engagement.

The thought of the night's commitments made her scowl.

"Dr. Linden?"

The voice was deep and oddly familiar. She turned to face the tall, handsome man who'd come up to her. He was not Sam the foreman. "Yes?"

"I'm Mitch Conrad, we spoke on the phone." He extended a hand, and she blinked in surprise. His name was Mitch, and his voice was—

But no, he couldn't be the man from the other night. That man had been an employee, a waiter or something, working the ball. She let him shake her hand, and watched his face intently for any sign of recognition in his stunning blue eyes.

There wasn't any. Instead, he seemed to be watching her face in much the same way she was watching his. "I, um, thought you had an appointment this afternoon," she said when she regained the power to speak.

"I did, but this is more important. I can't stand to see my longhorns suffer, and several of them are really feeling like hell right now."

She nodded in understanding. He felt the way she had as she'd watched her delicate tropical plants ailing. "I don't blame you."

"Do you want to see them?"

She nodded. "I'm not a vet, but I don't suppose it could hurt."

He took her elbow and led her into the barn where the sickest of the cows and steer were penned, each in an individual stall. The floor was spotless she noted. The place well lit and well ventilated. Windows on the sides were open, and fans built into the walls at either end kept a fresh breeze moving through the barn. It was cool inside, and smelled of hay and grain and cattle.

"This is Daisy. She's one of my best breeders," he said, stopping at the first stall. The cow was lying down, breathing heavily, but she turned her head, with its long, wide-set horns moving in slow motion, to look up at him. Her huge dark eyes seemed imploring.

Rosie had never thought of a cow as beautiful before, but this one was. And clearly in pain. "What kind of symptoms are they showing?" she asked. As she did, she glanced at the man, and saw that his eyes were almost as pain-filled as the cow's.

"They won't eat. Don't want to get up. We have to fight to get them on their feet and walk them around several times a day, and then they're off balance, staggering around. You can't let a cow lie, or they're history, though, so we get 'em up all the same. They'll drink if you coax 'em. And uh, well…"

"Scours?" she asked, because he seemed to have trouble saying it.

He nodded. "We're cleaning the stalls almost hourly."

"Dark or light?"

"Dark."

"And the vet can't find anything wrong?"

"Everything wrong, just can't pinpoint what, beyond that it's something in their digestive systems. That's why I called you."

Rosie looked out of the barn. "How much land do you have here, Mr. Conrad?"

"Five thousand acres, give or take. Several different pastures. We keep the heifers in one, steer in another, bulls are on their own when they aren't breeding. Bred cows stay in one, and fresh cows with their calves in still another."

She lifted her brows. "You use bulls?"

"You surprised?"

She shrugged her shoulders. "I thought it was more cost-efficient to use artificial insemination these days."

"It probably is, but we don't care much about profits around here. I prefer to let nature take its course. Like to see where my calves are coming from."

He either had so much money he didn't have to worry about it, or he honestly didn't care about getting rich off his cattle. Rosie wondered which it was. The Conrad family was known for its millions, but they'd made their fortunes in oil, not cattle. Besides, the Lindens were known to be a fairly rich bunch, too. She knew from experience that you couldn't tell much by a person's family.

"I don't suppose all the sick ones come from one pasture?" she asked.

"No. Two groups have been getting sick. Steers and breeders like Daisy here."

"Well then those are the pastures where we'll have to begin. How big are they?"

He bit his lip. "Big. It'll take some time. A lot

of time. I know you have a day job already, but I don't know where else to turn here.''

She nodded. As she did, Daisy struggled valiantly to her feet, and walked to the stall door, her head clearing the top of it, her nose almost touching Rosie's shoulder. Rosie looked at those thickly fringed eyes, and stroked the smooth neck. ''Poor thing. You don't feel well at all, do you?''

''I'm awfully afraid she's gonna lose her calf,'' Mitch said.

Rosie licked her lips and came to a decision. ''I have vacation time coming from the Gardens. I'll let them know tonight that I need to take it starting tomorrow, so I can be here full-time until we nail this thing.''

The man looked at her with his brows raised. ''You'd do that?''

''I can't stand to see anything suffer, either,'' she said. She glanced down at her clothes and sighed in misery. ''If I had my way I'd start right now, but in these clothes, I can't do more than survey the areas and figure out a plan of attack.''

''Don't apologize. You're already going above and beyond. Besides, there's a lot of area to cover. Just doing that much will take a while. Fortunately, we can do it from my pickup.''

She nodded, and he led her out of the barn to the truck, opened her door for her, and she got inside. Then he was behind the wheel, driving them over well-worn dirt tracks, pointing out pastures.

The place was incredible, lush and sprawling,

and so green it took her breath away. They drove over trails that skirted numerous meadows, some being used as pastures, others allowed to grow undisturbed. Wildflowers swayed gently in the breeze, and with the blue sky as backdrop—as blue as Mitch Conrad's eyes, she thought without warning—it was paradise.

She slid a sideways glance at him, just to see if those eyes were really that blue. He caught her staring, and didn't flinch. Just stared right back.

"This place is beautiful."

He smiled at her. "I know. I love it. My family is constantly pushing me to give it up and join them in the oil business, but you know, the thought of being cooped up in an office all day just about gives me hives."

She smiled. "And all that money doesn't even tempt you?"

"Not even a little. If I could give this place up just for money, I'd be no better than David Castlemane and his cronies. There's something just plain odd about his staff."

She nodded her agreement, recalling her odd encounter with Oliver Grimble at the ball. "You know that land he inherited borders the state park. It's an incredibly beautiful parcel, but more importantly, it's an ecosystem. It supports a lot of wildlife, a lot of plant life as well."

"Yet he's ready to sell it to a developer just to line his pockets. And he's already richer than God. It oughtta be a crime."

She smiled at his passion on the subject. "So I'm betting it would take a lot more than money to get you to part with the Double C."

"A *lot* more. My grandmother keeps telling me I'd have landed a prize of a woman by now if I'd just get rid of the ranch and go to work at Conrad Oil. But I've yet to find a woman worth that much of a sacrifice." He said it with a smile that hit her like a two-by-four to the chest. And their eyes locked and held for a long moment.

She finally managed to break away, catch her breath again. "Um…can you have your men move the two affected groups of cattle to another pasture for the time being?" She asked the question just to fill the silence and only belatedly realized it was a good one, but also an obvious move.

"Actually, I've got the men working on that already. They just need to beef up the fence around a couple of the vacant pastures. We hope to move the cattle into them before dark tonight.

"Good." She glanced at her watch, surprised that so much time had passed, mostly in companionable silence and a shared admiration of the natural beauty around the two of them. "I have to go. But I can be here first thing in the morning. Is 8:00 a.m. too early for you?"

"Not at all. I'll have two horses saddled and waiting. Uh, that is, if you ride. We can take ATVs if you'd rather. But we can't really get around the pastures in the truck."

"I can manage to stay on a horse, if you pick me out a nice, gentle one."

He nodded as he drove the truck down a small hill that spilled into the driveway, and right up to where her car was parked. "I've got just the mount for you. Is there anything else you'll need?"

She licked her lips, glanced at her watch, knew she was running out of time and regretted it deeply. She was enjoying this man, and knew she would enjoy the job as well. "Yeah, a whole new wardrobe," she muttered.

He frowned at her.

"Nothing," she said. "I will have to pick up some things before tomorrow though, and I'm a little short on time."

"I won't hold you up, then."

He got out of the truck, and came around to open her door for her, but she was already climbing down. From the nearby barn, she heard the ailing cow bellow soft and low. She felt the poor animal's suffering again. "Has the vet given them anything to ease the symptoms?"

"Yeah, some pink stuff. He says it's basically the same thing we humans take for stomach ache, only in the industrial-strength drum."

She smiled at that. "She got up by herself before we left," she said. "That must be a sign she's feeling at least a little better."

"Or maybe she just liked you." He took her elbow, and started to lead her toward her car. "You know, Doc, you seem awfully familiar to me. Is there any chance we've met before?''

She averted her eyes fast. ''I think I would remember you if we had.''

''It's the oddest thing. I don't suppose you have a sister.''

''Two sisters. Tara and Pheobe.''

''Ahh, so you're one of *those* Lindens,'' he nodded as he said it. ''I wondered.''

She lifted her brows. ''What is that supposed to mean?''

''Nothing. I just know of your family, is all.''

She let it pass, and he said no more.

So she was a Linden. Of the Greenlaurel Lindens. Which explained why she'd shown up for an appointment in a barn, dressed like a fashion model. She could not, *could not* be his Rosie from the rain storm and the garden shed. He knew about the Linden girls. Hell, his grandmother and their grandmother had been trying to match up a Conrad boy with a Linden girl since he was old enough to know the difference between boys and girls. His brothers had been fixed up with her sisters and he had heard the dirt. They were beautiful, but shallow as they came. Ultra concerned about social status, gossip and looking perfect. They went to the right schools, drove the right cars, wore the right clothes, and attended the right functions. They weren't *anything* like his earthy, unpretentious Rosie in the rain.

She would never have shown up in designer shoes to look at sick cows.

And still, the niggling familiarity gnawed at him. He supposed he could have just flat-out asked her. But then again, he wasn't exactly proud of the way he'd behaved with the mystery woman. So on the off chance she might be the one, and she didn't recognize him, he didn't see too much point in confessing his identity as the ravager of innocents in rainy gardens by night.

His telephone rang, cutting off his thoughts, and he picked up the barn extension.

"Mitch, darling, it's your grandmother," she said, as if he wouldn't recognize her voice. "How did the appointment with Dr. Linden go?"

He frowned at the phone, then looked around the barn, half expecting to see her peering down at him from the rafters. "She just left, Grandma. Your timing is...eerie."

She laughed softly. "Don't be silly. Was she helpful at all?"

"Not yet. But she's gonna take some time off work just to devote to this, so chances are she might end up being some help. Tell me, Grandma, why did you pick her?"

Her voice conveyed complete innocence. "Well she's the only botanist I know, dear. And I knew when I saw her at the Bluebonnet Ball that she might be just the person to—"

"She was at the Bluebonnet Ball?"

"Oh, that's right. You were out wandering the

grounds when she arrived. And she didn't stay long. Actually, I'd heard she was visiting the gardens when the storm hit, and got rather soaked."

Mitch swallowed hard. "Where did you hear that?"

"Well, her grandmother is a dear friend of mine you know. She said it ruined her gown, but then again, it was a rather poor choice. Emerald-green and a size too big."

It was *her*. It was his Rosie. His stomach knotted up, and he felt ill. "She, uh…she must have been having an off night."

"Not the first, I'm afraid. Though I understand she has agreed to let her mother and sisters make her over. It's for the best, really. If she wants any social standing at all, not to mention a worthy husband—"

"I have to go, Grandma. I'll keep you posted about the cattle, all right?"

"Darling, wait, I have a favor to ask you. And it's vitally important that you say yes."

He closed his eyes, praying it wouldn't be another setup.

"I need an escort tonight, dear. Now, don't say no. It's not a ball or an opening or anything like that. Just a simple dinner party at the home of a dear friend. Your brother Jeremy was going to take me, but he's had an emergency at the office and—"

"Gram, if this is another fix-up—"

"I swear to you, darling, it's not. It's a small, intimate affair. Please?"

Mitch sighed, and wished he had the willpower to refuse his grandmother anything she asked. But he didn't, and he knew it.

Rosie had limited funds and even less time. So she pulled her VW into a K-mart on the way home, and practically sprinted through the place, buying three pairs of jeans, a handful of five-dollar tank tops in various colors, a package of white ankle socks and a pair of no-name running shoes. The lines were long, though, and it took longer to get through the checkout than it had taken to hurl the items into her cart. Finally, she headed to the car with two plastic shopping bags, and drove straight to her office.

It was late. The staff had left. Just as well. She let herself in, opened the biggest desk drawer, tossed the bags inside, then closed and locked it. She hid the key in a potted male fern, patting a small amount of soil over it, and felt like she was getting away with the crime of the century.

She couldn't do her job while keeping to her end of the bargain with her family. And if it were just a matter of suffering through the inconvenience for a month, she'd have probably stuck it out, but there was more at stake now. Animals were suffering, and she had to be able to work if she was going to help them. She could not do that in designer clothes and flimsy, dressy shoes. *She couldn't.* That was all there was to it.

She drove home, pulling into the driveway with less than an hour to spare before the dinner she was being forced to attend with her well-meaning family.

It was a relief not to find anyone waiting in ambush at her cozy cottage. Instead, there was something far less intrusive; a note from Grandma Marjorie.

Welcome home, darling. I hope you enjoyed your day. Did you notice how differently people respond to you when you dress according to your true status? I'll bet you even carried yourself differently today. Be honest, you did, didn't you?

Sighing, she admitted, silently and to no one but herself, that Grams had a point. She had stood up straighter, held her chin higher and people had been falling over themselves to be nice to her all day long. Sighing, she returned her attention to the note.

Try to be patient, darling. One day is down, leaving only twenty-nine to go. They will pass quickly, and you will learn more about yourself as a result. Try not to be too impatient with your mother and sisters. They love you, and they truly mean well.

We'll pick you up at six for the dinner party. I've taken the liberty of laying out your clothes for the evening, along with a little gift I wanted you to have.

Love always, Grams

Rosie sighed, folded the note, and took it with her into the bedroom. There, she saw a red silk dress, with an A-line neck that ended in a collar that fastened at her nape. The back was bare. The bra made specially to go with the dress, lay beside it, and shoes sat on the floor beside the bed. There was a tiny velvet box with a bow on top resting on her pillow, and she reached for it, opened it and caught her breath.

A pair of earrings with huge teardrop shaped rubies sparkled up at her. Grams had owned them for years. Gosh, she was such a dear, dear woman. How could Rosie possibly disappoint her by begging off tonight, or refusing to wear what she suggested?

She couldn't. And she had a feeling her cagey grandmother knew it.

Chapter 9

"Oh, well, now that's much better," Mitch's grandmother said, standing back and admiring him.

She had wheedled and whined until he'd put on a suit and tie, and made him polish his good boots, which had been sitting in the back of his closet, unworn for so long they'd grown a coat of dust. They were stiff and uncomfortable. He far preferred his everyday boots which he'd worn until they were butter-soft and cozy.

"I thought this was just a casual dinner."

"Mitch, honey, do you even care if you ever find a good woman?"

He averted his eyes. "A good woman wouldn't care how shiny my boots were, Grandma C."

"No. She wouldn't. Not once she got to know you. But darlin' you have to draw her eye. You have to attract her notice. At a first meeting, there's nothing much to go on besides how a person looks. If you're ever gonna have any hope of finding Miss Right, you're gonna have to take my advice. Polish up the surface of that diamond inside you, or she'll walk right by and never notice it shining."

"You're a poet, Grandma. A true poet."

She smiled. "Now come along. You can drive my Lincoln."

"'Cause Miss Right would never see me shining from inside my pickup?"

"Now you're catching on."

He sighed, opened the door for her, then took her to the car and opened its door as well. "Do I dare ask just which Miss Right will be at this dinner tonight?"

She looked up at him from the passenger seat, eyes wide. "Whatever are you talking about, Mitch? This is just a casual dinner party."

"Right. I keep forgetting." He closed her door and went around to the driver's side. And then he headed for the dreaded dinner party.

He spotted her the second he walked in.

Rosie. No, no, he realized as he watched her across the room, it wasn't Rosie. It was Dr. Rosemary Linden. And even if the two were one and the same, they were still completely different. She wore red, elegant, figure-hugging red. Her legs were encased in silk and the matching shoes were spike-heeled and open-toed. Her hair was styled and sprayed so that it barely moved when she did. Her makeup was flawless and huge red stones dangled from her ears. She was standing between her two, equally flawless sisters, and she was more stunningly beautiful than either one of them. She held a drink in her hand, and she laughed at something one of them said, while they beamed their approval at her.

That wasn't Rosie. It wasn't the same woman he'd been making out with in the pouring rain, in the too-big dress and bare feet. And they couldn't both be real. At least, not in his experience, which with women, was admittedly scant.

She spotted him across the room, and her face was still for a moment, then she smiled and waved a cool, polite hello.

You'd have never known that she'd been soaking wet and trembling in his arms only a couple of nights ago.

Rosie had made up her mind on her way to the dinner that she would show them all she could be the woman they were trying to make her. They were overwhelming her with their advice and lectures. It wasn't that she didn't know how to be a socialite—it was that she didn't *want* to be. But she couldn't seem to get that message through to her sisters or her mother. So she had decided the best strategy would be to show them. If she could outshine the debs, out-phony the phonies, and out-socialize the socialites, she figured they would finally have to believe that she *could*. That her lifestyle was a choice, not a handicap.

So she'd been laughing and talking, and sipping champagne. She'd been standing properly, sitting the correct way, rising like a princess, and batting her eyes. And people were responding by milling around her like flies around fertilizer. Ridiculous.

And then, she spotted *him*. Mitch Conrad. He was on the opposite side of the room, watching her, and looking puzzled. She managed to wipe the surprise from her face and give him the same practiced smile she'd been giving everyone else. It took more effort to sustain it when he came walking toward her.

"Hello, Dr. Linden. I had no idea you'd be here tonight." He took her hand, then nodded hello to her sisters. "Tara, Phoebe. You're looking lovely as always."

"Hello, Mitch," Tara said. "How is your family?" Phoebe had only nodded in return, and then sidled away to seek more interesting company.

"Fine, fine. Grandma C is here with me." He nodded in her direction, and Tara looked, too, then gave the older woman a wave.

"I didn't know you and Mitch were acquainted," Tara said, turning her attention to Rosie. And there was something in her eyes. A spark of anger or a warning Rosie couldn't quite interpret.

"Actually, I was out at the Double C just today,"

Rosie admitted. "From the looks of things, I'll be spending most of the week there."

Tara's brows rose. "Really." The word dripped with disapproval.

"Something's been making the cattle sick," Rosie said, falling into a state of ease when discussing her work. "We think it may be something growing in the pastures. It could be a type of hemlock, but I just don't see cattle eating that. It would taste bitter and—" She stopped there, as her sister's forced smile became slightly pained instead. She was clearly boring Tara to tears.

"Well it was nice to see you again, Mitch," Tara said, leaping on the silence like a lizard on a cricket. "Please carry my love to your family." She took Rosie's arm. "I don't mean to pull you away, darling, but Jake was asking for a moment with you. Will you excuse us, Mitch?"

He inclined his head, and Rosie tried to keep smiling as her sister tugged her across the room.

"Tara, that was so rude!" she said when they were out of earshot.

Tara turned to her, a worried look on her face. "Listen, Rosemary, that man will never do."

"*What?*"

"Come on, honey, don't tell me you don't know about him." Rosie only frowned so Tara rushed on. "He's the black sheep of the Conrad clan. Won't have anything to do with the oil business, turns up his nose at his share of the billions, and instead, spends his time running a ranch that barely turns a profit.''

To Tara, Rosie knew, anything less than five hundred grand a year was flirting with poverty. So his ''barely turning a profit'' might actually mean he made a comfortable living. He certainly hadn't shown any qualms when offering to pay her handsomely for her work.

''Every *decent* woman who's dated him has dumped him in short order. He refuses to attend any social functions. He actually works with the cattle—hands-on, building fence and cleaning stalls. It's disgraceful, Rosemary. Don't get mixed up with him.''

''Thanks for the warning, Tara. God forbid the black sheep of the Linden family should get involved with the black sheep of the Conrad family. Next thing you know, we might have a whole flock of little rebel lambs running around, refusing to go to parties and insisting on earning their own livings. And where would we be then?''

Tara frowned, the sarcasm going right over her head. Rosie turned and walked back toward Mitch. He was in conversation with a crowd of others, but he saw her coming, she knew it when his eyes found hers and held them, even while he kept up his end of the discussion. The look made a shiver run up her spine.

''I'm telling you, he's a loser,'' Tara said, coming up behind her and whispering harshly into her ear. "He made a complete ass of himself at the Bluebonnet Ball."

Rosie stopped walking, frowned. "How?"

"Oh, he came slogging in from the gardens, soaking wet, tracking rainwater and dirt all the way across the ballroom floor. Looked like a drowned rat, and he was carrying beer of all things!"

A lump came into Rosie's throat. He was still looking into her eyes.

"I was worried when Jake admitted you'd been out in the rain, too, but he insisted you had been alone and left long before Mitch made his big, wet scene. Thank God. Goodness knows what a man like that might have done with you had he found you out there by yourself."

Suddenly Rosie didn't feel as if she could out-charm the society debs. She felt like a cold, wet, vulnerable dishrag, whose shameful little secret had been fully exposed. He knew perfectly well this persona she was wearing was nothing more than an act. He'd seen her in an ill-fitting dress, getting drunk on two beers and all but sleeping with a stranger in a garden shed.

She felt her face heat and tore her eyes from his.

"Dinner is served," someone announced.

Licking her lips, she turned and started toward the dining room, even while trying to work up her nerve to plead a headache and go home.

Mitch caught up to her, sliding his hand over her elbow. "Are you all right? You look...distressed all of the sudden."

She couldn't look at him. She couldn't. "I'm...fine."

"You don't look fine, Rosie."

She closed her eyes when he called her that. He knew it was her, he had to know. "You're right, I'm not feeling at all well." She tugged her elbow free, and hurried through the entryway doors.

Phoebe called her name, but she didn't stop. "I'm taking your car, Phoebe," she replied. "Please give my apologies to our hosts and see to it Grams gets home all right."

And then she was outside, breathing in the air, letting it cleanse and fill her. This was disastrous. And she had no idea what in the world she was going to do about it.

How could she face the man again, much less go to his ranch and spend hours on end with him every day for the next week or so?

She got into Phoebe's car, found the keys in their usual spot above the visor, and then drove as fast as she could legally drive, all the way back to her cottage.

She locked the door as soon as she was inside, kicked off the shoes, which were killing her anyway, and stripped away the expensive dress on her way to the bathroom. Then she ran a hot, deep bath and shut herself in her tiny bathroom to soak. She wasn't going to come out, she told herself, until she had an answer to her problem.

Eventually, her skin began to prune and the water cooled, and she was still no closer to knowing how to get out of the uncomfortable situation she'd somehow gotten herself into.

Maybe he *didn't* know. Maybe he hadn't recognized her. She supposed that was possible. It had been dark outside that night, and goodness knew she looked different now than she had then. The glasses were gone, and her hair was different.

But he called me Rosie!

He had to know. He had to.

And yet, she kept thinking of that poor, suffering cow with her big, brown eyes, and her own promise to help find the solution. She kept thinking about how much good the promised donation would do the botanical gardens. And above all she kept thinking that, despite everything else, she wanted to see him again.

She supposed she had her sister Tara to thank for that. According to her, Mitch Conrad was a black sheep...just like Rosie.

Chapter 10

Tara and Phoebe arrived before Rosie could finish her morning coffee, and they seemed pleased to find her wearing one of the impractical outfits they'd chosen for her. She'd even applied her own makeup, figuring she was better off putting on a light touch herself. If she didn't do it, her sisters would, and she'd end up wearing far more of the stuff than she wanted.

"You know, you don't need to dress me every morning," she said as she let them come in. "I'm not in grade school. I mastered buttons and zippers long ago."

"Don't be silly, Rosemary," Tara told her as she walked to the kitchen and helped herself to a cup of coffee. "We were worried about you after your hasty retreat from the dinner party last night. That Conrad man said you were feeling ill."

"I was."

"We tried to call," Phoebe told her, "but there was no answer. I wanted to come up and check on you, but Grams insisted you were fine and that we ought to let you be."

"She was right. I took a long soak in a hot bath, and it worked wonders."

Phoebe, who didn't drink coffee, rummaged in the fridge, emerging with a can of diet cola. Breakfast of champions, Rosie thought. "So what was it?" Phoebe asked. "Headache?"

"Yeah."

Tara eyed her as if she doubted it. Still, Rosie didn't think she knew her secret. If Jake had told Tara the true timing of Rosie's soaking wet departure from the ball—which must have been within a few minutes of Mitch's own—Tara would have put two and two together, and she wasn't the type to keep quiet about something like this. Jake must have done a fabulous job covering for Rosie. Leave it to Jake to be scrupulously trustworthy.

"Look, guys, I have to get an early start this morning," Rosie said, pushing those thoughts aside.

"Still going out to the Double C?" Tara asked.

Rosie nodded. "That's right."

Tara rolled her eyes. "He's a womanizer, Rosie. He'll use you for a few weeks and drop you like a hot potato or offend you so deeply that you drop him. That's what he does with women. God, ask anyone if you don't think his track record speaks for itself."

Rosie didn't really want to discuss Mitch Conrad with her sisters, so she snatched up a bag, irritated that it matched her suit, and headed for the door. "Lock up when you leave, okay?"

She didn't wait for a response.

Twenty minutes later she was in her office, with the door closed. She took a pair of jeans, a tank top, the running shoes and a pair of socks from the bag in her desk drawer, and stuffed them into her briefcase. Then she left again, heading straight to her favorite fast-food joint, where she used the rest room to change clothes.

As a final act of rebellion, she found a hair band, and pulled her lighter-and-curlier-than-before hair into a ponytail, and surveyed herself in the mirror with a sigh of satisfaction. She almost looked like herself again.

Finally, she continued her drive out to the Double C. If she had to face the man, knowing that he was the one, and that he probably knew who she was, at least she would do so at her best. Her feet practically sang in gratitude for the soft sneakers cushioning them.

* * *

Mitch was ready and waiting when she arrived. And he almost melted at the sight of her. She wore jeans and sneakers. He greeted her with a happy "Good morning" as she got out of her car. For some reason though, she couldn't seem to hold his gaze.

"You feeling better?" he asked.

"Fine." She licked her lips. "Look, you don't really need to come out with me. I'm sure you have things you'd rather be doing, and—"

"Nope."

"Oh." She glanced up, then away. "It's just that it seems silly for you to spend the day guiding me around the place. You've already shown me the parts in question. And if I need more directions, you could have someone else come along and—"

"What's going on, Rosie?" he asked. She fell silent. "What's changed since yesterday?"

"Nothing. Let's just...get on with this."

He sighed. "You finally figured out it was me, that night at the ball, didn't you?"

Her eyes fell closed, and her cheeks went pink. "I...wasn't sure you'd figured out it was me."

"I wasn't sure when I first saw you again. You were so different. The clothes, the hair."

She cleared her throat. "Not like the kind of woman who'd drink beer from a bottle and make out with a stranger in the dark?"

"Not like the woman I met in the gardens that night."

"That's what I said." She turned away from him and started toward the stables.

He caught up with her easily, fell into step beside her. "Rosie, I know I got out of line that night. I'm sorry for that."

She kept on walking.

"I came on too strong, and scared you away, and I've been kicking myself for it ever since. I wish I'd acted differently."

"The results would have been the same, Mitch. I don't sleep with men in rainstorms."

He stopped walking. "Damn, do you really think that's what I meant? That I wish I'd used a different approach so I could have taken it further?"

"Isn't it?"

"No." She just kept walking as he stood there trying to digest her words. He had to run a few steps to catch up. "What I meant was that I wished we'd just talked, maybe danced a little or something. Listen, I didn't react to you the way I did because I thought you were easy."

She shrugged. "Then it must have been the beer." She was at the stable now, where two horses stood saddled and ready near the hitching post in the front. "Which one is mine?"

He nodded toward the chestnut mare, and she climbed into the saddle before he could even offer her a leg up. He mounted his own horse, a spirited black gelding, and started off toward the north pasture. After they'd ridden in silence for a few minutes, he said, "It wasn't the beer."

"Mitch, can we not talk about this? It's really uncomfortable for me."

He clenched his jaw, sighed. "So what are we supposed to do, then? Pretend it never happened?"

"Works for me."

He didn't know how the hell he was supposed to do that. He hadn't been able to get her out of his mind since she'd vanished on him. And something—either gut instinct or stubborn pride—told him she couldn't forget it that easily, either.

"So what's with the new look?"

"How do you know it's new?"

He sighed. She was being stubborn. "If you hadn't needed your glasses, you wouldn't have worn them to the ball. So I'm guessing you recently got some contacts. Your hair is lighter, and curlier than before, and if you'd been in the habit of wearing makeup, you'd have certainly worn it that night."

She wouldn't look at him. "Is that the pasture where we planned to start?" she asked, pointing ahead.

"Yeah. The gate's open, we can ride right through."

She heeled her horse, riding ahead of him, then

easing the mare along the very edges of the pasture, where the grasses ended and small trees and brush grew up. "You don't fence off the wooded areas?" she asked.

"Not entirely. The cattle like the shade of the trees."

"Makes sense." She rode slowly, in the lead now, with him right behind her. Finally she stopped the horse, and climbed down, leading the mare as she walked along, slightly bent, peering at every weed, wildflower and clump of brush.

"My, uh, my grandmother thinks you're making yourself over to attract a rich, society husband. Is that true?"

Rosie's head snapped toward him. "Maybe I'm just making myself over so as not to attract men who think they can bed me in dirty sheds."

He lowered his head, because that shot hit dead on target. "I'd have never let it go that far, Rosie."

"You'd never have tried even that much with any of the other women there that night," she said. "You said it yourself, I was nothing like the *ladies* dancing in the ballroom."

"What I meant by that was that you were not a phony like those other women. That you were honest, unpretentious." He sighed. "But maybe I was wrong about that, huh? Probably just wishful thinking on my part. God knows it wouldn't be the first time."

She stood still for a long moment. Finally, she turned to face him, swallowed hard. "The truth is, I'm embarrassed by the way I behaved that night, and I'm taking it out on you. I shouldn't be. No one's to blame for my behavior but me. Still, Mitch, I really would be more comfortable if we could just forget it."

He stared into her eyes, stunned by her yet again. She was direct, pulled no punches and, apparently, was straight-up honest to boot. He liked that about her, and decided to respond in kind—with straight-up honesty. "To tell you the truth, Rosie Linden, I don't think I'll *ever* forget that night. For the record, I don't behave that way either, not as a rule. But you—there was just something about you that knocked me right outta my boots."

She averted her eyes and her face colored again. It sounded like a line, even to his own ears. He was blowing this, big time.

"All right," he said. "If you really want me to, I'll stop talking about it. For now, at least."

"Guess I'll take what I can get." She turned again, walked a few more steps, and then bent to her knees, releasing the horse's reins. She gripped a vine that was twisting around one of the fence posts, way down near its base, and tugged its roots from the soil. Then she unwound it carefully.

"What's that?" he asked.

"Ten to one, it's the source of your problem."

She held it out to him, and he saw its deep green leaves.

"What is it?"

"Atropa Belladonna," she said. "Its folk name is Deadly Nightshade. It's related to eggplant and tobacco—even contains nicotine. The berries that grow in the fall are only slightly toxic, but the leaves contain some pretty potent chemicals including atropine. It has a narcotic affect."

"So what do we do?" he asked, examining the plant.

"First, you call your vet, let him know what we've found. If he knows what's causing the trouble, he can more effectively treat the cattle that are already ill."

"And then?"

"And then, get every hand you can, round them up and bring them out here. We're going to have to go over every inch of this ranch, and it's gonna take more than the two of us to do it. But before they can begin, the men need to know what it is they're looking for."

He nodded, studying her for a long moment.

"What?"

"You, uh, you're really good at your job, aren't you?"

For the first time since she'd arrived, she smiled fully. "You know, I really am."

He smiled back. "You truly are different from

other women, Rosie. And I mean that as a compliment."

"Then I'll take it as one."

They mounted up and rode back to the main barn. Mitch asked his foreman to round up the men. They gathered outside the barn, twenty-two men, besides Mitch, with one small woman in the center of them, holding a plant up the way someone else might hold up a killer rattler they'd bagged.

"This is what we're looking for. It's known as Belladonna or Deadly Nightshade. It likes to cling to things as it grows, so you'll find it near outbuildings, twined around poles and fence posts, or other plants and trees. Wear your gloves, this stuff is highly toxic, and as sick as these cows are, I'm guessing you'll be handling a lot of it." She set the plant aside, accepting a wet cloth from Mitch and wiping her hands. "You need to pull it up by the roots, then put it into a trash bag, and move on. Get every plant you see."

The men nodded and muttered.

Mitch said, "Take a few bags each, so you don't have to keep coming back. When your bag gets full, tie it up and leave it along the fence line. We'll collect them all when we finish."

Rosie jumped in once again. "It's probably best not to take the horses," she said. "They might decide to nibble while you work, and end up as sick as the cattle."

"Good thinking," Mitch said. "Is everyone ready?"

Everyone was. The men paired up and headed out, several taking ATVs, others piling into pickups or setting off on foot. Mitch preferred to work with Rosie, and he couldn't deny his sigh of relief when she didn't object to his walking along beside her yet again.

"This way," he said, leading her right up to his own ATV, a tough-looking red four-wheeler. He climbed aboard and patted the seat behind him.

Looking doubtful, she got on. Mitch started the engine, shifted into gear with his foot, and the machine lurched forward. Rosie's arms closed around his waist, just as he had hoped they would, and he drove them back to the north pasture.

He noticed that the faster he drove, and the more bumps he managed to hit, the more tightly Rosie would cling to him. He was nowhere near honorable enough not to take advantage of that. He liked this woman. He wasn't sure who she was yet, or what she really wanted in life, much less in a man, but he knew what he wanted.

He wanted Rosie Linden.

So he squeezed the accelerator a little harder, and hit all the bumps and holes he could find along the way.

Chapter 11

Rosie spent the entire day working side by side with Mitch. The day grew hot, and the work was dirty. By the time noon rolled around she was sweaty and her hands were covered in soil, but she felt better than she had in ages. And during the entire time, he never brought up the subject of her indiscretion on the night of the ball again. He kept to his word. In fact, he was a perfect gentleman.

At lunchtime, he drove her back to his charming house on the teeth-jarring four-wheeler, and led her inside. "There's a bathroom through there if you want to wash up," he told her, pointing the way.

"Thanks." She took his suggestion, wondering if the fact that he hadn't hit on her again was a sign that he was no longer interested, or an attempt to convince her that he wasn't the womanizer people thought he was. She wished she knew.

When she returned, he led her through the house, and out through a set of sliding glass doors she hadn't seen before, onto a large concrete patio in the rear. Picnic tables were set up, and some of the men were already helping themselves to the food heaped on them. Platters of sandwiches, bowls of chips with dip and dewy pitchers of iced tea lined the tables.

She blinked at Mitch in surprise. "You didn't have time to do all this. Do you have a cook?"

He nodded, waving her to an empty spot on the bench. "Not full-time or anything. Just when things get really busy."

Rosie sat down, and Mitch sat beside her. It wasn't a fancy meal, but it was a pleasant one. And halfway through, Mitch's grandmother, Ida Conrad showed up. "There you are!" she said. "I should have known I'd find you out here."

Mitch got up and went to his grandmother, gave her a hug, and led her to a bench. "There are still some sandwiches left, if you're hungry," he said.

"I'm dining at the country club in an hour, dear. I just wanted to stop on the way by and see how your little project was going." She glanced down at Rosie. "Hello, dear. Have you managed to solve my grandson's problems yet?"

Rosie got to her feet to be polite, even as the foreman, Sam, paused in eating to yell, "Heck, it would take a team of shrinks to solve your grandson's problems. But she did manage to figure out what's been making the cattle sick."

Rosie laughed. She couldn't quite hold it back. Mitch sent her a look. "Oh, you think that's funny, do you?"

She shrugged, fought the lingering smile, and took his grandmother's hand. "Good to see you, too, Mrs. Conrad. We found Belladonna growing in some of the pastures, and I'm betting that's the problem."

"The woman's a genius," Sam called.

Ida ignored him. "Well, that was fast work."

"Not hardly," Mitch said. "Rosie's gonna be here all week, helping us find and pull up every single vine."

"I knew she could help you." Ida sighed. "Thank you, dear. You've no idea how upsetting this has been for poor Mitchell. He hasn't been himself since—why since the cows first started showing symptoms—the very morning after the ball, in fact." She leaned closer, speaking in a lower, conspiratorial tone to Rosie. "He was so out of sorts that I thought at first some female had finally managed to get under his skin." She smiled brightly as she said it. "But alas, just the cows again." Then she blinked at her grandson, and Rosie recognized the look of feigned innocence, having seen it so often in her own grandma's eyes. "Speaking of females, did you ever figure out the identity of the one you kept asking about after the ball? The girl in the green dress?"

Mitch jumped to his feet. "Uh, Grandma, I'd love to sit and gossip with you, but we really do have to get back to work."

"Of course, darling." She leaned up, pecked him on the cheek. "I'll be on my way."

"I'll walk you out," Rosie blurted, and when Mitch shot her a curious look she added, "I, uh, need to get some more sunblock out of my car. I'm starting to burn."

Ida smiled knowingly, hooked an arm through Rosie's and marched her away. As soon as they were out of earshot, Ida said, "You wanted a private word with me, yes?"

"Yes," Rosie said. "Mrs. Conrad, I know you're very close with my grandmother, so you're probably aware of the…the project my family has underway. The one to remake me."

She smiled. "I am aware of it. I've been wishing I had the pull with Mitch to do something similar, but he's far too headstrong. He'll never land a woman worthy of the Conrad name unless he changes his ways, I'm afraid."

Rosie frowned. "You'll forgive me for being

blunt, but according to gossip, he has no shortage of female companionship.''

Ida tipped her head to one side. "Only until he brings them here.'' She looked around the house and sighed. "This is hardly the lifestyle most suitable women would find tempting. When the wind blows just right, the scent of cattle just wafts over the entire place.'' She shook her head. "No, every time my grandson even begins to get interested in a female, she takes one look at this ranch, and him mucking about with his cattle, and drops him like the proverbial day-old fish. The poor boy has been jilted more times than I can count. I'm afraid he's all but given up on females.''

She smiled at Rosie. "But my hope was renewed when I saw how utterly forlorn he was after the ball. Some girl in green had his head spinning, and he didn't know who she was or how to find her. But I've veered off the subject. You wanted to ask me not to tell your grandmother about the way you're dressed today. Correct?''

Rosie shook herself back to the subject at hand. "You're too smart for me,'' she said. "That's exactly what I wanted to ask you. My family means well, but what they don't realize is that I can't do my job in designer clothes and impractical shoes. I did give my word that I'd let them use me as their personal fashion doll for a month, but that was before I knew I'd be taking on this project for Mitch.''

Ida sighed dramatically, looking Rosie up and down, from her dirt-stained denim knees to her untidy ponytail. "I can certainly see the logic in dressing down for this job," she said. "I think your grandmother would, too, dear. But I'll give you this much—unless she asks me directly, I won't breathe a word. All right?"

"I can't ask for more than that. Thank you, Mrs. Conrad."

"You're more than welcome, child."

As she watched the woman go, Rosie thought about what she had learned. Of course, most of it should probably be taken with a grain of salt. Mitch was obviously much beloved by his grandmother. But it did make sense, when she put it all together. He never saw any single woman for more than a few weeks at a time, that was factual enough. But if they'd been dumping him, rather than the other way around, and because of his lifestyle and income, instead of some horrible behavior on his part, then he might not be the player Tara assumed he was. It was kind of sad, when she thought about it, to think that he'd repeatedly fallen for women who would not have him because of who he was. He loved his ranch. He loved his cattle. What was so awful about that?

Of course, Ida Conrad had made a point to mention, more than once, that it was a "suitable" woman she had in mind for Mitch. Not that it mattered to Rosie.

On the third day of the project, Mitch and Rosie had completed work in the first pasture and were moving on to the second, when an ATV came roaring up to where they knelt, tugging up vines by the roots. Sam got off and came running toward them.

"What's wrong?" Mitch could tell by his face that something was happening.

"It's Daisy. The calf is coming."

"Now? It's early yet!"

"I know, and she's still weak, but she's ready, Mitch. I've already called Dr. Wallace. He's out on an emergency call, but he'll get here as soon as he can."

Mitch turned to Rosie. "I have to—"

"Let's go," she said.

He frowned a little. "It's not a neat process, Rosie."

She looked at her soiled hands. "Like *this* has been, you mean? Let's just go."

With a nod, he got on his ATV. Rosie jumped on behind him and held on as they bounded back to the barn.

Daisy bellowed at him even as he walked in. Hell, the poor thing was just starting to get her strength back after being so sick from the toxic weeds. He wasn't sure she'd get through this. "It's all right, girl,'' he told her, rushing past her stall to the washroom off the rear of the barn. There he rolled up his sleeves and scrubbed his hands with antiseptic soap in a large stainless steel sink. Rosie did as he did, without being told. He pulled on a pair of latex gloves from a dispenser mounted to the wall. She did likewise. When they emerged, and returned to the stall, Sam was standing beside the animal, talking to her.

"Go ahead and wash up, Sam," Mitch said. "Any word from the vet?"

"They reached him by mobile phone. He'll be out as soon as he can."

Rosie walked into the stall, too, stroking the cow's neck and face. "There now, we're all here for you, girl. You'll be all right."

Sam dashed back to the washroom. Mitch walked to the back of the cow to check her progress. "Ahh, hell…"

"What is it?" Rosie asked.

"We have forefeet and a nose visible." He called to Sam as the foreman came back through the barn. "How long has she been like this?"

"The last time she was checked was 8:00 a.m. It was the new kid, Mitch. I don't think he realized how close she was. He didn't know to check her for dilation."

Mitch closed his eyes. "I should've checked her

myself. Dammit, she could have been like this all day.''

The cow moaned softly, down deep, and just let herself drop. She landed heavily on her side in the soft hay, breathing fast.

''She seems exhausted already,'' Rosie said.

''Which means she's been struggling to push this calf out for a while now.'' Mitch crouched behind her. ''If we can't get the little one out, it won't survive. Daisy might not either way. We have to help her.''

''How?'' Rosie asked. She was kneeling now, at the cow's side. She stroked her gently.

''When she pushes, we pull,'' Mitch said. ''Sam, give me a hand back here. Rosie, put your hands down low on her belly. When it feels like she's trying to push, tell us.''

She did so. Then, frowning at the gloves, she peeled them off and replaced her hands on the cow's distended underbelly. Rosie waited, her expression intense. She was utterly focused, concentrating fully on the animal. ''Now!''

Mitch gripped the slippery forelegs and pulled, gently but steadily. The nose emerged just a little farther.

''Okay, stop. Wait,'' Rosie said. She stroked Daisy, spoke to her. ''What a good girl you are. You can do this. Yes, you can. You'll be all right. Okay, she's pushing again!''

Mitch kept up the pressure, just enough to keep the calf where it was, then pulled some more when Rosie gave the word. The nose emerged farther. The forelegs were out enough now so that Sam could get a grip, too.

The pushing and pulling went on and on. For two hours they worked with the calf, gaining only inches, and still no sign of the vet. The head was out, but the widest part of the calf was at the front shoulders, and the poor mother was worn out.

"She's barely pushing anymore, Mitch," Rosie said, "but the contractions are almost constant." The cow flung her head down on the hay, rolling her eyes and panting.

Mitch and Sam pulled still harder, not letting up now, knowing they had stretched this down to the wire. It had to be now or never. Finally the calf's shoulders came clear.

The slippery baby slid out in a rush, and Mitch and Sam stumbled backward with the sudden release. They quickly righted themselves and leaned over the newborn.

"It's not moving," Rosie said. "Mitch, is it...?"

Mitch pried the little jaws open and cleared its mouth. Then he rubbed the little body hard. Finally, a hoarse bleat emerged. The baby blinked its huge brown eyes, and bleated again, and then it started trying to get up.

Sam got up, peeled off his gloves and ran out of the stall.

"How's Daisy doing?" Mitch asked.

"She wants to see her baby."

He looked away from the calf, to see Daisy, lifting her head, looking toward where he was with the calf. He picked the little one up in his arms, and carried it to where its mother could reach it, to lick the newborn clean. Then he peeled off his gloves and stood there, watching.

"Is she going to be all right?" Rosie asked, getting to her feet as well.

"I think so." As he said it, the little calf stood up, fell down again, then tried a second time. As he did, the valiant mother struggled to her feet, and then stood while her calf found his way to her udder and began nursing for the first time. "Yep, I think they're both gonna be just fine." He smiled, glancing down at Rosie.

She had hay in her hair, and tears on her cheeks.

"Are you crying?" he asked, amazed.

"Well of course I'm crying. I've...never seen anything that scary—or that beautiful—in my whole life." And without a word of warning, she turned right into his arms. He closed them around her automatically, and hers twisted around his waist.

He held her there for a long moment, and when she lifted her head to look up at him, he couldn't keep himself from kissing her. It was long, and slow, and tender. His lips melded with hers, moved over them, and she let them part gently when he urged her to. Her body pressed to his and she held on tight. Every part of her returned the kiss. Every part of him relished it in a way he'd never relished a simple kiss in his life. He tasted her tears, and he knew that this woman was the only woman in the world he wanted. Ever.

"Ahem."

They drew apart almost guiltily. Sam had returned with a pail of clean, slightly warm water, which he set down in front of Daisy. Daisy drank deeply, and someone from outside shouted, "The vet's here!"

Mitch met Rosie's eyes, returned her smile, and felt arrows piercing his heart.

Chapter 12

All week long, Mitch got to spend all day, every day, with Rosie Linden, and frankly, the more time he spent with her, the harder he fell. She was funny, she was smart and she was honest.

He even let his grandmother drag him to social functions and gatherings every night of the week, because without fail, Rosie would be there, as well. But not the same Rosie he knew by day. A different woman entirely, dressed to the nines and perfectly made-up, constantly flanked by her sisters, or her mother, or her grandmother, or all four. They watched her constantly, and he'd taken note of the disapproving glances he received whenever they caught him paying undue attention to her.

He was completely confused as to what he was supposed to do, how he was supposed to proceed. And finally, in desperation, he decided to ask the one person who might be able to help.

"My boy, you are working far too hard," Grandma C said as she stared across the table at him. He'd invited her to dinner at her favorite French restaurant, and he suspected that she already knew why. "You look exhausted."

"It's not the work. I'm used to work. It's…"

"It's Rosemary Linden," she said, guessing correctly.

He sighed. "I know perfectly well you've been conspiring to throw us together," he said. "And for once I don't even mind. I like her. I might even more than like her. But I just don't think I can stand to see this thing end up like all those other times."

"Why not?"

He frowned at her.

"What's different about this time than all those other times, darling?"

Mitch thought hard. "*She* is. She's what's different. It means more this time."

Grandma Ida smiled and nodded. "You're in love with the girl."

He looked away, shaking his head. "I haven't even been around her long enough for—"

"Oh, don't be ridiculous, Mitch. Love doesn't depend on time."

"I just...I don't know what she wants."

"She wants the same things any other woman wants."

He sighed. "That's what I'm afraid of, I guess."

"You needn't be. Listen, Mitchell, let me help you. There's a ball at the Somers' estate this Saturday night. Far more formal than the Bluebonnet Ball, this is white tie and tails. I know for a fact that your Rosemary will be going."

His head came up fast. "She will?"

"Yes. And it will be the perfect opportunity for you to show her that you can outshine the most polished gentlemen in this entire state. *If* you'll let me help you."

He sighed. White tie and tails were not his thing. But if it would help him win Rosie—hell, if he had to change in order to keep this woman in his life, then he could change. He would. She meant that much to him. And he realized, with a little surprise, that no other woman ever had.

"But, Rosemary, darling," Grandma Marjorie pleaded. "This ball is the event of the summer!"

"Like every other event you've insisted I attend?" Rosie asked. She was tired and she was bored with the nightly excursions. If not for Mitch's inevitable presence at them, they'd have been unbearable. She'd finished her work with Mitch out at the Double C now. His sick cattle were healthy again, and his pastures were free of Deadly Night-shade. His men could recognize the plant on sight now, and would be on constant guard against new growth.

Rosie was battling a feeling of depression and knowing full well it was because she no longer had reason to spend her days with Mitch Conrad.

"Mitch is going to be at this ball, you know."

"He is?" Her head snapped up.

"I knew it!" Grandma said. "You *are* interested in Mitchell Conrad."

Rosie shrugged, and averted her eyes. "Everyone else in this family keeps telling me he's all wrong, completely unsuitable."

"Yes, well, I've lived a good deal longer than any of them and I have it on good authority that he's working hard to make himself perfectly suitable."

Rosie couldn't imagine what on earth that meant. "I can't believe he's going. He positively *hates* those sorts of things."

"Perhaps he does, dear, but he's a Conrad. He has a certain image to uphold, and goodness knows it's long past time he settled down with a suitable woman."

There was that phrase again. "I wish someone would tell me exactly what 'suitable' might mean."

Grandma shrugged. "To land a man from a fam-ily like the Conrads, a woman has to put forth some—extra effort. That's all. Exactly the way we've been coaching you to do all along. It's all about appearances, dear.''

Rosie pouted. She disliked putting on airs, and had suffered through it reluctantly for her family's sake. But her heart had never been in it. Still, she wanted to regain Mitch's notice. Aside from that one, soul-shattering kiss in the barn, he hadn't made an inappropriate move. Damn him. Maybe it was because she wasn't ''suitable.''

''Let me get you ready for the ball,'' Grandma Marjorie went on. ''Oh, darling, with what I have in mind that man won't know what hit him when he sees you there. He already likes you. This ball could be the night you show him that you are exactly the kind of woman he's waited all his life to find.''

She searched her grandmother's face. ''You... really think so?''

''His grandmother is one of my best friends, darling. I know so.''

Sighing, Rosie nodded.

It was sheer hell, she thought as they prepared her. A corset so tight she could barely breathe, long white gloves and three people working on her hair all at the same time were enough to make her scream. And the gown—oh, God the gown. She might not like pretense, but she didn't think anyone with a Y chromosome could have found fault with the gown.

When they finished with her, and allowed her a glimpse in the full-length mirror, Rosie almost wept. She felt like Cinderella. The gown had layers of sheer white, with something woven into the fabric that made it glitter. Its sweetheart neckline, combined with the corset, gave her cleavage she'd never known she had, and the full skirt made her feel feminine and beautiful. Her neck seemed longer and more graceful than it ever had, and her hair was piled up with curling bits allowed to drape around her face. Diamonds dangled from her ears and encircled her throat.

"Is that really me?"

No, a little voice inside her whispered.

"Yes," said Tara, while her mother and Phoebe and Grams nodded in agreement.

Mitch's collar chafed, the cummerbund was awkward and the tails felt ridiculous. The shoes were so shiny they blinded him when the light hit them just so, and he was bored to tears with the stunningly dressed people at the ball. Rosie still hadn't arrived, and he was beginning to think he'd been tricked.

But then she showed up, and every eye in the room turned toward her when she walked in. She stood in the wide archway at one end of the ballroom, and Mitch suddenly realized he'd stopped breathing. "My God," he whispered.

A lot of people were whispering, he noticed all at once. And a lot of men were staring at her as hard as he was. There was no time to lose. He all but ran across the room, even as a crowd of people closed in around her, and he forgot all the manners Grandma had been trying to pound into his head, as he shouldered his way through her admirers to get to her.

And then he was there, with no one in between them, and she was staring at him, and he forgot to breathe all over again.

"Hi, Mitch," she said.

"I...you..." He clenched his jaw, cleared his throat, and started over. "You look incredible."

She smiled. "Thank you."

"Dance?"

She nodded, and he took her hand and led her onto the dance floor. Then he pulled her into his arms and he held her close. He inhaled her scent, and he absorbed her warmth, and he knew that no matter what he had to do, it would be worth it to keep this woman by his side. His hands rested at the small of her back. Hers twined around his neck. She rested her body against his, and he felt as if they were one person, their hearts beating in perfect time.

"I'm so glad you're here," he told her.

"Me, too."

"I've missed you, Rosie."

"I've missed you, too, Mitch."

"We need to talk."

She nodded against his chest. "Yes. It's high time."

When the music ended, he didn't let her go. Instead, he drew her outside, into the rose garden, where other couples wandered, or sat in intimate silence. He found an isolated spot, with a small bench and eased her onto it. Then, still standing, he cleared his throat he said, "I'm thinking about selling the ranch."

Rosie blinked at him as if she were stunned.

"I could join my father and brothers at Conrad Oil. I'd make a ton of money there and—"

She jumped to her feet. "Mitch, what the hell are you talking about?"

He blinked. "Don't worry. I mean, I wouldn't let it go to land developers the way David Castlemane and his creepy assistants are doing with the land he inherited. I think that's a crying shame. No, I'd find someone who wanted to use the land, keep the ranch going. And then I could—"

She backed away from him, shaking her head slowly. "I thought I was starting to know you, Mitch. My God, when you said we had to talk, I thought you were going to—" She bit her lip, not finishing her sentence. "But the man telling me

he's made this ridiculous decision isn't the man I
just spent the past week with. God, why would you
even consider doing something like this? You told
me you'd never do it. That there was nothing worth
enough to you that you'd give up your ranch for it.
Nothing.''

"I finally found something," he said. He drew a
breath, and reaching out, closed his hands on her
shoulders. "I need to make this change," he said.
"Because I want to be the kind of man a woman
like Rosemary Linden could consider…marrying.''

She blinked at him, but didn't say a word. And
then to his utter shock and surprise, tears welled up
in her eyes.

"Oh, Mitch…"

"You're crying. God, I messed this up. I
wanted—''

She held up a hand to stop him. Then she turned,
and ran away. On the way, she almost collided with
his grandmother, whom, he thought, had deliberately placed herself in Rosie's path. She spoke to
her quickly, briefly, and then she continued out the
door.

Mitch went after her, but his grandmother
stopped him.

"Gram, not now. I have to—''

"What on earth did you do to that girl, Mitchell
Conrad?" Grandma asked.

"I asked her to marry me.''

Her scowl faded. "Oh? That's lovely! And… what did she say?"

He shook his head. "I think her retreat probably says it all." His heart was crushed, and he hung his head.

"Don't be so sure about that, darling. She told me not to let you leave. Said to tell you she'd be back with her answer."

He looked up slowly, his stomach knotting. "Is she trying to kill me or just drive me insane?"

"I guess there's only one way to find out. Get me some punch, dear, and go find a safe place to pace."

Chapter 13

Mitch did as his grandmother suggested. He paced. Rosie was gone for nearly an hour, and every minute ticked by with excruciating slowness.

He tried looking over the ballroom, with its chandeliers and white-tie wearing waiters, and champagne fountain. He'd never been to, or even heard of, an event this formal before. He tried listening to the string quartet with its classical music. He tried watching the other couples dancing and talking and avoiding him like the plague.

Nothing worked to ease the ache, or take the sharp edge off the anticipation. He was dying!

And then, she made her entrance. And what an entrance it was. She appeared in the archway, right where she had been before. Only this time, she was wearing a pair of jeans, and a pretty silk blouse that buttoned down the front. No jewelry, and her face was scrubbed clean. Her hair was loose and fell around her shoulders softly, its recently acquired curls having relaxed into more natural-looking waves. He remembered seeing it blow in the Texas breeze when they'd gone out on horseback together. He remembered seeing her, smeared in dirt and sweat and laughing about it.

She spoke to the tuxedoed fellow Mitch thought of as "the butler" and she seemed to be insistent on whatever it was she said. The butler finally nodded, cleared his throat and announced her. "Ms. Rosie Linden."

Anyone who hadn't already been staring at her, turned to do so now. People gaped, and whispered to each other as Rosie stood there smiling.

Then, she walked right up to Mitch, never hesitating, even when her sister Tara asked in a loud whisper just what the hell she thought she was doing, while Tara's fiancé, Jake, smiled approvingly at his future sister-in-law.

"Rosie," Mitch said as she eased up close to him and slid her arms around his neck. "What in the world are you up to?"

"Dancing with you…uh, that is, I will be, once you make yourself 'suitable.'" She pulled her arms from around his neck, tugged his white tie loose, and tossed it to the floor. Then she unbuttoned the tailed jacket, and threw it aside as well. Reaching her arms around his waist, which turned him on to no end, she unfastened the cummerbund, and let it drop to the floor. "Kick off those shoes, cowboy."

He obeyed, catching on now, or he hoped to God he was. Then he wrapped her up tight, and held her close, dancing her around the room in his sock feet. And she said, "Now, about that sorry excuse for a marriage proposal...." She let her voice trail off.

"God, Rosie, don't keep me in suspense. You're killing me with this."

"Well, I have a few conditions, is all. First and foremost, there is no way in hell you're gonna sell that ranch, or join up with any family business. You love that ranch. I love it, too, you know."

"You do?"

"Oh, yeah. You know, my family has been trying to make me over, so I'd be good enough for a suitable man. But I don't want a suitable man. I want you, Mitchell Conrad. And the only thing you have to promise me is that you will never, ever ask me to pretend to be something I'm not."

"Why would I do that when I'm head over heels in love with the woman you are?"

She smiled, and kissed him full on the mouth.

Mitch tugged her locket from his pants pocket, snapped it around her neck. "I've been meaning to give this back to you,'' he said. ''I fell in love with the little girl inside it the first time I saw her.''

She touched the little heart at the end of the chain. ''I'm glad you gave it back to me, Mitch. I'm gonna need that free spot in the other side, to hold our wedding picture.''

He kissed her long and hard, and he didn't give a damn that it was a kiss far too intimate to be shared in polite company.

* * * * *

A MATTER OF DUTY

Eileen Wilks

This is for all the quiet heroes—
the soldiers and the bureaucrats, the clerks,
the secretaries and the sailors. Postal workers.
Embassy personnel. People who process forms
as well as those who handle M-16s. People in
uniform and out, whose work goes unseen
by the rest of the country. Thank you.

Chapter 1

"The Belles of Texas Historic Society proudly announces their annual Bluebonnet Ball, to be held at the Silverwood Estate this Saturday. All proceeds will go to support the Greenlaurel State Park and Preserve. For more information, contact…"

Aiden Swift paused just inside the wide entry. The ballroom was large, lavish and crowded. People milled around the tables that lined three out of four walls and flooded the open area in the center that would later be used for dancing. A band occupied the dais against the fourth wall; chandeliers sparkled overhead.

He didn't see the face he was searching for—a face he hadn't seen in over twelve years. He *did* automatically catalog the exits.

"French doors at the back open into the gardens," the woman beside him murmured. "There's a door to the kitchen in the interior wall at the back. It leads to a short hall, no exits but the kitchen and the ballroom."

Aiden smiled down at her. He didn't need to look down far to meet her eyes. Dr. Alexis Sullivan was a long, lean blonde only a few inches below his own six feet. "I'm glad you haven't forgotten everything I taught you."

"However unnecessary it may be for you now," Alex agreed.

And it was, of course. But habits that had kept him alive for over twelve years weren't likely to evaporate overnight.

"Now that the two of you have found the best spots for defense or evacuation if we come under attack," the man on the other side of Alex said dryly, "shall we find our table?"

Alex gave a ladylike snort. "As if you didn't do the same thing."

In unspoken agreement, the three of them moved on into the crowded ballroom. Aiden collected a flute of champagne from a passing waiter as he listened to the playful bickering the other two enjoyed. An outside observer might think Alex and

Jared didn't behave like proper newlyweds, but Aiden could hear the exhilaration underlying the words they batted back and forth. To his eyes they were clearly intoxicated by each other, made giddy by the sheer improbability of the happiness they'd found.

Not that many people were likely to call either of them giddy. Jared Sullivan was too damned big, for one thing. A good man in a fight, Aiden suspected, though he'd never worked with him. And never would, he reminded himself. He was out of the game now. The idea still seemed vaguely unreal.

"Alexis, that dress is fabulous. Where did you find it?" A plump blond woman with diamonds almost as impressive as her barely contained breasts put a hand on Alex's arm, stopping her. Aiden and Jared perforce stopped, too.

"New York," Alex said. "Molly, this—"

"I should have known. And is that also where you found your second gorgeous escort? Too greedy, love! You're not allowed to keep them *both.*" So saying, she linked her arm in Aiden's, slanting him a roguish smile out of eyes that didn't take any of this seriously.

Pretty eyes they were, too, even if they were twenty years older than his. "Am I being kidnapped?" he asked mildly.

"But of course. Resistance is futile."

"Molly," Alex said firmly, "this is Aiden Swift, an old friend and my guest, not my escort. Aiden, your abductor is Molly Dupois. Her husband's name is Rex Dupois. He's the silver-haired man heading this way with a frown on his face."

"So he is," Molly said, sounding pleased. "I thought I might pry him loose from his boring old business discussions, but I didn't expect it to work so quickly." She patted Aiden on the arm. "You are *excellent* ammunition, sweetie."

"I've been used," he said sadly. "Used and cast aside."

When the older man joined them, however, so did a couple of others, and it didn't take long for the conversation to veer into the realms Molly deplored. The ball was a charity event, after all, sponsored and attended by people with money. People who had lost some of that money after news broke about the World Bank Heist. The subject was bound to come up again and again.

Aiden listened. He had good reason to be interested in what the people of Greenlaurel, Texas thought, discussed and argued about. But he couldn't keep his attention wholly on the conversation. He kept scanning those around him, looking for one particular face.

Maybe she wasn't here. Maybe Georgia Ann had been wrong about that.

"You mark my words," one man was saying,

his pointed chin jutting out belligerently. "This global economy nonsense will be the ruin of our nation. If all it takes to plunge the markets into chaos is one bank losing a fraction of its holdings—"

"A fraction! One bank!" a tall, elderly woman exclaimed. "Benny, we're talking about the World Bank and hundreds of billions of dollars."

"Exaggerated," another man scoffed. "We all know the media sensationalizes things. The first reports said that only five billion or so had been siphoned off."

"Only five billion?" The tall woman shuddered. "When I think of what terrorists can do with that kind of money—"

"We don't know that it's terrorists."

"Come on, Jessie, of course it is. A damned well-organized bunch they are, too. To systematically drain accounts at the World Bank the way they did, they have to be damned good."

"And no one really knows how they did it, either. That's spooky. I mean, if the bankers can't even tell how much money is missing, or how it was removed—"

"It's the Internet," a plump, red-faced man asserted loudly. "Banks have no business being on the Internet. Everyone knows you can't stop hackers. What we need are laws that keep banks off the Internet."

For a few seconds everyone seemed stunned to silence by such firmly stated idiocy. Hard to know, Aiden thought as he sipped his champagne, how to explain to someone who didn't already grasp it that there was a difference between hackers and the highly sophisticated economic trickery that the media had dubbed the World Bank Heist.

Aiden returned to scanning the crowd. Suddenly, he caught a glimpse of a slim form with shining black hair. A door closed quietly on the rest of the world, sounds fading from his awareness as he stared…and she turned, providing him with her profile.

A girl. A pretty, laughing girl, perhaps twenty years old. The wrong age, the wrong face.

The world crashed back in on him. Voices, movement, scents—his mind sorted these automatically and made a coherent whole of them easily enough. His interior landscape was more confusing. Relief mingled with disappointment, with dread and anticipation and guilt in a miasma he'd almost grown used to since reaching the decision to come to Greenlaurel. Almost.

The good news, he supposed, was that he was coming back to life. For the past couple of years he'd been all but dead emotionally. His curiosity had saved him—it had been the one itch that had never gone away completely, the one tie that kept him anchored in his own humanity, even at the worst.

The bad news was that he had no idea what to do when these waves of feeling broke over him.

The silver-haired man whose arm Molly had claimed after abandoning Aiden's was speaking. "I don't think speculation helps at this point. When reports vary so widely, all we can do is wait and hope that the experts figure it out soon."

Molly's husband, Aiden had soon realized, was running for local office—county commissioner. He was a quiet, rather self-important man with a good grasp of the way national issues were likely to affect the local economy.

"Well, I for one have the utmost confidence in the experts," Molly announced, "considering that it's Jake Ingram who is conducting the investigation. That man is so smart it's scary."

For some reason this statement, too, created a small, awkward silence. Aiden's curiosity itched. What about Jake Ingram made everyone uncomfortable?

The lights dimmed, brightened, then dimmed and brightened again. "That's the signal for the dancing," Molly told Aiden, smiling. "It will be starting soon. The first dance is for singles, but you save me one of the later dances, hear?"

With a glance, Alex collected Aiden and Jared.

The three of them broke away and headed for their own table.

"Why does Jake Ingram's name strike people temporarily dumb?" he asked. "High intelligence does put some people off and he's reputed to be a genius, but he's also a local boy. That ought to reassure people."

It was Jared who answered. "Jake was adopted. There have been a few jokes—at least, I think they were meant as jokes—but the laughter comes across more nervous than amused."

"Ah." Another story had stolen a few headlines from the ongoing revelations about the World Bank Heist. Originally broken by a tabloid reporter— M.H. Cantrell—the story was highly sensational. Cantrell claimed to have copies of official documents about a government program called "Code Proteus" that, nearly forty years ago, had used human embryos to dabble in genetic engineering. The reporter further claimed that the human results of this experimentation could have been adopted by families all over the country.

Aiden shook his head. Cantrell claimed a lot of things, some of them mutually contradictory. A few more reputable publications were starting to investigate, though. "I suppose adoptees between thirty and thirty-five years old are getting funny looks these days."

"I imagine so. It must be rough. I wonder if Ingram is here tonight.'' Alex looked around as they reached their table.

So did Aiden, but he wasn't hunting for a financial genius. He didn't find what he was looking for, but his gaze did pause, arrested, on a couple who looked vaguely familiar. Well, perhaps not the man. He was somewhere between fifty and sixty, with thick gray hair and the kind of face you forget minutes after seeing it. The woman was more memorable. She reminded him of a ferret—narrow in face and body, sleek and intense.

Dammit, he'd seen her face before somewhere. Not in connection with any of his assignments, though. That much he was sure of. His life had depended on his memory for faces too often for him to be wrong there. But somewhere...

''Something wrong?'' Alex asked.

She and Jared were already sitting down. Aiden pulled out a chair and found a smile for her. He knew how to look relaxed, no matter how tightly strung he might be, but he suspected he wasn't fooling Alex. ''What you are tactfully trying to ask is whether I just saw her. No, I had a brief tussle with a memory that won't quite rise to the surface.''

''Okay. Next question. Are you sorry you came?''

Aiden shrugged. ''Not yet, anyway.'' He had all sorts of logical arguments for picking Greenlaurel to start his new life, but he wouldn't pretend logic

had truly directed him. Yet neither could he talk
about the compulsion that had brought him here
tonight.

The sounds of the band tuning up slid through
all the conversations. The dancing would start any
second. The lights hadn't been dimmed yet, but
they would be soon. He pushed to his feet again.
"I'm going to reconnoiter."

"There you are!" a cheerful voice announced.

He turned. An older woman, permanently
blond—no gray would ever be allowed to appear
on Georgia Ann's head—swept up to the table. She
wore a sequined jacket over a pale blue gown that
went straight to her ankles. Her makeup was flawless, her smile Auntie-Mame wide.

"Alex, Jared, so good to see you." She took Aiden's hands in hers. "Such a mob! Which is wonderful for the belles, of course, or at least for the
charity we're sponsoring this year, but I thought I'd
never find you."

He considered and discarded a dozen evasions.
"Is she here?"

"Oh, my dear. Haven't you seen her yet? I
thought—well, never mind. Yes, she's at my table.
And the singles' dance is about to start."

"And your table is…?"

"Across the room, between the windows."

He saw the windows, and there were several tables in that general area. But, although most people

had taken their seats, a small knot of people still stood in the middle of the dance floor, blocking his view. He took an impatient step forward. A bald man laughed at something another man said and moved aside. And he saw her.

Hair flowing like a midnight river down her back. Slim arms, shoulders held so straight it would be easy to overlook how delicate they were. Skin that made him think of sunrise. Eyes as dark as her hair...but that came from memory. He was too far to see the color of her eyes from here, or the little mole on her neck, or the crooked incisor that showed only when she laughed.

God, he wanted to hear her laugh again. His dusky fairy child, the woman he'd once planned to marry...the woman he had left two weeks before the wedding. His lips parted and his breath carried her name. "Noelle."

Chapter 2

Noelle pretended to listen to Mrs. Porter's account of her recent surgical adventure and wondered why hiding had such a bad rep. Hiding out at home seemed like a much better idea than facing down the gossip. Why had she let Georgia Ann talk her into this?

There was a lot of pretending going on tonight. While she pretended a serene disregard for what others said about her, others pretended they didn't see her. Ed Eames, for example. She'd known Ed for—what, maybe fifteen years? Something like that. Since the first time she lived in Greenlaurel, anyway, when she was a teenager. Yet he'd hustled his wife across the room a few minutes ago so he wouldn't have to speak to her.

He wasn't the only one. The parents of one of her students had done the same thing. The mother of a former student hadn't bothered to pretend— she'd deliberately turned her back on Noelle. It could be worse, she supposed. They could all be like Amber Heffinger, oozing sympathy and watching avidly, hoping Noelle would do or say something crazy.

Or they might all look at her with the pity she'd seen tonight in an old friend's eyes.

There were a few who treated her as they always had, though. Mrs. Porter for one. That thought made Noelle feel guilty, and she forced her attention back to the saga of the gall bladder. Over Mrs. Porter's shoulder she caught a glimpse of a smiling, smooth-faced man with dishwater blond hair and eyes so blue the color jumped out at her even from a distance. He was moving between the tables several feet away.

Oh, God. He was coming toward her.

She simply was not going to deal with this. Not with the whole room looking on. Abruptly she stood. "Excuse me. I have to visit the ladies' room."

"But, my dear, they're about to start the dancing. The singles' dance is first."

Sure enough, the lights went down. All the better to make her escape. "I'm not booked for this one, so it won't matter.'' She dredged up a smile for Mrs. Porter. ''I'll be right back.''

She'd taken two steps away from the table when a man's hand fell on her shoulder. Feelings shot through her like an electric charge—fear and fury, plus something less definable. She went rigid.

He spoke her name and her world tilted.

Slowly she turned, stunned by disbelief. This wasn't the man she'd seen heading her way, the smiling man she'd wanted so badly to avoid. This man's eyes were dark, not a laughing blue. He was all angles, not smooth at all. His dark hair was brushed back from a widow's peak, and the bones of his face seemed to strain against his skin. And he wasn't smiling.

Aiden. *Aiden* was here.

Noelle didn't hear the waltz begin. She knew only the feel of his hand wrapped around hers, impossibly familiar after so long. Her feet, left without guidance from her shock-blanked brain, followed as he urged her out onto the dance floor. He pulled her close and started to move.

His suit jacket was smooth. The hand at her waist was warm; she felt each finger distinctly. And she smelled him—not his cologne, for he didn't wear any, but a subtle blend of soap and man that dived deep into the underside of her mind, where thought couldn't reach. Oh, she knew that scent! Ambushed by the most primitive part of her brain, Noelle lost her grip on the division between past and present.

Just so had he held her once, when they danced to another song. Just so had the world faded, leaving the two of them alone in their magical bubble. Her heart, still in sync with present reality, beat against her chest like a trapped bird, fast and frantic. Everything else slowed to the sweet, adagio rhythm of desire.

He bent his head and murmured close to her ear. "You're so beautiful still. Looking at you hurts my heart."

His *heart?* Was he claiming to have one, then? Anger rippled through her and she shook off the temporal dislocation like a dog shedding water. God, she'd let him sweep her off to dance as if she had no mind, no will—no right to despise him. Her body turned from limp pliancy to stiff refusal. "What are you doing here?"

"Making a fool of myself, most likely."

"That would be fair. You made a fool out of me twelve years ago." She was aware of the other couples on the floor, and of a strong desire to hit him. Or weep. "You aren't limping."

His eyes were hooded now, hiding his thoughts. "My right leg will never be as strong as the left, but it holds up well enough in normal use."

"I suppose I shouldn't be surprised that you just

showed up this way. You aren't in the habit of warning your victims.''

He winced. ''I've handled this badly. I didn't mean to launch a surprise attack, I just…I wanted to see you. Speak to you.''

''Some people use telephones for that.''

''I suppose Georgia Ann would have given me your number,'' he admitted, ''if I'd asked. I couldn't imagine just picking up the phone and calling, though I—what is it?''

She'd dropped her hand from his waist and stopped moving. All around them couples glided in three-quarter time, the men in their dark suits like so many exclamation points circling the colorful statements made by the women's bright silks and glitter.

''Georgia Ann? She knew?'' Noelle's voice rose. ''She knew you'd be here tonight?''

''Ah…I asked her not to say anything. She didn't—Noelle!''

If he followed, she didn't know. She was too busy shoving her way through all those swirling, happy dancers, then rushing past tables where the faces swinging her way passed in a blur. Someone tried to stop her—a woman, her unfamiliar face tilted up, the sense of her words as blurred as Noelle's vision. Noelle could only shake her head and pull away, instinct driving her to the French doors at the back of the ballroom. It wasn't until

she stepped out onto the flagstone patio and the cool
night air swam over her face that she realized her
cheeks were wet.

That hadn't gone well.

Aiden stood alone on the dance floor, the focus
of dozens of curious eyes, and wondered what he
was supposed to do now. Go after her and apologize? Try to make her listen to explanations that,
from her point of view, were twelve years too late?
Leave the ball entirely?

He thought of everything he'd meant to tell her,
the questions he'd wanted to ask, the yearning to
know what she'd done, what had been done to her
and who she'd become in the years since he'd for-
feited the right to ask those questions. And he
thought of the strain he'd seen on her face before
even she knew he was there.

In the end he fell back on training and went after
more information. Georgia Ann was sitting in his
chair at the table where his friends waited. He
stopped beside her, his face expressionless.

She looked up at him, her eyebrows lifted as if
asking a question. "That didn't go well."

The echo of his own thoughts brought the ghost
of a smile to his face. "No, it didn't. Care to tell
me why?"

"I'm not a mind reader. You'd better ask
Noelle."

"You're involved somehow. She ran off when she realized you'd known I would be here."

"Oh. Oh, dear." The older woman looked distressed. She glanced at Alex and Jared, who were politely pretending not to listen. "She's jumping to conclusions, but I can't say that I blame her."

"There's a great deal you haven't told me."

"I wanted you to hear about it from her, but...." She sighed. "Depending on who you believe, Noelle is either being persecuted by her ex-husband...or else she's stalking him."

Noelle headed for the koi pool, one of her favorite spots on the estate. But the winding paths, lit by small spotlights, were too inviting. Others had been lured outside. The bench near the pool was claimed by a couple who, occupied with each other, never noticed her hurry past.

A huge cottonwood anchored the west end of the grounds. At its roots lay the white garden. In summer it would be magnificent by moonlight, with night-blooming clematis, thorn apple, phlox, Japanese iris and moonflower. This early in the season only the narcissus had made an appearance, nodding their white heads at the moon.

By the time Noelle sank onto the wrought-iron bench that faced the garden, her tears had stopped. She wiped her cheeks, sighed, and contemplated the logistics of leaving the ball without returning to the ballroom.

She ought to write a book, she thought with weary humor, on how to make a fool of yourself in public. Running off the dance floor was not going to convince anyone of her stability, was it? Too many of the people at the ball knew what had happened—or not happened—twelve years ago. Some of them would have recognized Aiden. No doubt word was already spreading that his sudden return had overset her.

No doubt there was some truth in that, too. Dammit.

Now that she'd stopped moving, she was chilly. Her dress wasn't exactly designed for warmth. She rubbed her bare arms, noticed that her neck and shoulder muscles were rigid with tension, and began rubbing them.

"Pretty as a picture," a man said. "Moonlight suits you."

She froze. Slowly her arms fell as she turned to her left. "Go away, Greg."

He didn't, of course. He came right up to the bench where she sat and propped one foot on it, leaning over her. And smiling. "I know it shook you up to see your old flame again, sweetheart, but you really have to get a grip on your emotions. You created a lot of talk, and that's the last thing you need right now."

She wanted to hit him—no, she wanted to pick up something large and heavy and smash him. But as satisfying at that would be, it wouldn't help. She needed to get away, just get up and walk away before he somehow turned this encounter into more ammo in the bizarre war he was waging.

Only she didn't think her legs would hold her. "Why are you doing this?" she whispered. "Why, Greg? You've gone to so much trouble to make people think it's me. But it isn't. It's you. We both know that, but I can't understand why."

"Noelle." He shook his head sadly. "I know you believe that's true. You need professional help, sweetheart. I'm asking…no, I'm begging you to get that help."

She looked at him more in wonder than anger. The smile had slipped from his face and the concern in his eyes looked utterly genuine. "Even now, with no one else around, you won't drop the act. Maybe you can't. I've never understood how your mind works."

"Noelle, you are delusional." He laid a hand on her shoulder. "You don't trust me, but there are others—"

"Take your hand off me."

His fingers tightened. "Others who are worried. People who care about you. If you can't listen to me, listen to them."

"I told you to remove your hand. I don't want you touching me."

"Don't upset yourself," he said soothingly, and squeezed her shoulder. The caress would have looked like simple affection, had anyone been there to see. But it would be a wonder if she didn't have bruises tomorrow. "I would never hurt you."

"The lady told you to remove your hand," Aiden said.

Greg jolted. His hand dropped and he straightened, turning around.

Aiden was a dark, almost invisible figure beneath the spreading edges of the cottonwood, where little light reached. He stepped forward, stopping a few feet away, his gaze fixed on Greg. His face, underlit by the spots that flanked the path, held no expression.

Greg smiled. "Ah! Aiden Swift. My ex-wife's ex-lover. I don't think we've met."

Aiden didn't move, didn't speak. There was nothing threatening about his expression or his stance—he just stood there looking at Greg. Noelle had no idea why a chill went down her spine.

She stood. "Greg, you should go now."

"And leave the two of you alone?" He glanced at her, still smiling. "Well, why not? It's the tactful thing to do. I'm sure I'll see you around, Swift."

Still Aiden didn't respond. Greg's lips tightened. He spoke to Noelle. "A man of few words, your former lover. I guess it wasn't his conversation or his manners that appealed to you. Not that I'm criticizing. There's nothing wrong with having a healthy sex drive. That's one of the things I always liked—''

"Go." Aiden started toward him. "Now."

"I'll leave the two of you to catch up," Greg said hastily, and, at last, he left.

All of a sudden her legs were shaky. Noelle sat down and tried to catch her breath. How absurd she was, being frightened by a look in a man's eyes. Aiden wouldn't have really hit Greg…would he?

Chapter 3

Aiden watched the man he'd wanted to kill move off down the path, watched until Greg Snowden was out of sight. There was a fine tremor in his hands, the aftermath of a clean, hot rage such as he hadn't felt in years. Abruptly he asked, "Has he always done that?"

"What?"

"Taken swipes at you when he was mad at someone he didn't dare go up against."

"Oh." She smoothed her skirt, not looking at him. "Sometimes. People don't usually realize that's what he's doing. He's clever about that sort of thing."

"Smart bullies can cause more damage than the

stupid ones.'' They could find ways to hurt the unseen places, where healing comes slowly if it comes at all. Yet even the smart ones weren't always satisfied with mental cruelty. He looked at her delicate, averted profile, partly hidden by the fall of her hair, and swallowed sickness. "Did he ever hit you?"

Now she looked up. Her lips curved, but it was irony, not humor, behind that smile. "Oh, no. Someone might have found out, and Greg cares deeply about what others think. I sometimes wonder if the mirror is empty when he looks in it. All he has of himself is what other people reflect back at him.''

Had she reflected more truth than the man could handle? Aiden noticed that his hands had closed in fists and forced them to relax. He was steady again physically, uncertain in every other way. "I want to help.''

Her shoulders straightened and her glance was wary. "I don't need any help.''

"Don't you?" He came and sat beside her, his legs spread, his hands clasped between them and his head down. Now that he was alone with her, he didn't know how to begin. "Why did you run away?''

"What, can't you guess?''

Her voice was mocking, but he couldn't tell which of them she mocked. He thought of the laughing, open girl she'd once been, and wanted to hit someone...but maybe it was his own face that needed bloodying. "You sound bitter. That's new."

She shrugged.

"Is it my fault?"

"Yours?" She stood and took a few quick steps if she couldn't be still another second. "Don't make yourself too important. It's been twelve years. Of course I've changed, and of course the way you left me played some part in that. But my marriage played a bigger part."

"You ran away because you thought Georgia Ann arranged for me to come here tonight to distract you from your obsession with your ex-husband."

She flinched. "I don't want to talk about that."

"She doesn't believe it, Noelle."

"She doesn't *want* to believe it. There's a difference."

"Don't you want to know the truth?"

"Actually, I'm the only one who *does* know the truth. Greg has always been convincing, and he—he's arranged things to make me look bad."

"I want to help," he repeated.

"And I don't want your help." She turned away and touched a tiny new leaf on a bush still mostly winter-bare. For a long moment neither of them spoke.

Finally he had to ask. "Do you want me to leave?"

She sighed. "No. Apparently there's more anger left in me than I'd realized. But you didn't come to Greenlaurel to talk about my ex-husband, and I don't want to discuss him. Why are you here?"

She was braver than he was, to speak so easily of leaving and pain, time and change. He tried to be as honest as she had been, but though he knew what he needed—the sense of it pulsed inside him, bright and mute—confusion lay like a heavy fog between that beacon and everything else. "I've retired from the service. For good this time, and voluntarily. I want to live in Greenlaurel, and I needed to see you. I've never forgotten you."

She tilted her head to one side. "Is it conscience? Do you want me to tell you I forgive you? You asked me to once, but you weren't around to find out what my answer was."

He remembered. God, he did remember—the next-to-last sentence in the note he'd left her had been only two words long: "Forgive me."

He thought of the man he'd been back then, and his mouth twisted. "I had no right to ask you for forgiveness. I regretted that I'd hurt you, I regretted my own pain, but I didn't regret leaving. Not really. A man who's making a noble sacrifice can justify all sorts of things." He snorted softly. "I was an arrogant bastard."

"Something of a bastard, maybe. But I'd say you were more desperate than arrogant."

He couldn't keep his surprise from showing.

"Did you think I didn't understand that?" She shook her head, sending ripples through the long, straight silk of her hair. "I was young, but I wasn't blind. You didn't want to be in Greenlaurel. You didn't want to be a civilian at all. I knew that. You were trying to make the best of things, but that was because you thought you had no choice. Once you had that choice back…" She shrugged.

Pride was capable of amazing regeneration. Slice it, dice it, burn or bury it, and still it came back. He didn't like learning that she'd thought of him as desperate. "I didn't lie to you. I had to leave. The situation was urgent, and duty left me no choice."

"A matter of duty. That's what you said called you away. 'I could not love thee, dear, so much,'" she quoted softly, "'Lov'd I not honor more.' But you didn't come back, Aiden."

This was it. This was the question he'd been waiting for—though she hadn't quite phrased it as a question. "There were things I couldn't tell you then. I wrote that I'd been recalled to service. That service wasn't with the army."

"What? You mean you lied about—"

"No. God, no." He walked closer, restraining himself at the last moment from reaching for her. "I'd been in the army. But I was recruited by another agency. A secret one connected to the CIA. I didn't—"

"Oh, good grief." She stared at him in disgust. "Is that the best you can do? You were a spy, called away on a secret mission...one that lasted twelve years. I've heard better stories from guys looking for a pickup in a bar." She turned and walked away.

Aiden shook his head, then surprised himself by smiling. How many times over the years had he imagined telling her the truth? "You aren't following the script," he told her, his longer legs catching him up with her easily. "You're supposed to be stunned, maybe a little disbelieving, upset that I put duty before you. But impressed. You left that out entirely."

She didn't look at him, but she chuckled. Noelle had the most distinctive chuckle he had ever heard—a low, burbling sound, as if humor was a fountain bubbling over. "That's better. For a minute there I thought you were serious."

"I am," he responded. "I know you don't believe me, but I'm not going to lie. Not even if you would buy a lie more easily than the truth. I won't keep trying to convince you, though, not until I can document what I say. Fortunately," he added, "you won't have to take my word for it, though I don't have the proof on me right now. Where are we going, anyway?"

It was more or less a rhetorical question. He could see where they were headed—to the west side of the house, which lay in darkness. He could guess where she meant to go from there.

She shot him a quick, dubious glance. "I'm going to the parking lot. I don't know where you're going."

"With you, of course. There aren't any lights on this side of the house."

"I stopped being afraid of the darkness a few years ago," she said dryly. "I hardly ever need the night-light anymore."

Yet sometimes there really were monsters hiding in the darkness. Aiden had hunted some of them and been lucky to survive the encounters. "No doubt I'm using an overblown protective instinct as an excuse to stay with you."

She entranced him by chuckling again.

"I understand you're teaching now."

"Sophomore and senior English."

"Brave woman." He realized with some surprise that he felt good. Really good, light and happy. None of this had gone the way he'd planned, but for the moment she wasn't running or trying to push him away. She was willing to walk and talk with him. "When I think of what I was like at that age, I have to subscribe to the bunghole theory of raising adolescent males."

"The bunghole theory?"

"Put 'em in a barrel, nail it shut and shovel what

they need through the bunghole. Let them out around, say, age twenty-five.''

She laughed. It was even better than her chuckle. ''I think you'd have a hard time selling that one to the school board. Some of the parents might back you, though.''

''So how did you end up teaching teens? You were teaching third grade before.'' The path led them into the shadow of the big house. Aiden had been careful not to gaze at the better-lit areas, so his eyes were partially adapted to the darkness. Not that he expected trouble. It was automatic.

''There was an opening, and I applied for it. It was an impulse, but it's worked out well.''

''Impulse can be another name for instinct sometimes.''

''Well, I like to think so, of course. Considering how often I act on impulse.'' She stopped. They'd reached a gate in the iron fence, and she reached for the latch. ''But I have to admit that sometimes impulse is another name for stupidity. When I—oh, no.'' She jiggled the latch. ''It's locked.''

''Let me see.'' He moved up, gently nudging her aside.

''I can tell when a gate is locked. The padlock is a clue.''

''I'm good with locks.'' Not that he had his tools with him, but it was unlikely they'd use a combination lock on a gate, and he had his ballpoint pen.

He pulled out the tiny flashlight attached to his key chain and aimed it at the lock. Very basic. It would be even easier, of course, to just vault the fence, but he didn't think Noelle would care to climb it in her dress.

He put his keys back, pulled out the pen and disassembled it. Taped to the ink cartridge was what looked like a long steel toothpick. He removed it. "What's the best part of teaching sophomore and senior English?"

"The kids," she said promptly. "They have so much energy, and it's so scattered. Every day is a collision course with extremes. They're altruistic, selfish, sincere, affected. And emotional." Her voice held wry humor. "I can relate."

He probed the padlock with his "toothpick." "When did you start worrying so much about being emotional?"

"I...it's not that I worry about it. I'm aware that it can create problems, that's all."

"So can breathing, in some circumstances. You're apologizing for something that's as natural for you as breathing, too. Stop it." With a click felt rather than heard, the tumbler gave way. "Here we go." He removed the padlock and swung the gate open.

"You did it!"

He smiled. "Maybe I've been a burglar all these years instead of a spy."

"I hope you're kidding this time." She walked through the gate.

He closed it, put the padlock back and slipped his lock pick into his pocket with the remains of the ballpoint pen. She was waiting for him. Though they were still in shadow, the front of the building was brightly lit, and enough light leaked around the corner of the building that he could see her smiling impishly, her head cocked to one side. Time slipped. His breath caught as, for a second, he was with the Noelle he'd once loved—young, playful, bubbling over with optimism and zest for life.

"You realize I'm making a break for it," she said.

"Not going back to get your things?" She must have brought a purse, he thought, and some kind of wrap. Her dress was long and layered and looked black in the dimness, though he knew it was really a dark blue. But the layers were thin, the fit was slim, and the top dipped low and was held up by straps no wider than his lock pick. She must be chilly.

"Georgia Ann will figure out that I've decamped and take my purse home with her. I can get it from her later."

He slipped off his jacket and stepped close so he could place it on her shoulders. "Will you accept a ride, or should I hotwire your car?"

She laughed, a low gurgle. "Another of your

skills? It won't be needed this time. One of the parking attendants is a student of mine. He'll let me have my keys without the ticket. Though I guess he'll have to take an I.O.U. on his tip.''

She was so close. Her perfume was light, with misty floral notes mingling with something green and herbal. He felt dizzy. How easy it would be to bend his head and taste that smiling mouth....

She turned away abruptly and started walking. ''Did you mean what you said earlier?''

''These days I generally mean what I say.'' She couldn't know what a luxury it was to speak the truth. He meant to indulge in it for the next fifty or sixty years.

''About moving to Greenlaurel, I mean. About staying here.''

''Yes, that's my plan.''

''But why? I mean, your parents live on the east coast—''

''My father does. My mother died five years ago.''

''Oh!'' She stopped and put a hand on his arm. ''I'm so sorry.''

''She'd been ill. Cancer. At first we thought the treatments were working, but all at once...'' A knot in his throat stopped his voice. He swallowed. He'd made it home before she died, but it had been a near thing. ''She went very quickly.''

"If she didn't suffer long, that's good. But you suffered."

His eyes watered. Embarrassed, he blinked rapidly, wondering what had happened to the control that had kept him alive so long. "My father's doing well." He started walking again, and they rounded the corner of the building. "He talks about retiring, but I don't think he's serious. He's seeing a woman he and my mother were friends with, someone he's known for years."

"Good for him."

"I think she is, yes." He was glad his father wasn't pulling into himself, but the whole business made Aiden feel unsettled.

"They say that people who have been happily married are the most likely to remarry if they lose their spouse. They know how wonderful it can be."

She'd either sensed or guessed at his disquiet. It made him feel odd. Visible. He wasn't used to that. But it wasn't a bad feeling, he decided.

They negotiated for the release of her car keys. The parking attendant—senior English, Noelle whispered to Aiden—wanted to bring the car around to her the way he was supposed to, but Noelle was in a hurry. She was nervous about waiting out front, Aiden realized. She wanted to escape without speaking to anyone.

How bad had things been for her? Georgia Ann had been frustratingly vague.

Once Noelle had her keys, she told him goodnight quite firmly. He smiled. "I'll walk you to your car."

"Aiden," she said, frustrated. "I don't want to be rude, but it's been a difficult evening. I don't want company."

"Then I'll follow you to your car. That overdeveloped protective instinct, you understand. I'm helpless against it." Her ex-husband was here at the estate. She said he had never hit her. Maybe not, but he'd found other ways to do his damage. For whatever good it might do, Aiden would see her safely bestowed in her car with the doors locked and the windows up.

Then, of course, he would follow her home. But she didn't have to know about that.

She huffed out an impatient breath. "I'd forgotten how stubborn you are. All right. Just don't— don't *talk* to me."

So he smiled again and walked with her in silence.

Music followed them, muted by the walls of the house, fading as they crossed from the paved drive to the parking lot, where their feet crunched pleasantly on gravel. The air was crisp and still, the sky clear. She still wore his jacket, hung over her shoulders like an oddly tailored cape.

That pleased him, as did her quiet acceptance of his company. Unwilling acceptance, he supposed, yet her presence was a gift that, however grudged, soothed him. She'd taken a step or two along the road to forgiveness, he thought. No telling how far along that road she would be willing or able to travel, but he was intensely grateful for those few steps.

"Aiden," she said suddenly, her voice low. "Why did you never so much as call?"

"At first, because I left the country the same night I left you. For some time after that I was operating under deep cover."

He felt more than saw her quick glance. She didn't say anything, which he decided to take as some sort of progress. She wasn't calling him a liar, at least.

"Well, we're here," she said after a moment. "My car's the dark green sedan with the...oh, my God."

She stopped. He did, too. Someone had scrawled obscenities over the windshield, hood and driver's side of the car.

Chapter 4

The ugly words had been painted in white. Even in the dim light, they showed up vividly against the dark green paint.

That was wrong, Noelle thought. That was just wrong, to use white for such filth. "I've only had it a year. It's the first car I ever bought new, and now…" Her voice quivered. She bit her lip. Don't lose it. That's what he wants. Though why…no, she told herself firmly. Speculate later. Right now just…just hang on.

Aiden rubbed a knuckle across one letter, drawing a clean path through it. "Shoe polish. If it's removed quickly, it shouldn't damage the finish. We need to get the police out here right away, though. My cell phone's in my car. Come on." He took her arm.

"No!" She pulled free. "No police."

"Noelle, this needs to be reported."

"I've tried that. You don't understand." A fine tremor shook her. "Somehow he'll make everyone think I wrote those words. That I'm sick, sick enough to write that just so I can blame him. You don't know what it's like. What *he's* like."

He looked at her without speaking for a moment, then loosened his tie, pulled it off and began unbuttoning his shirt.

"What in the world are you doing?"

"Saving the paint, I hope." And, bare-chested, he used his dress shirt like a rag to wipe the ugly words away. When he was finished he glanced at it. "I'm afraid I'll need my jacket back."

They ended up at a truck stop on the interstate. Noelle wasn't sure how. She never agreed to go with him, yet somehow she found herself in his car with the heater going and Debussy playing on the stereo.

It was just that she was so tired, she thought. And he was so determined. At least he didn't try to talk to her. She leaned her head against the headrest, closed her eyes and did her best not to think.

The truckstop was bright and noisy and about half-full. Their waitress was a fortyish woman named Frankie who obviously itched with curiosity.

Noelle couldn't blame her. She and Aiden weren't exactly dressed like the rest of the clientele.

Especially Aiden. Noelle's lips curved as she fought off another fit of giggles.

"I'm glad you're feeling better, even if it is at my expense."

"Sorry," she said insincerely, and grinned. "You look very buff."

At first the manager had refused to let Aiden in. No shirt, no shoes, no service, and he didn't consider a suit jacket an acceptable substitute for a shirt. So Aiden had bought a T-shirt from the little gift section attached to the truckstop. It was violently purple, at least one size too small, with yellow lettering that read, UFOs Are Real. The Air Force Doesn't Exist.

"Buff, huh?" He put his elbow on the table and flexed his biceps, making the muscles strain against the sleeve in an interesting way. "Maybe I'll give up my plan to become a respectable businessman and start training for Mr. Universe."

"Not quite that buff." She was still grinning as the waitress put two mugs in front of them and filled them with coffee.

"You guys been at that fancy ball over at Silverwood?" the woman asked.

Aiden nodded.

"I won't ask what you've been doin' that left *one* of you without a shirt." She winked. "Just tell me one thing. Was that crazy woman there? You know, the one that's been after her ex-husband. That real estate guy. My cousin Maryanne works at the Snipshop, and he gets his hair cut there. She knows *all* about it.''

Noelle went light-headed, leaving her feeling fey and giddy. ''Oh, yes. She was there. Her ex was, too. *And* her former fiancé. It was quite a show.''

''What? What did she do?''

''She was dancing with the man she used to be engaged to years ago. Maybe you heard about that? He dumped her just before the wedding.''

The waitress clucked sympathetically. ''And—?''

''She went tearing out of the ballroom all of a sudden. Right in the middle of the dance. And you know what?'' Noelle leaned toward the other woman, who obligingly bent closer. ''Her ex-husband went after her.''

''He did? Well, I expect he wanted to see if she was okay. Maryanne says he's real worried about her.''

Noelle nodded darkly. ''That's what he says, all right. He just oozes concern. You know what I think? I think he's the one who's after her. He's making it look like she's crazy.''

''I dunno. Maryanne says he's awful nice. Always stops to talk with her, and he's not even her customer. She does nails, see. Does a real good job.

See?'' She held out the hand that wasn't gripping the coffeepot. The nails were dark red, inhumanly long and perfect.

''Frankie,'' said the man in the booth behind Aiden, ''you gonna gossip all night, or can I have some more of that coffee?''

The waitress rolled her eyes and went away.

''You may not need much help,'' Aiden said. ''You handled that very well.''

Noelle shrugged. The giddiness had drained out, leaving her feeling flat. What was she doing, sitting here drinking coffee with this man? Maybe she really was crazy. Self destructive.

He sipped from his mug. ''This is definitely truckstop coffee. Are you up to talking about it now? I'm getting some idea of what you're up against, but I'm short on facts.''

''Didn't Georgia Ann fill you in?''

''There wasn't much time, and she kept saying she wanted me to hear the details from you. She said it started with harassing phone calls.''

Noelle picked up the paper that had covered her straw and started pleating it. Why not tell him? She'd told her story to so many people…the police, whose cynical eyes suggested they didn't believe anyone. Friends, whose eyes reflected their struggle with disbelief…a struggle many of them had lost. It couldn't hurt more to see these doubts in Aiden's eyes than it had to find them in Georgia Ann's. He didn't matter. Not anymore.

"About a month ago I started getting nuisance calls," she began. "Hang-ups at first. They always occurred at midnight or later. Untraceable, which probably means they were made from a cell phone. After about a week of that, they changed from hang-ups to the heavy breather bit. Such a cliché. I told him that once, before I stopped answering my phone at night."

"Did you know it was Greg?"

"Oh, not then. He didn't even cross my mind at first. I've hardly seen or spoken to him since the divorce."

"Georgia Ann said you were the one who filed. Did he oppose the divorce? Was he upset? Angry?"

"He wasn't crazy about the timing. He'd had a couple of deals go sour and didn't see why I couldn't wait a year or two to give him a chance to recover financially."

"Did he contest the divorce?"

"No, he was willing enough to see the last of me. There were some squabbles over the division of property, but it was pretty civilized. My lawyer talked to his lawyer, that sort of thing."

"How much property are we talking about?"

Back and forth she folded the straw paper, making tiny pleats. So far he seemed to be taking her at her word, but she hadn't gotten to the more outlandish aspects yet. "I didn't ask for part of his business, just my share of the house. He wanted it. I didn't, but he couldn't buy me out without selling one of his other properties. He wasn't happy about that, but my parents had put up the down payment as our wedding present. I wasn't going to let him just keep it. Besides, we could have sold the house and split the proceeds."

He thrummed his fingers once on the table. "The man you've described sounds selfish and greedy, but not obsessed."

"He doesn't, does he?" She shook her head. "I understand why people don't think Greg's stalking me. I have trouble believing it myself half the time."

"I understand he's engaged to someone else now."

She gave him a quick glance. Georgia Ann would have told him that. She wondered how much else her old friend had said. "That's part of it."

"Tell me the rest."

The straw paper was completely folded up. She laid it on the table and smoothed it out again. "It's been over a year since the divorce. Fifteen months. Why would he suddenly become obsessed with me? He…I could swear he doesn't care enough to stalk me. Yet he *is*."

"You've seen him hanging around your house at night."

"Yes." She cupped her mug with both hands, hoping to draw some of its warmth inside. "About a week after the calls started I saw him across the street, staring at my house. He was there for nearly thirty minutes. It was…spooky. I saw him several times after that. Not just my house. I'd turn around, and he'd be there—at the grocery store, or coming out of the bank, or driving past when I left the school."

"Was that when you reported the harassment to the police?"

"Not then. What was I supposed to tell them? That my ex-husband went to the grocery store the same time I did? That I was getting harassing phone calls and was sure it was him?" She shook her head violently. "I did call the police after the break-in. I wish I hadn't."

"Break-in?" he repeated sharply. "Georgia Ann didn't mention that. What happened?"

"About two weeks ago, I woke up a little after midnight. There was someone in the house—I could hear him moving around. The phone was in the kitchen, so I couldn't call—oh, yes," she said with a flash of wry humor at his expression. "I can see you have the same opinion of that as the officer who came out. I've got a cell phone now and keep it charged and by my bed. I didn't then."

"Tell me you didn't go looking for the intruder yourself."

"I didn't. I was too terrified to move. But I heard him leave, so I dashed to the kitchen. The back door was wide open. Naturally I looked outside."

He shook his head.

"I saw him. Greg. From the back, but it—it looked like him. Size, build, hair—and I know that was his windbreaker. I bought it for him. And that's what I told the police. I told them about the other things, too. Only…" She looked down and saw that she'd shredded the straw paper. She didn't even remember picking it up again. "At the time I saw him running away from my house, Greg was at a party with about thirty people. The district attorney alibied him. Among others."

"The obvious answer is that he gave someone his jacket. Someone with the same height and build."

She blinked and smiled in sudden gratitude. He was still with her—still accepting what she said. "I thought so, too. And the police didn't dismiss the idea entirely, not until…"

His eyebrows lifted. "There's more?"

"Two days after the break-in I received a letter. Typewritten, not a computer printout. The police were quite pleased about that. It said…" She started to reach for her coffee, but her hand trembled, so she hid it in her lap. This was the hard part, the part when he would be jolted into doubt. She would see it in his eyes—the incredulity, the hunt for some reasonable explanation...an explanation she wouldn't be able to supply, because what was happening made no sense to her, either.

Get it over with, she told herself. "The letter said that I was his, would always be his. A lot of stuff like that. Greg's name was at the bottom, but it was typed, too."

"What did the police say?"

"Like I said, they were very pleased it had been typed. They even found the typewriter it had been written on. Unfortunately, it turned out to be the one I keep at school."

Chapter 5

At three o'clock the next afternoon, Aiden drove down a tree-lined street in an older section of town. He'd slept well last night and woken this morning with an eagerness he hadn't experienced in years.

Last night he'd kissed Noelle.

A quick brush of the lips, that was all. He'd driven her back to her car, checked it out for surprises even less pleasant than the obscenities that had been scrawled across it earlier. Then he'd told her good-night. And he'd kissed her.

She'd stepped back immediately, her eyes wide. But she hadn't slapped him or told him he was slime. She hadn't said a word, in fact, just turned away and climbed into her car, and he didn't know if that was good or bad. But after twelve years, he'd kissed Noelle again.

And now he was going to see her. He was as foolishly delighted and jittery as any schoolboy with a crush.

On the seat beside him was a folder. He'd rather bring her flowers, but there were things she needed more than flowers right now. Information, for one. Greg Snowden was a clever bastard. The frame was as subtle as it was preposterous, not least because there seemed no reason for it. But Aiden had gone up against men brighter and more ruthless than Snowden.

A phone call early this morning had netted the contents of the folder, which he'd taken with him to the newspaper morgue, the courthouse and the police station. After leaving the station, he'd driven past Snowden's home—the house where he and Noelle had lived as man and wife for six years. That, too, provided information, but of a more personal sort.

It lay in one of the newest, most exclusive developments. The house itself was big and modern, swallowing almost all of the small lot, and looked ready for the camera crew from some "home beautiful" magazine. The brick was dark red, the trim white, the landscaping immaculate. Aiden couldn't picture Noelle living there. It was tasteful, expensive and absolutely generic.

The house she'd bought after the divorce was different. Aiden found himself smiling as he pulled up in front. This house was surrounded by enough trees to make up a small woods. It sat on a double lot, badly overgrown, with bushes crowding trees and what had once been gardens, overwhelmed by invaders. It was a tall, narrow, golden house that had been cobbled together from amber stones set higgledy-piggledy, and looked like just the place for a friendly witch.

He recognized the cars in the drive: Noelle's green sedan and Georgia Ann's long white Cadillac. Acting on impulse, he went to the side door instead of the front, stepped up on the small stoop and looked through the screen door. The two women were sitting at a small round table in a cozy kitchen.

Noelle didn't know why she suddenly looked at the door. She hadn't heard anything, but all at once she turned her head and there he was. Aiden looked up and their eyes met through the mesh of the screen. Her heart lurched in a single startled thump.

"Well, look who's here," Georgia Ann said. "Come on in, Aiden, it isn't latched."

Noelle swallowed and stood as Aiden pushed open the screen door. "I have some coffee, if you'd like. Or a soft drink."

"Coffee would be great." The wooden floor

creaked beneath his feet when he entered. It badly
needed refinishing. He smiled, looking around her
little kitchen. The counters were red ceramic tile,
shiny and new and cluttered. The cabinets were ancient and battered. She'd started redoing things, but
had a ways to go still. "Nice house. Where's the
black cat?"

She poured the last of the coffee into a blue mug.
"His Majesty is taking one of his afternoon naps,
I believe."

"You mean you really do have a black cat?" He
accepted the mug. Their fingers brushed.

"Not entirely. He has a white spot on his belly
and one white paw." Aiden looked rested. She re-
sented him for it, after the restless night she'd spent,
which had been mostly his fault.

He'd believed her. Or at least his doubts hadn't
shown—that's what she'd told herself later, undone
by his trust and by the brief touch of his lips. She
couldn't know, after all these years, what emotions
Aiden was able to hide—or to fake. Greg had
taught her that some people could simulate whatever feelings served their purpose.

And yet Aiden's kiss had felt so honest...and
familiar.

After twelve years, it shouldn't have been familiar. After the way he'd left her, it shouldn't have
electrified her. Her fear, though—the sudden snap

of terror that had sent her scuttling to her car—that had been entirely appropriate.

She studied his face. There were lines there that hadn't existed twelve years before, crow's feet marking his eyes and grooves along his cheeks. She'd noticed them last night. She hadn't noticed the thin line of scar tissue running from just below his ear to beneath his jaw.

"I'll bet you do a brisk business at Halloween." He sipped the coffee, his eyes never leaving hers.

"Good guess. I went through six bags of candy." She retreated to the table, wanting to put something solid between them. "Have a seat."

Georgia Ann smiled at him. "How are you, dear? I've been trying to apologize to this hardheaded young woman for springing you on her without warning—which was entirely necessary, after all. I was barely able to drag her to the ball as it was."

"That's one way of putting it," Noelle said dryly. "Another perspective is that you came over to ask me a lot of nosy questions and chew me out for having thought that you doubted me."

Georgia Ann chuckled. "It's all in how we look at things, isn't it? So tell me, Aiden. How do you look at this mess Noelle is in?"

"As a concerted campaign to discredit her, or—worst case scenario—have her committed."

"Well." Noelle's fingers gripped the handle of

her mug so tightly it was a wonder it didn't break. "You don't mince words."

He put a file folder on the table and slid it to her. "I can't help you by dealing in half-truths. I've gathered some data on your ex-husband that's pretty interesting. Have a look."

"You told me you wanted to help, but you seem to have forgotten what I said."

His eyes crinkled at the corners. "I don't see how you're going to stop me. Though you can make it more difficult, of course."

"I don't need—"

"Noelle," Georgia Ann said sternly. "What makes you think any of us get through life without help? It is an absurd arrogance to think you must always be the one to help others."

She didn't think she was too arrogant to accept help. But to accept it from this man...she bit her lip and opened the folder. "Who is this?" She picked up the photograph that lay on top. "It looks so much like Greg, but it isn't him."

"Douglas Snowden. A cousin on his father's side."

"Oh, yes. Greg mentioned him, but we've never met. He lives in California."

"That's where Greg's parents live, isn't it?" Georgia Ann asked, holding out her hand for the photo.

Noelle handed it to her. "Yes. Aiden, do you

think…could he be the man I saw leaving after the break-in?''

"Possibly. He's in Texas now, not California.''

"How do you know that?''

"Credit card usage.''

"But you can't…'' Her voice trailed off. Obviously he had. Why was he doing all this? Why was he here, in her kitchen? It seemed unreal.

"If you look at the rest of the papers you'll find a credit report and a list of Snowden's assets. Put the two together, and we get a picture of a man paddling like crazy in very deep financial waters.''

Noelle frowned as she looked at the credit report. How had Aiden gotten this? And the list of assets—surely most of that was confidential. "I don't see his land listed.''

"The strip mall on Governor Street he owns an interest in? That's on the third page. It has a lien against it,'' he added. "A big one.''

"No, he owns about a hundred acres outside of town. His uncle left it to him. Greg thought he had it sold a couple years ago to a New Jersey company, but the deal fell through.''

Georgia Ann shook her head. "Are you sure? The man lies about a lot of things.''

"Oh, he lied about this, too,'' Noelle said. "He pretended he didn't know why they wanted the land. I didn't figure it out until I read that the county had turned down a request by a New Jersey firm to build a toxic waste disposal site. Greg ranted about shortsighted bureaucrats for days.''

Aiden's gaze sharpened. ''According to the property tax rolls, he doesn't own the land now.'' He reclaimed the folder and scanned a couple of the pages. ''There haven't been any large deposits in any of his accounts in the past six months that aren't accounted for. If he sold the land, either it was more than six months ago, or he didn't get paid. I'll check into it.''

''I can't believe how much he's lost in the markets.''

''He's been buying on margin. When the World Bank Heist precipitated a stock market crash, he had to put up his interest in the strip mall as collateral for a loan. He's got a huge balloon note on it due next year.''

Noelle sighed. Poor Greg. Money meant too much to him. It was one of the mirrors he used to see himself, the way he created the persona he thought the world would admire. ''But what does this have to do with me?''

Georgia Ann put down the photograph she'd been studying. ''Most crimes are committed for money.''

Aiden nodded. ''That's right. I'm convinced money is the motive here, not some twisted obsession with Noelle.''

''That fits what I know of Greg,'' Noelle said

slowly. "But I'm not responsible for his debts, and there's nothing of mine he can touch. I don't see how he can get money out of making me look nuts."

"I don't know yet, either. We'll keep digging until we get that figured out. In the meantime, we need to start casting doubt on the rumors he's been spreading."

"Good idea," she said dryly, crossing her forearms on the table. "How?"

He smiled. "I'll move in with you."

The legs of her chair scraped as she pushed to her feet. "What? Have you decided I really am crazy?"

Aiden watched Noelle pace. His mouth was dry, his stomach tight with anxiety. So much depended on how he handled this... Noelle was easy to read, but understanding the emotions that flashed across her face was harder. Hell, he didn't even understand his own surges of feeling. Like right now, when he longed with every cell in his body to go to her, put his arms around her....

Georgia Ann beamed at her. "Don't you see? It's perfect! Aiden will be here if Greg tries to break in again, or plant something here, or makes any more of those nasty phone calls. Best of all, Greg can't make everyone believe you're obsessed with him if you have a hunk like Aiden living with you. Before long, everyone will believe you were in love with

Aiden all along and never did do any of those
things.''

Noelle threw up her hands. ''Matchmaking,
Georgia Ann?''

''Nonsense,'' the older woman said airily. ''Not
that I can see a thing in the world wrong with you
and Aiden getting reacquainted.''

''Don't.'' Noelle paced over to the counter, then
spun around, her hair flying in her face. She shoved
it back. ''Do you remember what happened the last
time you played Cupid in my life?''

Georgia Ann looked uncomfortable. ''That's not
at all the same thing.''

''What happened?'' Aiden asked.

''I married Greg.''

''Not a sterling recommendation.'' He stood and
crossed to her. ''You look ready to fly apart.''

''Who, me? Known far and wide as the essence
of calm, cool and collected?''

''Noelle,'' Georgia Ann said, ''I wish you
wouldn't mock yourself.''

''That was supposed to be humor.''

''After what he did to you…'' Georgia Ann
brooded for a moment, then said to Aiden, ''It's not
just what he's been doing lately, though God knows
that's horrible. Her job is in jeopardy—hush, dear,''
she said when Noelle tried to interrupt. ''If Aiden
is going to help, he needs to know what you're up

against. The principal is a spineless worm," she informed Aiden.

Noelle's smile was strained. "Thank you, love, but Mr. Harding is in a difficult position. People don't want their children being taught by a crazy woman."

Georgia Ann waved that aside. "He's a worm. But the fact is, the rumors started even before the divorce."

"What do you mean?" Aiden asked.

"Greg played tricks on her before. Nasty tricks. He'd talk about how he loved Noelle's spontaneity, her emotional nature, and then recount these little incidents. It's hard to describe how he did it, but…I remember one time he talked about Noelle throwing a sponge at him in a temper fit. Such a little thing! But somehow he created this image of a woman hovering on the edge of a breakdown, all the while sounding as if he was trying to persuade me she was fine."

"He's good at that," Noelle said in a flat voice.

Georgia Ann nodded unhappily. "I'll admit that I didn't see what he was doing at first. He had a lot of people thinking she was—well, delicate. And he set up oddities."

"What sort of oddities?" Aiden looked back and forth between the women.

It was Noelle that answered. "Little things. Weird things. Once he moved all the furniture around in the living room while I was at school. The next day he moved everything back—and denied it had ever been changed.'' Her mouth twisted. ''He was very concerned. Urged me to 'see someone' about my problems.''

Anger filled Aiden. He held himself still so he wouldn't explode and frighten her, and kept his voice carefully level. ''Was he trying to make you think you were crazy?''

''I don't know. Maybe. Or maybe it was all done for the benefit of our friends and neighbors. We were on the edge of divorce by then, and he wanted them to think I was the damaged one, not him.''

She sighed and started pacing. ''Not long before I moved out he told me that an old friend of mine had called. He said she was in town and staying with Beth—Beth Randolph, a teacher I work with. I called Beth. She had no idea what I was talking about. And Greg, of course, just looked blank when I confronted him.

''He dropped a word in Beth's ear later,'' she added bitterly as she circled the room. ''I wasn't there, but I gather from what she said later that he was very *reassuring*. Told her not to worry too much about these little lapses of mine, that they didn't mean anything, and anyway, he was sure I was getting better.''

''Thereby insuring that Beth did worry, and remember the incident,'' Georgia Ann said. ''Naturally, Noelle stopped believing anything Greg said. But that created problems, too, because sometimes the messages were genuine. There was one from her principal..." The older woman shook her head.

"But it stopped!" Noelle flung her hands up without stopping her restless circuit of the room. "After the divorce he stopped playing those games. He'd gotten what he wanted. A lot of people believed I was the damaged one, not him. So why has he started doing it again? Why?"

"I don't know. But there's a reason." The calculated campaign of terror that had been waged against her made Aiden sick, and some of that sickness was pure, blind rage. But his fury wouldn't help her. "I'm going to find that reason and stop him."

"How?" She stopped suddenly. She stood with her arms stiff, lifted slightly from her sides as if she wanted to take flight. Her fists were clenched, her chin lifted. "By moving in with me?"

Aiden looked at her delicate face, her fierce posture and thought of an injured hawk. This wasn't the girl he'd remembered for so long, the girl he'd come back to find. This woman was wary, cynical, distrustful—and she had reason to be.

She was also much stronger than that vanished girl. He felt a pang of loss...and the stir of fascination. Was it the memory he wanted to protect, or the woman in front of him? "I'll do whatever it takes."

Georgia Ann stood and carried her coffee cup to the sink. "Listen to the man. In one day he's accomplished more than the police have in two weeks."

Noelle's glance at the older woman held affection and exasperation, but it was Aiden she spoke to. "Yesterday at this time you were a memory, and not an especially happy one. I didn't expect to ever see you again. Now you think I should let you move in with me?"

He'd already pushed too hard. "All right. Skip that part. We could still pretend to be involved. The best way to persuade people you aren't hung up on your ex-husband is to give them something else to talk about, and the best way to prove he's up to something is to catch him in the act. I'm good at that sort of thing." He touched her arm lightly. "Think about it, at least."

Georgia Ann spoke cheerily. "I'd better be going, kids. You don't need me around to mediate your argument."

"We're not arguing," Aiden said.

"You will be. Or else you'll be doing something that really doesn't require a third party." The older woman collected her purse, gave Noelle a kiss on the cheek and advised her not to cut off her nose to spite her face. Then she was gone.

"Do you want rules?" Aiden asked reluctantly. "A promise that I won't touch you, except in public, to persuade people we're involved?"

"I don't know what I want." She drifted over to the door and looked out through the screen. After a moment she said, "I bought this house six months ago, using what Greg paid me for my share of our house."

"It's a great house. Maybe you'd give me a tour sometime."

She nodded, but absently, her gaze on the jumbled growth outside. "I've started planning, but there's so much to decide, so much to do. Should I keep the Englemann daisies out front? They're lovely in the spring, but can be invasive. They've pretty much taken over the bed by the driveway, and I'd like a mixed daisy garden there, I think. I want paths in the little woodland section, but I may need to thin it first. There's escarpment oak, live oak, sumac and juniper. Which do I keep? Then the persimmon out back isn't doing well...."

She turned to face him, gesturing widely. "My life is like my yard right now. Overgrown in places, neglected, needing time and attention. I don't know what I want. How can I? It's only been a year since I divorced Greg. I've barely started rebuilding."

"He really did a job on you."

"I allowed him to, I suppose." Her smile flickered. "I'm nothing if not stubborn. By my first anniversary I realized my marriage had problems. It took me another five years to admit I couldn't fix them.''

''One person alone can't make a marriage work. It takes two.''

''So I've learned. Did you?'' When he looked at her blankly, she clarified her question. ''Did you ever marry?''

That she wanted to know made his chest feel suddenly loose and warm with hope. ''There was only one woman I ever wanted to marry, and I destroyed what I might have had with her. After that, my job made that kind of commitment unwise.''

''Aiden...'' Her voice trailed off. She shook her head.

He nodded at the table. ''You haven't looked at everything in the folder.''

Her eyes questioned him even as her feet moved, taking her to the table. She opened the folder, turned over the pages one at a time. The last item in the folder was a check stub. She picked it up. Her eyes widened.

Aiden couldn't read it from here, of course, but he knew what it said. It was from the Central Intelligence Agency, payable to Aiden B. Swift. ''So,'' she said after a moment. ''What does the B stand for?''

''Bond.''

''You're kidding.''

He shook his head. "Afraid not. It's a family name, actually—my mother's maiden name."

She looked down at the piece of paper in her hand, biting her lip. "I should have believed you. I'm sorry."

"You've every reason to doubt what a man says."

"But I don't want to be like that!" Her voice was low, intense. "I don't want Greg's lies casting their shadow on everyone else I know. I don't want him to have that much power over me."

He took a deep breath. This woman needed honesty more than anything else, but it was hard. "You've got reason to distrust me. I didn't tell you the truth about myself twelve years ago. But I give you my promise now, Noelle. I'll speak only the truth to you." And with a last, brief pain he let go of the girl he'd loved so long ago. It was the woman in front of him he gave his promise to. "Let me help."

Slowly she nodded.

Chapter 6

For the next five days, Aiden kept his promises—those he'd given or implied, and one Noelle hadn't asked him for. The one about not touching her except when they were in public.

He came over after school and helped her dig, weed and compost two of the front beds. He took her to the Italian restaurant, a popular Chinese place and the movies. Saturday afternoon they went to a busy nursery, where she bought sacks of mulch and two flats of annuals for the beds they'd prepared. In public he was cheerful, attentive, touching her now and then in the casually proprietary way of a lover—and they were always in public. On display.

When he wasn't asking her questions about Greg,

they talked of all sorts of things. Gardening. Foreign affairs and foreign countries, many of which he'd visited, though he said nothing about his reasons for being in those places.

They spoke carefully about Georgia Ann and a few others he'd known in Greenlaurel twelve years ago—carefully, because that was mined territory. The questions she didn't ask pressed on her, but Noelle wasn't ready to risk explosions, not yet. They talked about the World Bank Heist and cats, the kids she taught and the annoying and strangely similar thought processes of administrators—those in high schools, and those in what he called The Company.

He said very little about what he'd done over the past twelve years, and even less about his plans for the future. And she didn't ask. Every night when he brought her home, he said good-night. And that was all he did.

Noelle knew she should be grateful for that. But it had been a long time since she'd been touched the way a man touches a woman he desires. It had been even longer, she gradually realized, since she'd wanted to be touched. Like a foot that has fallen asleep, part of her was coming back to life. She was all pins and needles, wobbling between numbness and sensation. And it hurt.

On Saturday they'd played tennis. At least, they started to. It took only a few serves for Noelle to realize that Aiden had never held a tennis racket in his life. She'd stalked up to the net and demanded to know why he'd lied.

"I didn't," he said mildly. "I asked if you still liked to play tennis. You said you did, and I suggested we try the courts at the country club, since I bought a membership. Very public."

The local country club wasn't terribly expensive or exclusive, but buying a membership there sounded very permanent. And not much like Aiden. When had he done that? Why?

But she never could bring herself to ask the important questions. "I still don't see why didn't you tell me you'd never played before."

He grinned. "Well, it was bound to be blindingly obvious." His amusement faded quickly, though. "There's more to lying than words, Noelle. A successful lie is lived, not just spoken. I know too much about that. I've done it over and over and I'm sick of lies. But I...my habits are all wrong. I've lost the trick of revealing myself. Even when I don't or can't tell you everything, though, I won't deceive you."

He'd touched her cheek lightly then, and it hadn't seemed like one of his public touches. She'd stared at him, her heart hammering, her confusion so vast she hadn't known she was going to speak until she heard herself say, "I'll teach you." Then she'd stammered, "Tennis, I mean. I'll teach you how to play tennis."

So she'd given him an impromptu tennis lesson, and somehow they'd veered from the serious to the silly. They'd played—lighthearted, laughing, with neither of them thinking about putting on any kind of show for whoever might be watching. Or so it seemed to her later, when she thought about it.

It wasn't until she lay in her bed Sunday night listening to the rain on the roof that she'd understood the rest of his reasons for not telling her he didn't know how to play tennis. The part he hadn't put into words.

He wanted her to look at his actions for truth, not just his words.

So what, she asked herself, did his actions speak of? An honorable man, she decided. One who wanted redemption more than forgiveness—redemption being earned by acts, not apologies. A man who was interested in her, she thought. Who maybe cared about her...but not a man in love. No, she knew how Aiden acted when he was in love.

But there were so many kinds of love.

If only, she thought, but the two words trailed off into a confusion of memory and pain. She remembered a man who had swept into her life like a thunderstorm, a passionate man who had needed her desperately. Aiden had just been discharged from the army when he showed up in Greenlaurel—or so she'd believed at the time. Wounded in the line of duty, mustered out on a medical discharge, hating the turn his life had taken and unsure how to make a life as a civilian.

They were out of step, she thought. Always out of step. Twelve years ago Aiden had been the one swamped by confusion, while Noelle had been carried along on the high tide of certainty. With the cheerful arrogance of youth, she'd been sure her love could heal him, confident they could build a new life together so wonderful that he wouldn't grieve for what he'd lost.

She'd been hopelessly wrong about that, hadn't she?

Now Aiden was the one with his feet firmly planted. He seemed to know what he wanted from himself and his life. And she was the one floundering in the morass she'd made of her life…and her heart.

Rain washed the roof, the trees, the window near her bed, a damp benediction soaking quietly into the ground. And for a very long time all she could think, lying there all pins and needles in her soft and empty bed, was, *if only*….

Aiden was reflecting on the nature of hopeless causes as compared to difficult tasks when a waitress set chips and salsa in front of him. He glanced at his watch. Noelle should be here soon. She'd had some kind of meeting to attend at the high school before joining him here. She wasn't happy about his choice of restaurants.

He'd arrived early to claim a table. Noelle had warned him that Hot Peppers would be crowded. A number of Rotary Club members ate here before their meeting every Monday.

That was why he'd picked Hot Peppers for their sixth date. Snowden was in the Rotary Club.

At that moment, Aiden's target was scooping salsa up with a tortilla chip and laughing. His pretty, dark-haired fiancée sat next to him; there were two other couples at the table. Aiden was watching him openly.

It was time to start applying pressure. A frightened man, like a hare startled from cover, was easier to bring down.

Aiden sampled some of the salsa Snowden was enjoying. Too much cilantro, he decided, but it had a nice bite. He ought to be feeling some satisfaction. He'd made progress today. But then, he'd never doubted he'd be able to find out what Snowden was up to, and put a stop to it. It was his ability to gain Noelle's trust he doubted.

She'd relaxed with him some over the past five days, but there was a guarded quality to her still. She never talked about what had been between them before. And she never asked him why he hadn't come back for her.

Snowden turned half-around in his chair, speaking to someone at the next table and putting his back to Aiden. So far he'd pretended not to notice the way Aiden was watching him.

He looked relaxed. His suit jacket was draped over the back of his chair, and he'd loosened his tie. His hair was a little shaggy in back, as if he'd missed his last trim. According to Noelle that was part of the packaging. Snowden's stylist had learned to cut his hair so he would always look a week or two late for a trim. He thought that made him look more trustworthy, and it fit the image of a country boy turned self-made man.

The latter, at least, was true. If you used an elastic definition of "man," and counted success in dollars.

Snowden had moved to Greenlaurel about a year after Aiden left, but was regarded as a local because his family had lived here until he was ten. Noelle had met her ex-husband's family exactly once. They could have been the poster family for dysfunctional—an alcoholic father, a manipulative martyr of a mother and an older sister who spent most of her time in rehab or prison. His parents lived in California and never left the state. This suited their son very well, as it allowed him to re-create them in a better guise for his audience in Greenlaurel.

Over the past five days, Aiden had questioned

Noelle frequently about her ex-husband. Georgia Ann, too. From others he'd gathered impressions more indirectly. He needed to know what the man craved, what he feared, what he believed about himself and the world. Facts, impressions and Noelle's dearly bought knowledge had added up to one basic truth: Gregory Snowden was a pathological liar.

He was also a very good one, which was rare. Most people liked him, and those who didn't weren't sure why. One comment seemed to sum up that reaction: the man was just too good to be true.

Aiden scooped up more salsa with a chip and smiled like a shark at his target, who was doing the same thing. This time Aiden managed to catch his eye. The man's hand froze. Salsa dribbled onto the tablecloth.

Aiden's smile widened ever so slightly. Then, for some reason, his attention veered to the front of the restaurant.

Noelle was there. She was talking to the hostess, her smile flashing. It fled when she looked around the restaurant and saw Greg.

Aiden's throat tightened. Sounds around him faded and colors sharpened as he watched the slim, dusky woman making her way toward him. Her back was very straight. She was wearing chinos and a thin sweater the color of the sea near Barbados. Her hair was braided neatly, which meant she'd come straight here from school. Noelle always wore her hair braided or pulled back to teach, and she always set it free as soon as she got home.

Had he fallen in love in only six days? Or had he simply never stopped loving her?

The girl she'd once been hadn't vanished, after all. She was still there inside Noelle, just as a tree's center still exists no matter how many wooden coats it grows over the years. Yesterday Aiden had laughed with that girl over his inability to hit a tennis ball over the net. The day before that, he'd glimpsed her in Noelle's eyes when she bought candytuft and blue daisies.

It was the whole woman he was in love with, the woman she was today—but those glimpses were precious.

He stood up for her. That was eagerness as much as manners. The boy in him was no more dead than the girl in her.

"Greg will be over at some point," she said as she took her seat. "He won't be able to resist the chance to poke at me, maybe find out what's going on. But that's why we're here, isn't it?"

"I know this is unpleasant for you. I'm sorry for that."

"I'm not so weak I can't handle an encounter with my ex-husband."

"You're not weak at all."

Their gazes snagged. He didn't know what she

saw in his eyes. He wasn't sure what he found in hers, either. Longing? Wariness? Then she looked away and began talking about one of her students, who had been the subject of the meeting. Aiden didn't mind. It was pleasant to sit and listen while she shared her day with him. It was more than pleasant to watch her.

Her hands were small. She kept her nails short, with only a small crescent of white tipping each finger. He imagined the feel of those small hands on his body. There was the mole on her neck that he'd remembered, right where he wanted to put his mouth.

He reminded himself to be patient. Much as he craved her body, it wouldn't be enough. The past still lay between him and everything else he wanted from her. The past, and all those questions she'd never asked.

He waited until after they'd eaten to share his day. It was good news, but he wanted her all to himself for a while, without the shadowy presence of her ex-husband. When the waitress had removed their plates he said, "I found the missing money."

"The missing…oh, the money Greg got for selling the land, you mean? What did he do with it?"

"Three months ago he sold the land to Frederick Abrams for a dollar and other considerations."

"A dollar! That doesn't make sense."

"The 'other considerations' will tell the real

story, once I find out what those were. I haven't had time to find out much about Abrams, except that he's in the phone book under 'attorneys.' What do you know about him?''

"That's him sitting with Greg." She nodded slightly in that direction. "The African-American with the long chin. He and Greg are pretty good friends. He's quite well off, active in local politics—served on the school board two years ago, and he's a county commissioner now. His wife's name is Laura. She teaches at the high school with me."

"You don't like her."

"I didn't say that."

"You didn't have to." Noelle never had learned how to hide or deceive. It was one of the things he loved about her. "If you'd liked her, it would have shown in your face, your voice. Does she have access to your typewriter at school?"

Her eyes squinched up unhappily. "I suppose. I guess it must be someone at the school who typed that letter, but…it's hard to believe Laura would do something like that."

"Her husband is involved with…uh-oh. Company coming." Snowden's party had broken up, and he and his fiancée were headed their way.

Chapter 7

The fiancée was a pretty girl of twenty-two or three—a bit young for Snowden, but Aiden had noticed that some men repeated themselves. If their first wife was twenty-two when they got married, the second one would be about that age, too.

She was short, thin and stylish. Her clothes were sophisticated, and her dark brown hair had been cropped and gelled so that the ends stuck out here and there, artfully ragged. Yet somehow she looked like a little girl playing dress-up. Maybe it was the round face or the round, uncertain eyes.

She and Snowden were holding hands. He spoke first, which didn't surprise Aiden. "Swift." He nodded. "I don't think you've met my fiancée, Janee Albright. Janee, this is Aiden Swift. You, ah, already know Noelle.''

The young woman nodded stiffly. Aiden murmured something appropriate, and waited to see what tack the man would take.

He started by aiming a sad smile at Noelle. ''I don't want to intrude, but I was hoping…perhaps you're ready to let the past go. It would mean a lot to me if we could be friends.''

''It would mean a lot to me if I never had to see or speak to you again. Unfortunately, we live in the same town, so that isn't likely.''

''Ouch. Noelle, now that you've found someone new, can't you forgive me for doing the same? Let go of old grievances?''

''Oh, I've let go. But you keep piling up new ones.''

''That is so unfair!'' Janee burst out.

''Sweetheart,'' Greg began.

''But it's just wrong!'' She glared at Noelle. ''You wanted the divorce—and you took him for everything you could, too! Demanding that *ridiculous* amount of money for the house, and getting half his investments—''

''I didn't get a penny of Greg's investments. I had trouble keeping his hands out of my retirement fund.''

Janee rolled her eyes. ''Oh, right. Just like you haven't been writing yourself little letters and telling horrible stories about Greg breaking into your house—when everyone *knows* he was at a party with me and a hundred other people."

"Actually, yes," Noelle said dryly. "Just like that."

"Darling." Greg smiled at the woman bristling at his side. "Every man should have such a charming champion. But Noelle is...well, we have to make allowances. I'm not sure she knows what she's doing. That it's intentional."

"I think she knows exactly what she's doing." Janee nodded twice. "I don't think she's fragile or unbalanced. She's just *mean*. And jealous. She found out about you running for office and realized she'd thrown away the kind of status she's always craved."

Noelle craved status? Snowden was damned good, Aiden thought. Even knowing what he did about the man, it was hard to fault his performance.

"Janee, sweetheart." His chuckle held a hint of embarrassment. "I'm running for county commissioner, not president."

Bingo. The puzzle pieces fell into place with all the inevitability of falling dominoes. It was all Aiden could do to keep from grinning. A quick glance at Noelle told him he needed to distract Snowden, or that lovely, transparent face would give the game away.

"Still," Aiden said blandly, "county commissioner is an important position locally. Possibly a stepping stone for bigger and better things, too, if you're inclined that way. Is this a recent decision?''

It was Janee who answered, carried along by the exhilaration a normally timid woman feels when swept away by a cause. ''He's been considering it for ages, but he just today officially declared his candidacy.'' She hooked her arm through his. ''We're celebrating. And I do not appreciate you spoiling this moment for us.''

Although the ''you'' in her speech clearly referred to Noelle, Aiden chose to assume he was included. ''I see. You'd rather that we didn't come over to your table in a restaurant and publicly accuse you of mean-spirited behavior?''

Janee's mouth opened—and closed again. She flushed a miserable shade of red. ''I'm sorry. I didn't…I wasn't thinking.''

Snowden patted her hand. ''You're allowed to be partisan on my behalf, sweetheart. Though perhaps…a little more thinking before speaking next time?''

Patronizing bastard. Aiden glanced at Noelle. ''I don't think I want any dessert. How about you…sweetheart?''

There was a tiny twitch at the corners of Noelle's lips. ''Not tonight. Darling.''

Greg was too smooth to ignore such a hint, and took himself and his embarrassed fiancée away. Aiden exchanged a glance with Noelle. She fairly brimmed with excitement, but held herself in until he'd collected and paid the check.

They stepped out into a musty gold world, the air infused with the failing light of sunset. The parking lot was populated by cars; not a soul was in sight.

Noelle walked beside him, her legs swinging out in long, excited strides. "You know what this means, don't you?"

"That your ex-husband's bride-to-be is an earnest little twit?"

She laughed. "That, too. Though I can't help feeling sorry for her. Aiden, the county commissioners are the body that voted down the toxic waste dump two years ago!"

"Quite a coincidence that Snowden would decide to run for that position, isn't it?"

She snorted. A snort from his delicate fairy lady.

"And you're the only one who knows he nearly sold the land to the waste disposal company before."

"Yes!" She stopped and grabbed his hands. "That's why he's so determined to make me look like a vindictive madwoman, so no one will believe a word I say about him after he's elected."

"He's banking a lot on winning an election."

"Oh, he'll get in." Bitterness touched her voice. "You've seen how well-liked he is. Everyone knows him, or knows who he is. But Aiden, how can they do this? Frederick Abrams is already a county commissioner, so he'll be helping Greg push the approval through, but if the land's in his name—''

"It won't be." How she sparkled. He squeezed her hands. "I'll bet dollars to doughnuts the land is now held by a corporation which, with some digging, will turn out to be owned by Abrams and dear old Greg. Though if they're smart, they've buried their ownership behind two or three other dummy corporations.''

She shook her head. "I don't understand how all that works. But I don't have to, do I? I've got you to figure things out. And you have. I didn't think it was possible, but you've done it.''

She stretched up and kissed him on the mouth.

It was an impulse. He knew that. Relief had made her reckless, but she didn't intend more than a quick kiss, brimming with gratitude. Pride should have held him back if honor wouldn't, but he could no more keep himself from grabbing her and diving into that kiss than he could have stopped the sun in its path.

Her lips were soft. The shock of her body against his jolted through him, bright and sweet, and the taste of her swam inside him like wine. And she trembled. That almost stopped him—the sudden jab of conscience, a stab in the gut. Did she shake with passion or fear?

Then she opened her mouth to him, and his mind crashed.

The dying sun was warm on his eyelids. The woman in his arms was warmer, and more dear. Her fingers dug into his arm, then fastened themselves at the back of his neck, holding his mouth to hers. He made a happy captive.

The blat of a car horn made them both jump. Someone yelled, "Get a room!" Another voice called, "Or at least a back seat!" Aiden heard laughter—young male voices—and the screech of tires as the car pulled away.

Noelle stiffened. "Give me a minute," he whispered against her hair. A long tremor went through her, and he stroked her back with a hand that trembled, hoping to soothe both of them. He could feel the hammer of his heart, and his mouth was dry from the chemical and emotional backlash.

Dear God. He was in a parking lot. Exposed. Anyone could have walked right up to him just now and slid a knife between his ribs. He wouldn't have noticed until the blade went in.

Apparently he was getting the hang of civilian life. Though most civilians probably didn't worry about getting knifed in the back when they kissed a beautiful woman. A woman who still trembled ever so slightly in his arms. "It's all right," he said to both of them, rubbing his hand up and down her spine.

Her chuckle was muffled by his shoulder. "Says who?"

"If you'd wanted me to make sense, you shouldn't have kissed me that way."

Slowly she drew back. Her eyes were heavy, her lips slightly swollen from his kiss. "I don't know what makes sense anymore. Aiden…" She touched his lips lightly. "Come home with me tonight."

There was a roaring in his ears. Now—tonight— heaven help him, he'd been sure she wasn't even close to being ready for this. Now she was inviting him. And he…he had surely lost his mind, because he said, "I had little choice but to leave you when I did. After that assignment ended, though, I could have come back. I didn't dare."

Her eyes went dark and blank. She'd shut herself away even before she pulled out of his arms, step-ping back two paces, putting every kind of distance between them. And staring, staring at him all the while, with no expression at all on her face.

"Do you want to know why? If you won't ask, will you at least let me tell you?"

She bit her bottom lip hard enough to drain both blood and color from it. Then shook her head, turned and walked slowly to her car.

* * *

Noelle stood in her moon-washed kitchen glaring at the answering machine. The sound of someone breathing hard came clearly over the machine's speaker. It was five minutes after one in the morning.

The phone had rung just as she finally dozed off. She'd almost answered it, visions of family disasters running through her brain, but at the last minute she'd remembered to let the machine pick up. Sure enough, it was Greg or his cousin. Hard to tell one heavy breather from another.

She had a stupid urge to pick up the phone and tell him she knew what he was up to. That Aiden was going to stop him.

Click. He'd hung up. That didn't take long, she thought with grim satisfaction. Panting into an answering machine probably wasn't much fun.

She'd come downstairs in her nightgown. It was thin, mint-green and sleeveless, and her arms were cold. Chilly, angry and wide-awake, she drifted past the window over the sink. The full moon peered through the lacework branches of the old elm, flooding her yard with silvery light. There was more light outside than in tonight.

How could she have done that to Aiden? Or to herself?

Noelle hugged her chilly arms closer. First she'd

kissed him as if she'd given up air. Then she'd asked him to come home with her.

A euphemism, that. She'd meant *come to bed with me*. She'd meant *I don't need air as much as I need you right now*. And he'd known it.

He had wanted to talk. To tell her why he'd left and never returned. Not a phone call, not a letter— for twelve years all she'd had of him was that accursed note he'd left her. The one that claimed to love her.

He obviously had no idea what the word meant.

Noelle paced the length of the kitchen, turned, stopped and smacked her palm against the wall. Hard. It stung.

The heck with this. She wanted to yank weeds out by the roots. Pull them out and lay their little corpses on the ground. So what if it was the middle of the night? She needed to get her hands dirty.

Moving fast now, she sped to the little laundry room off the kitchen. A moment later she left the house wearing her nightgown, a brown corduroy jacket, an ancient pair of sandals and her gardening gloves.

The ground would still be damp from last night's rain, she thought as she stepped onto the back porch. And the border by the west fence definitely needed work. She'd start there. Now, where had she left her trowel? Oh, yes, on the window ledge. She grabbed it and—

The wooden step up to the porch creaked.

She spun around, her mouth opening in a scream that didn't quite happen. "Oh." Her breath gusted out. Her heart was dancing in her chest, silly beast, but it was her stomach her hand went to, as if to hold in the fear. "My God, Aiden, you scared me. What are you doing here?"

"Watching." He stepped closer. In the moonlight there was no color to him, only light and shadows. "And the last thing I expected to see was you being an idiot!"

"You're angry," she said, almost as surprised by that as by his presence.

"Damned right I'm angry. You've got better sense. *Surely* you've got better sense than to wander around outside after midnight when you know Snowden is after you."

"But not to injure me," she pointed out reasonably. "He wants to make me look crazy. Attacking me would work against him."

"He wants to keep you from screwing up his deal." He gripped her shoulders. She had the idea he wanted to shake her, and was restraining himself. "One way to do that is to make sure no one believes a word you say about him. Or he can make sure you can't say anything, period."

Fear fluttered up her throat. "You don't mean—you can't think he—that he would try to kill me!"

"I don't know. Neither do you. That's the point." Now he did give her shoulders a little wake-up shake. "People are seeing us as a couple. That's the last thing he wants—he's got to keep everyone convinced you're unhinged about him for the next several months. He's nervous, he's going to do something to get things going his way again, and *we don't know what that will be.*"

She stood very still. Her heartbeat settled as she stared up at him in a kind of wonder. "That's why you're here, isn't it? You're watching over me. Were you planning to spend the night in my back-yard?"

He hesitated, then dropped his hands. "You didn't want me to move in. I can understand that."

"Have you been here all along? Every night?"

"It's no big deal, Noelle. No one has seen me. You wouldn't have seen me tonight if I hadn't wanted you to."

He'd *meant* to scare her when he stepped on the squeaky step. "When do you sleep?"

"In the daytime, obviously. I'm no superhero. Look, Noelle—"

"It rained last night."

"You'll have noticed that I didn't melt. Look, you have to work tomorrow. You'd better go in, get some sleep. Don't worry about Snowden. I can't watch the front and back both, but amateurs never use the front door when they're trying to sneak into a place."

She had a sudden image of a series of hit men, spies and assassins politely using her front door to break in, that being more professional. She bit her lip to keep from giggling. "This is the sort of thing you've been doing, isn't it? Watching, finding things out. Only the people you've been watching have been a lot scarier than Greg."

"He's no pro," he assured her. "He won't get to you."

Aiden had spent the past five nights watching her house. Keeping her safe. When no one else had believed her, not really—even Georgia Ann had had her doubts, however staunchly she suppressed them. Aiden had accepted everything she told him. Completely. And when she wouldn't let him keep an eye on her inside her house, he'd simply done so from the outside. Without a word to her about it.

This was no effort to win her admiration, or even her forgiveness. This was…heroism. Quiet, uncounting of cost, and without glory. Noelle's eyes stung with sudden tears. "Why didn't you let me know you were out here?"

"I..." he stopped, rubbing the back of his neck. "To tell the truth, it never occurred to me."

The watcher didn't inform the watched. Not in his world, the one he'd lived in for so many years. "Aiden," she asked quietly, "why didn't you come back? Or call, or...anything."

He took a quick step towards her. Stopped. "I didn't dare."

"Tell me."

Chapter 8

At some point while Aiden was talking, the wind came to play. It teased the hem of Noelle's nightgown and tangled the ends of her hair. Her toes grew cold. That was okay. The rest of her was warm enough, especially the side next to Aiden. They were sitting on the wooden porch, their feet on the first step.

Until the assignment that had nearly crippled him, Aiden had been what he called ''one of the grunts''—part of an elite team with military training who operated as a covert strike force. His injury had put an end to that. While he'd recovered enough to function well in any normal situation, the sort of situations the strike force handled were far from normal. He'd come to Greenlaurel thinking that part of his life was over, and he'd fallen in love.

That part had been true, just as Noelle had always believed. He *had* loved her.

Two weeks before their wedding, while Noelle was out of town, visiting her parents, he'd gotten a call. The assignment that had ended his career had belatedly birthed some repercussions. He'd had some kind of special knowledge—perhaps of the people involved; he didn't say—that made him the best one to deal with those repercussions. And so he'd left.

He'd handled the job so well that the agency decided to keep him on in another capacity. One in which he would operate more independently. One that meant he'd spend months, possibly years, under deep cover. And so he'd never come back, never contacted Noelle again...because he'd loved her.

Just not enough.

That had been hard to hear, hard to accept. Aiden had loved her enough not to want her waiting for him, never knowing where he was, what he was doing or if he would return. Enough, too, that he'd feared seeing her again, afraid he'd try to keep some kind of relationship going in spite of everything. The effort might have gotten him killed. In such a life, distraction could be deadly.

But he hadn't loved her enough to give up that life.

Deep cover. She'd heard the phrase, had a vague idea of what it meant. Aiden had lived it. His work hadn't been Hollywood derring-do, but the quiet, ongoing submersion of his own personality in a series of adopted roles.

"What was it like?" she asked, knowing he couldn't tell her specifics. That he'd never be able to speak of much that he'd done these past twelve years.

He was leaning forward, his hands clasped between his knees. "Like skydiving, in a way. Or war. Long stretches of discomfort, boredom and painstaking attention to detail, punctuated by moments of sheer terror."

"It sounds horrible."

"It was and it wasn't. For a long time," he said, looking out at the quiet night, "I loved it. Don't be picturing me as some sort of selfless hero. It wasn't like that. Those moments of terror…they were also some of the best times. When everything comes together at once, and everything depends on you and you *act*…there's this heightened consciousness. Like a prolonged adrenaline rush, or seeing Rome for the first time, or…I don't know how to put it. Life shines more brightly."

"Do you miss it?"

"No. No, I stayed in it too long. I stopped loving

it a long time before I left. That was stubbornness, in part. And there was a need...but finally I had to get out. Noelle..." He shifted to face her more directly. "Why was it so hard to ask?"

"I didn't want to forgive you. Not really." She tipped her head back, her heart constricting with painful self-knowledge. "I thought I already had, but there was this angry little corner of my heart...it was easier to hold on to that anger. I was so hurt when you left. For a long time I was sure you'd be back. That I'd at least hear from you. When I didn't..."

She made a small sound, half-pain, half-amusement. "I did something stupid. I married Greg. Oh, no, you don't," she said, seeing the expression on his face. "You made some mistakes, but you don't get to claim responsibility for mine. There are plenty of ways to deal with pain that don't involve rushing into marriage."

His voice was tense, constricted. "Would you have married him if I hadn't left that way?"

Amusement sparked briefly. "No, I'd have married you, remember?" Then she sighed. "I can forgive the big mistakes, it seems. I've forgiven myself for marrying Greg. I've forgiven you for leaving me. But I *stayed* with him...I lost so many pieces of myself. No, I gave them up. With all the little choices I made day after day after day, I gave away pieces of myself. I don't know how to forgive myself for that. It makes me feel sick." She put a hand on her stomach. "Literally. When I get close to those feelings my stomach ties itself up in a black, greasy knot."

"You married Snowden about a year after I left. Then, about a year after you divorced him, I showed up. Must feel like a really wicked version of déjà vu. Great timing I've got."

That startled a laugh out of her. She leaned her chin on her upthrust knees, looking out at the silver and black mystery the moon made of her yard. "Amazing timing. You know what I told myself when I met Greg and things got serious?"

"What?"

"That it was like riding a horse. Get thrown, and you have to get back on right away. Can you imagine that? Comparing romance to falling off a horse."

"The principle is sound. You just got back on the wrong horse."

Something in his voice made her look at him. He was sitting with one leg cocked, one stretched out down the steps. Moonlight fell squarely on his face. He was smiling, his gaze very steady.

"You're scaring me," she said.

"I'll wait if I have to. Years, if that's what you need." He reached for her hand, which was clasped around her knee. For some reason she let him take it. "But I'd rather not."

Noelle was watching him with her eyes wide open when he kissed her.

Sometime later, it was she who took his hand and led him into her house and up the stairs to her bed.

The lamp on the bedside table glowed. The covers were jumbled and the room smelled faintly of the lavender she'd spritzed on her pillow in her earlier, futile attempt at serenity. Her heart thundered in her chest. For tonight, she'd given up on serenity, certainty, safety. She only wanted Aiden.

He cupped her face in both hands and kissed her. She slid her arms around his waist, and life seemed to burst and pop in every cell. Fizzy with delight, she leaned her head back and laughed.

"Yes?" he murmured, kissing her neck.

"I just remembered what I'm wearing. If ever a woman wasn't dressed for seduction, it's me."

He took the edges of her grungy old jacket in his hands and slid it from her shoulders. "You are beautiful."

And she looked in his eyes, and saw that she was.

There was so much to discover. Noelle hadn't expected this to feel so new—scary, trembly new. But so many years had passed, so much experience. They weren't the same two people who had made love with such fumbling urgency twelve years ago. Though he remembered the places she liked to be touched, his touch was different—more certain, and subtly more generous. His hand trembled when he cupped her naked breast.

There were bumps of familiarity, too. When they lay in a tangle of arms and legs and she nuzzled the column of his neck, his scent shot straight to the back of her brain. Time compressed, collapsed, and it might have been yesterday when she last lay with him, skin to skin.

Too soon, urgency overrode both memory and discovery. She gasped when he pushed inside her; he groaned. Sheer physical glory smothered thought as he began to thrust. Lost in motion, she let her body answer his, and the breathless race continued until her body bucked and her hands fell, limp and open, to her sides. Letting go. Letting go of everything.

Afterward, she lay close and warm and exhausted in the curve of his body in a bedroom that was dark once more. Strange, so strange, she thought, to have the weight of his arm draped over her ribs and feel a hard, hairy leg against her thigh. Her sleepy mind couldn't encompass the steps that had led from *alone* to this, much less grapple with the question of tomorrow.

His breath was soft on her hair. "I love you, Noelle."

Her mind went blank and astonished and she said nothing, nothing at all.

After a moment he kissed her gently, as if she

were the one needing comfort for her silence. And in spite of everything, she soon dropped off the edge of the world into sleep.

The next day passed in a blur. The morning was a mad scramble, because she'd forgotten to set her alarm. Aiden fixed coffee while she showered. There was barely time for a toothpaste-flavored kiss at the door. And that, blast the man, was the moment he picked to tell her he hoped to finalize a deal on the business he was buying.

"What?" she demanded. "What business? What kind of deal?"

"I'll tell you tonight. You're going to be late if you don't leave. Besides, I want to surprise you."

As if she hadn't had enough surprises in her life lately. But he just chuckled at her expression and gave her a little pat on the bottom, which made her want to kiss him again, or maybe hit him.

She should have been seriously drowsy that day, tense with doubts and questions. And she *was* distracted, but sleep lost to lovemaking seemed to render her silly instead of grouchy, filled with a fond patience for even the most difficult of her students. She'd heard that sleep deprivation could induce altered states of consciousness. Hers was certainly peculiar that day. She floated through the hours on impenetrable clouds of serenity, a mood as irrational as it was lovely.

She was in love. Desperately, hopelessly in love—still, or all over again. And he loved her. She didn't doubt that. Aiden would never have used the words if he hadn't meant them.

He'd loved her before. And left anyway. And she didn't care, she told herself in those few moments when reality nudged its way through the euphoric clouds. Whatever happened tomorrow would happen. For now, she was happy. When the last bell rang, she gathered her tote and fled out the door as eagerly as any of her students.

Her mood did suffer a few dents when she swung through the supermarket to pick up ingredients for lasagna. Greenlaurel wasn't such a small town that everyone really knew everyone else, but Noelle had taught at the only high school for several years now. Add students and relatives of students to the social circle she'd inhabited with her relentlessly social ex-husband, and it was rare for her to go anywhere that she didn't run into a lot of people she knew.

That had been a mixed blessing lately, given her recent notoriety. Today was no different—if anything, it seemed worse than usual. There were false smiles, sidelong glances and those telling moments of silence when conversation stops because its object has just come into view.

To top it all off, she ended up in line ahead of Meredith Upjohn. Meredith was the secretary at the high school and desperately needed to have more going on in her life, judging by the amount of attention she gave to other people's business.

She also tittered. "Imagine running into you here!" she said, as if the supermarket were some exotic locale. "Looks like you're cooking tonight."

"Lasagna," Noelle said, wishing she could snub the woman. But the secretary could make life difficult for a teacher she considered snobby.

"Cooking for two?" Meredith asked coyly. "I declare, Noelle, I think you are so brave! Though I worry about you, too."

"That is so typical of you. Your concern for others is endless."

"I've always said that God didn't put us here to be islands. Speaking of which, dear, I feel I have to give you a little warning."

"I'd rather you didn't."

"We don't always want what's good for us, do we? And I *do* understand how you might be swept off your feet. I've seen your new boyfriend—or perhaps I should call him your old boyfriend? I swear, that man could melt any female with just a glance! But looks aren't everything, you know."

"I agree." Noelle began unloading her cart, wishing the checker would hurry up with the woman ahead of her so she could escape. "I hope your allergies aren't giving you too much trouble, given the wet spring we've been having."

But her attempted diversion failed. Meredith abandoned the vague warnings intended to provoke Noelle's curiosity, and got straight to the nitty-gritty: the rumors she'd heard about Aiden, who was leading Noelle on. He'd *bragged* about it, my dear, so dreadful! She didn't like to carry tales— she said—but she'd heard the story from ever so many people, and where there's smoke there's fire, isn't there? Meredith did so hate to see Noelle hurt when it seemed she was just getting over the breakup of her marriage.

By the time Noelle pulled out her debit card to pay for her groceries, she was simmering. No amount of rebuttal would help. Not with Meredith. When the woman started hinting about Aiden's money troubles, she exploded. "For heaven's sake! You don't know any more about Aiden's finances than about—well, about anything else to do with him!"

Meredith bristled. "Don't shoot the messenger! I'm just telling you—"

"A lot of nonsense. And I'd appreciate it if you didn't bother, next time. By the way," she said as she grabbed her sack, "was it by any chance Laura Abrams who filled your head with this hogwash?"

"Why, I—that is, she may have said something, but I don't…"

Noelle walked away without hearing the rest. Greg again, she fumed. Aiden had said he'd try something soon, and this was it, apparently. She wasn't sure what Greg's goal was, aside from making trouble. Maybe he thought she would believe the rumors and break up with Aiden. Could he be that foolish? Or maybe this was just the start, and he had something else planned.

Georgia Ann's big Cadillac was pulling into a space across from Noelle's car. Good, Noelle thought, tossing her sack in the open window of her own car. She wanted to vent.

The older woman was so preoccupied she didn't even see Noelle coming toward her. Noelle had to call out her name to get her to stop.

She jumped like she'd been goosed. "Oh, Noelle, I—I didn't see you there."

Noelle took in the guilty look at Georgia Ann's face and forgot her anger. Georgia Ann only looked guilty when she was worried. "What's wrong?"

"Oh, nothing. At least, I think it's nothing—no, I'm sure it is."

"Georgia Ann, you're really worried about something. Can't I help?"

"I don't know if I should say anything. But if I don't..." She bit her lip, a sign of real distraction, since she hated to chew off her lipstick. "Oh, Noelle, I just came from Wood's pharmacy. Aiden and Greg were there, sitting together in one of the booths at the back, near the soda fountain."

Noelle blinked. "And that upset you? There

could be any number of reasons for them to sit together. Aiden might be warning Greg to lay off, or—or Greg might be trying out some of his lies. Aiden won't believe him," she assured her friend. "He knows what Greg is like."

"Greg was writing out a check. He handed it to Aiden. Noelle, it looked...it looked very much as if he were paying Aiden off. I haven't paid much attention to the rumors about Aiden—"

"You've heard them, too?"

"I was hoping you hadn't," Georgia Ann said unhappily. "I felt sure they were Greg's doing, only then I saw him and Aiden and I thought...but that has to be absurd. Doesn't it? Aiden wouldn't take money from Greg to—to seduce and abandon you."

Noelle stood frozen. The buzzing in her head made her dizzy. Shock, she thought. I'm in shock. And then: I'm not that much of an idiot, am I?

Then she was walking—running—to her car, with Georgia Ann's questions falling away behind her.

Aiden left the booth where Snowden was finishing his coffee in a glow of satisfaction. The man's check was tucked in his pocket. A nice little bonus, he thought, and grinned.

His grin died when he pushed open the drugstore door and saw Noelle running toward him.

Hell. He'd known Georgia Ann had spotted him and Snowden, but he'd thought he would have time to get to Noelle first. His stomach knotted sickly and he stopped moving, waiting stiffly for her accusations.

"Why didn't you tell me?" she cried—and threw her arms around him.

"I…" Automatically, his arms closed around her. "I can explain," he started again, but ran out of words, completely baffled.

She wasn't crying, or demanding explanations. She was hugging him.

"You don't have to," she said, leaning back to smile at him. "Or rather, you do need to explain some things, but not the way you're thinking. I know I have some trust issues, but you do, too, it seems. Or is it just habit?" She shook her head. "Why didn't you tell me you'd set up some kind of sting to trap Greg?"

"You—you figured it out." Dazed, Aiden did the one thing that made sense. He tightened his arms around her. "I don't understand. How did you know?"

She was smiling at him, sunny and confident. "There was no good reason for you to take money from Greg. That left bad reasons, only you wouldn't *do* that. So the only thing left was some kind of trap—but one you set for him, not for me." More shyly she added, "You wouldn't hurt me. I know that."

"No," he said. "Never." And did the next thing that made sense, which was to kiss her.

Their embrace was interrupted almost immediately, however. Two policemen needed them to move away from the door. They had Snowden with them. He was in handcuffs, and he was not happy.

"We'll take it from here," one of them told Aiden cheerfully. "Don't forget to bring the wire by the station when you get a chance."

Snowden glared at Aiden, then saw Noelle and started cursing.

"Here, now, none of that," the other officer said, and gave his bound arms a little jerk. "Watch your step. Wouldn't want you to fall down and mess up your face."

Noelle giggled, then put her hand over her mouth as if shocked by herself. "So what did you do?" she demanded as the cops and their prisoner moved toward the patrol car. "It involved a wire."

"I'd set up this sting days ago, before we learned what he was up to. I've been dropping some hints here and there that I needed money. And..." He grimaced. Noelle wasn't going to like this part. "That membership I bought at the country club. That was so I'd have access to some of his buddies. I, ah, led them to believe I was stringing you along. Using you. I know how to sound like scum," he finished grimly. "Snowden is a good liar, but a poor crook. He bought my story, and approached me with an offer."

"What kind of an offer? Why didn't you *tell* me?"

"He paid me to set up one of his little incidents. One that would make you look pretty well around the bend." Snowden had meant this one to take place publicly, with maximum humiliation for Noelle. Aiden's lips tightened. "After which I was supposed to dump you."

"That—that scumbag." Noelle watched, scowling, as the cops loaded her ex-husband in the patrol car. "Is it wrong to be this happy that Greg is going to be thrown in jail?"

Aiden snorted. "Is that a rhetorical question?"

Her smile returned, impish this time. "Maybe it is. You still haven't explained why I didn't know anything about all this."

"Partly it was habit," he admitted. "I'm not used to talking about an operation. And I didn't want to get your hopes up—the cops weren't exactly enthused at first, until a friend of a friend gave them a call and asked them to cooperate. And then..." He smiled ruefully and touched her cheek. "I'm sorry, love, but you're lousy at deception. If you'd known what was going on last night when we saw Snowden, you'd have given yourself away."

She chewed on her lip a moment. "All right. I guess. But don't do it again."

"I don't plan to. Noelle…" Amazement, tender and aching, floated up. "You stunned me, you know. With your trust."

She took a deep, shaky breath, letting it out slowly. "Of course I trust you. I love you."

Happiness bloomed in him, whole and complete. "I know."

"You what?" Half-laughing, half-angry, she poked him in the side. "What kind of response is that? I didn't know myself until this morning."

"I knew it when we made love." He kissed her tenderly, as he had last night after frightening her with his own declaration. "But I didn't think you were ready to admit it to either of us. I hurt you badly once."

She didn't answer in words, but with another kiss—flavored with forgiveness. This one went on for a very long time. Finally he made himself pull away. "Come on," he said, taking her hand. "I've something to show you."

"Something to do with that business you're buying?" Her voice was light, happy.

"Good guess. I did need money, but I got it the old-fashioned way—I saved like crazy, then borrowed a ridiculous amount of money from the bank."

"So what business did you buy?"

"The newspaper."

"The *Gazette?*" She stopped, shook her head, then grinned. "I think you're the crazy one. What do you know about running a paper?"

"Not much," he admitted. "Though I hope my business degree will be of some use, I have a lot to learn. I *have* been a journalist, believe it or not. Three times. It was a cover identity, of course, but I had to actually write some stories to look good in the role. I liked it," he said simply. "And after twelve years of secrets and lies, I'm ready to spend the next thirty or forty years uncovering secrets, and printing the truth."

She squeezed his hand and they walked on. "Is Greg's arrest going to be in the paper?"

"When a declared candidate for local office gets arrested, the paper has to print that."

"Good."

"There's something else I'd like to put in the paper soon." His heart pounded and his mouth was dry. He was terrified. He pushed on anyway. "An engagement notice. For us."

She walked on in silence, and his heart sank. It's too soon, he told himself. He was an idiot. He'd wait, give her more time...

"I don't think so," she said, stopping at the corner where the light was red. "A marriage notice, now, that would be fine. But I have a condition." She smiled and looped her arms around his neck.

"No more big weddings for me. The first one never happened, and the second one was a mistake. It's either the justice of the peace or Las Vegas this time."

His heart was expanding, growing enormous. Like the silly grin on his face. "Only one question left, then. Do you need to go back to your house for anything, or can we go straight to the airport?"

*   *   *   *   *

INVITING TROUBLE

Anne Marie Winston

For Trinabean and Lisabelle,
with all my love.

Chapter 1

"I heard Renata Brownley is adopted."

"So is Jake Ingram, and I know for a fact that he was adopted when he was older. Maybe he's one of them."

The voices behind her were conspiratorial whispers, and Katherine Davenport looked around in annoyance. Ever since the news had broken that successful genetic experiments had occurred during the mid-1960s the nation, and Greenlaurel, Texas in particular, had been abuzz with concern. Rumor had it that the resulting children, with heaven only knew what kind of strange genetic enhancements—or defects—that might show up in the future, had been placed in adoptive homes. Those children would be

young adults now and it seemed anyone who had
been adopted during the years in question was being singled out as some kind of possible freak.
Hype abounded and one unconfirmed source even
had speculated that one or more of the children had
been placed with adoptive families in central
Texas…in or near the town of Greenlaurel.

"Devina McClanahan, you should have your
hide tanned for spreading rumors," Kate said
sharply. "Your own grandmother and Renata's
have been best friends since before you were
born."

The young blonde tossed her head and smiled at
her companions, all silly, vapid debs who needed a
good kick in the ass, in Kate's opinion. "Kate's a
little cranky," she said sweetly, "because she
doesn't know where on earth she's going to find
someone to dance with her in a few minutes." Her
friends tittered and Devina, satisfied that her dig
had been appreciated, turned and swept away with
her little entourage in tow.

The comment might have been spiteful, but there
was needle-sharp accuracy in it and Kate had to
steel herself not to squirm. It was true, she didn't
have a partner for the upcoming singles' dance, and
she had less than no idea where she might find one.

She felt like a hooker, all decked out in the shining copper gown with its bodice of intricate jet
beadwork that her grandmother had insisted she

wear to the annual Bluebonnet Ball thrown by the Belles of Texas Historical Society. It actually wasn't bad compared to some of the other revealing dresses she'd seen, but Kate didn't even want to be here, much less be half-dressed in something that could pass for a fancy nightie.

She'd managed to get to the ripe old age of twenty-five without ever attending the ball, but this year she'd sucked it up and let her grandmother con her into attending. This year, she had a mission, and if she had to dress like a tart and fawn over a couple of geezers to accomplish her goal, she'd survive.

"Katherine! Would you please come over here? There's someone I'd like you to meet." The voice was sweet and silvery, and Kate sighed with relief. Oh, good. If she was busy with some guest of her grandmother's, maybe she could get out of the obligatory singles' dance, the notorious first dance of the Bluebonnet Ball for which every single person in the room had to find a partner. God, please just let her live through the evening without finding some man's hand on her ass. Which, come to think of it, was darn near hanging out due to the low vee-cut back of the copper dress.

She took several of her customary long strides before she remembered that her dress was slit up the side to mid-thigh, and she reduced her pace to a slow and stupid ladylike sway. As she crossed to Irma Davenport's side, she caught her grandmother's eye and the amusement she saw there made her own lips curve in wry chagrin.

"Guess you haven't managed to turn me into a lady yet," she said to her grandmother.

Irma shook her head, smiling fondly. "Apparently not. Although every man in the room is probably thanking you for those big steps you were taking."

Kate laughed. "Sorry. I didn't think about it until too late. If you'd let me wear jeans and boots, that wouldn't have happened."

Her grandmother cast her a look of mock-disapproval.

Just then, the bandleader announced that the singles' dance would be starting and instructed everyone to find a partner. The strains of the orchestra's music began to drift through the room and the volume of noise increased in direct proportion as every single person was pounced on and dragged to the dance floor.

Kate ducked her head and stepped a pace behind her grandmother, hoping no one would notice her. "So where's this person you want to introduce me to?" she asked. Maybe if she appeared to be deep in conversation no one would butt in.

"Right here, dear." Irma waved a hand at a space behind Kate and she turned to find herself face-to-face with a tuxedo-clad male chest in a crisply pleated white shirt. Damn. Sometimes her height, which she insisted was five foot without her boots, was a real disadvantage.

She was just about to look up when Devina's shrill voice cut through the crowd. "Kate Davenport! No hiding behind your grandmother allowed! You're a single so get on out here and find a partner."

Kate felt a tide of heat sweep up her neck and into her face as what seemed like every head in the room turned her way. Still, she managed an answer, pouring on an even thicker accent than she usually had as she turned to face Devina. "I'm coming, Viney, honey. I didn't want all the fellas fighting over me before you had a chance to snag a partner."

Devina's eyes widened in shock and her mouth set in a thin line.

Ha! It might be mean to be satisfied that she'd bested that brat, but she didn't care. Then she realized anew that every person within earshot was staring at her. Oh, no. Now she couldn't hide. Panic rose. She was going to have to go out there and dance with...who knew? One of the desperate men circling the fringes of the floor waiting for the girls who hadn't been asked yet to step forward.

"Katherine?" Her grandmother's voice broke into her dismayed thoughts.

"Yes?" She couldn't take her eyes away from

what promised to be certain disaster on the dance floor.

"This is David. He's new in town. Would you please dance with him and tell him a little bit about Greenlaurel?"

Belatedly, Kate recalled her grandmother had been trying to introduce her to someone. She turned back and gave the tall man standing beside her grandmother a distracted smile that reached as high as his bow tie. "Sure. Come on."

Saved, was all she could think as she grabbed the man's hand and began to tow him toward the dance floor. Mentally blessing her grandmother, she didn't even realize until they reached the dance floor that he'd drawn even with her and readjusted her grip, tucking her hand into the crook of his elbow.

Her grandmother's guest swung her easily into the rhythm of the opening dance, one big hand engulfing her much smaller one, and his other hand settled firmly against the exposed skin at the small of her back. An unexpected thrill of sheer sexual awareness caught her breath in her chest. Startled, she tilted her head back and got her first really good look at him.

Wow! His eyes were a clear blue, so pale that they looked nearly silver in the low lights of the ballroom. Dark rings around the irises made them even more striking, as did thick dark lashes and twin slashes of brows many shades deeper than his sandy hair. A cleft in his chin emphasized his square jaw. He was much taller than she, with wide shoulders and trim hips, and she could feel rock-hard muscle in the strong arms that held her so easily.

He was smiling down at her, and for the first time in her life, she understood the true meaning of sheer magnetic attraction.

"Thank you for saving me, Katherine," he said. "After your grandmother explained the singles' dance, it dawned on me that I didn't know one woman, single or otherwise, in the entire room except for her."

It was the last thing she'd expected from this god—an admission that he'd been worried about the dance, too—and she felt herself relax immediately. "You can call me Kate. And it was a mutual save." She laughed, tilting her head back to look up at him. "I've been dreading this dance since Gram talked me into attending this shindig."

His eyes crinkled into slits of amusement. His teeth were white and even, except for one eyetooth that overlapped its neighbor. She focused on that small imperfection, finding it unexpectedly charming. "I bet. If I had to do this every year, I might go out and shoot myself to relieve my misery."

Kate chuckled. "To be honest, this is the first time I've ever let Gram drag me to the ball."

His eyebrows rose. "You're kidding. I assumed

this was an inescapable part of being one of the Belles of the Historical Society.''

She nodded. ''It is. Fortunately, I'm not one of them, or I swear *I'd* go out and shoot myself.''

He laughed aloud, a deep chuckle that drew sidelong glances from couples around them, and swung her in a tight circle that brought her close against him, wrapping the skirt of her dress around his legs for an instant before the satiny fabric slid free. ''So tell me about Greenlaurel. This is my first visit to the area.''

''Are you from Texas?''

He nodded. ''I was born near Lubbock but I live in L.A. now.''

''So you're a city boy?'' she said teasingly.

He shrugged. ''You could say that.''

''In some ways, Greenlaurel is your typical small town, in others it's quite unique and charming,'' she told him. ''We have our own hospital, a Historical Society and an annual rodeo. Have you ever been to a rodeo?''

He nodded. ''An interesting experience.'' He dipped her backward again, and she was briefly amazed at how easily she was able to follow his steps. He made her feel as if she could really dance—a minor miracle considering that the amount of time she'd spent on a dance floor could be measured in minutes. Then he said, ''So your grandmother tells me your family has a ranch.''

She nodded. "A cow-calf operation. Right now it's branding season. My three brothers managed to get out of coming to the ball because they've been branding all day with Daddy." She frowned. "I usually help, but not today."

"You work outside with your brothers?" He sounded curious but not condemnatory, and she found herself warming to him even more.

"I do. I'm a pretty good hand if I do say so myself."

"And you enjoy it?" David studied her face as he spoke.

She nodded again. "I love being outdoors. I help around the ranch as much as I can, but I'm in school, too, so that keeps me away from it some. I've been working on my degree one or two courses at a time."

"What are you studying?"

"Forestry." She waited for him to smile, or laugh, or give her a verbal pat on the head like so many of the men she knew.

But all he said was, "Sounds like a good career path for someone who likes working outdoors."

She could really like this guy, Kate realized. He didn't appear to have a chauvinistic bone in his body. Then she felt a stab of guilt. Her grandmother would say she was monopolizing the conversation—and she'd be right. "So what type of work do you do?"

He grinned. "You'll be bored silly. I started out as a financial consultant."

He was right. But she pretended interest. "And what, exactly, does a financial consultant do?"

"Advise people on fiscal matters, stock purchases, that sort of thing. I've branched out a bit and now I look for businesses that aren't doing well. I buy them, make them profitable and resell them."

Now it was her turn to look surprised. "I'd say that's a bit more than simply financial consulting."

He nodded. "A bit. But it hardly makes for interesting conversation. Tell me more about Greenlaurel."

"Well," she said, "we have an absolutely lovely state park. I hope to work there some day. It's very close to our ranch. In fact, there's only one property between the two."

He nodded. "I've heard a little bit about it. It's considered quite a jewel in the state park system's crown, isn't it?"

"Yes. Unfortunately, the man who owns the property next to the park passed away recently and his heir is planning to sell it to a group that intends to develop it."

David's eyebrows rose. "And that's a problem because...?"

"Right now, the undeveloped land acts as an easement for wildlife between the park and our ranch," she explained. "It essentially doubles the habitat for any number of species. That access will be cut off if it's developed. Not to mention the stress that noise and pollution will place on the park's ecosystem—" She broke off. "Sorry. I should be bending the ear of the county commissioners, not you."

He was giving her his full attention and she felt her enthusiasm return. "Why the county commissioners?"

"Because they're considering a rezoning proposal right now." She got steamed just thinking about it. "They're looking for some fast cash and not thinking about the long-term impact of developing that tract of land."

He was quiet for a moment, and she wondered if she'd bored him to death. But then he said, "Perhaps if I'm in town long enough, you'd consent to giving me a guided tour."

"Sure," she said. Her pulse sped up at the thought of seeing him again and she had to rein in the pleasure the idea evoked.

Then David drew her closer. She felt the heat of his body, the press of his chest against her, and his hand slid a tiny bit south of her waist. His hand was large and warm on her bare skin, and surprisingly tough for an office worker. She had a hollow feeling in her belly and it was harder than it should have been to breathe. She cleared her throat. "Uh, David?"

He bent his head so that his lips nearly brushed her temple. "Kate. I'm glad you needed a partner."

Totally flustered by the warmth of his breath tickling her ear, she could barely think. "So am I."

"Will you dance with me again?"

She nodded. "All right." There was such a tightly wound coil of expectancy in her chest that she thought she might just snap in two, and her hands shook slightly.

David's mouth was against her temple. "When the ball is over, would you like to go somewhere more private with me for a drink?"

She was so caught up in sheer sensation that his words didn't register for a moment. When they did, an ugly realization doused every bit of the sensual interest with which she'd burned. This guy was hitting on her. And she, dope that she was, had nearly succumbed without a peep, just because he had a slick delivery and a hot body.

Immediately, she stiffened and pulled back. "No, thank you," she said crisply. "I believe it's time I checked on my grandmother. Thank you for the dance."

There was a moment of silence during which he studied her face. Then his hands slid away from her and he indicated that she should precede him off the floor.

"My pleasure," he said quietly. "It was nice to meet you, Kate."

His calm response took a little of the wind out of her sails, but as she turned to move off the dance floor, a memory of the naive girl she'd once been paraded through her thoughts. How stupid could she be?

Once before, not long after she'd gotten out of high school, she'd met a slick, attractive man from the city. He'd been a seemingly worldly banker on temporary assignment in Greenlaurel, and she'd been a young college student in a rural community. When Nolan Hatcher had evinced interest, she'd been so smitten it had never occurred to her to say no. But one day, she'd heard him in his office with a colleague, laughing at her inexperience, her unfeminine behavior and her hick manner of dress and speech.

The memory still had the power to bring a flush of mortified heat to her face. How could she have forgotten that lesson, she asked herself angrily. David was clearly a city boy with city attitudes and morals. She'd have to be insane to get involved with him, regardless of how tempting he was to her hormones.

Spotting her grandmother holding court with several of her friends at a table in the center of the ballroom, Kate made a beeline for her.

As she steamed toward the table, she nearly collided with a dark-haired woman rushing in the opposite direction. The woman swung around with a sound of distress and Kate was surprised to see the sheen of tears in her dark eyes.

"Are you all right?" she asked, steadying the other woman by cradling her elbow.

"I'm—I—I have to go." And the pretty woman wrenched her arm free from Kate's grasp and scurried away.

Kate looked after her for a second, openmouthed. She nearly went after the woman, who clearly hadn't been thinking straight. But then David said, "Do you think she needs assistance?"

Kate turned and glared at him. "Not from you." And she resumed her march toward her grandmother's table.

"Here," she said to Irma. "I danced with your guest."

"Wonderful." Her grandmother's voice was serene despite Kate's abruptness. "And did you two get along well?"

"Just fine." She wasn't about to regale her grandmother with her idiocy and the man's suspect invitation.

"Lovely. You can introduce him around the room in a moment. Have a seat, dear." Irma turned to her friends as Kate sank into the seat at her side, leaving David to stand. "Ladies, I would like to present an acquaintance from Los Angeles, David

Castlemane. David, this is Marjorie Linden, Ida Conrad and Georgia Ann Montgomery.''

Castlemane?

"It's a pleasure, ladies." David stepped forward and bowed over each of their hands.

"Castlemane?" Kate demanded. "You're John Castlemane's son?"

He nodded, clearly unperturbed by her attitude. "Yes."

"You're the man who inherited the land we just were discussing."

"Yes." His voice was calm.

"And you conveniently neglected to mention it." Her tone could have frozen oil.

Kate turned to her grandmother, doing her best not to lose her temper. "Why didn't you tell me who he was?"

Irma's face was innocent. "I did, dear. You must not have caught his last name."

"Apparently not." Kate gritted her teeth. "And why would you ask *me* to introduce him to people? You know how I feel about that land deal."

Irma spread her hands as if her request made perfect sense. "Well, you're going to be haranguing people about it all night, aren't you? This way, David can hear all your objections and meet the commissioners at the same time."

Chapter 2

David watched in fascination as Kate's face registered shock, horror, and finally, a growing fury. Holy hell. She might be small, but he certainly wouldn't want to be on the receiving end of that temper.

He'd assumed she already knew who he was. When Irma Davenport introduced them so casually, David had just figured she'd already spoken to Kate about him, as she had to him of her granddaughter. He'd begun to wonder about it as she'd spoken of the land development, but he hadn't wanted to risk spoiling the mood by asking her more.

Now, however, it was quite apparent from Kate Davenport's striking face that she'd had no idea

who he was. Her whole lovely little body was rigid
and her tiny fists clenched at her sides. She was so
petite it was hard to take her anger seriously, until
you got a look at her eyes—and then the force of
her personality hit you over the head and you forgot
all about her size. In her mind, she was a giant, and
she made you believe it, too.

Kate had narrowed her eyes and was glaring at
her grandmother.

Irma arched an eyebrow and smiled back
sweetly, and two identical sets of brown eyes
locked as the women engaged in a silent battle of
wills. For a moment, everyone froze.

"Oh, dear," said Georgia Ann mildly. "Katherine, mind your manners."

"I am," said Kate through gritted teeth. "I
haven't strangled her yet, have I?"

But David wasn't fooled. Kate might be full of
fire and as headstrong as they came, but she was
no match for the steel spine Irma Davenport hid
beneath her genteel manners and warm hospitality.
Clearly, Mrs. Davenport had defined stubborn years
before Kate was ever born.

And she'd passed it on to her granddaughter.
Watching the two, he felt sheer pity for the men of
the Davenport family.

Finally, the standoff ended as Kate spoke, making no effort to disguise her anger. "All right,
Gram. I'll introduce your guest around."

"He's not just my guest," said her grandmother. "I've spoken with your father and he's invited David to stay at the ranch for the next two weeks. We'd like you to show him his land and the whole area."

Kate's expression was stony, and he gave her marks for hiding the shock the second announcement had to have given her. "Surely you're joking."

"Not at all." Irma bestowed a beaming smile on Kate.

"But that's—that's—just inviting trouble!"

"Don't be silly," Kate's grandmother told her. "Who better to show him around than someone who knows the land so well and treasures it as you do?"

Kate was silent again. He could practically see the gears in her head whirring around and the gleam of calculation that lit her eyes. A gleam he didn't trust further than the space that separated them. Finally, she sent her grandmother a brilliant smile. "All right. I'd be more than happy to introduce David to the land."

Irma blinked. Then her own eyes narrowed in a manner so like her granddaughter's that David knew instantly where Kate had gotten that particular mannerism from. "Thank you, Katharine. I hope I can depend on you to be a good hostess."

Kate smiled at her grandmother, showing enough

teeth to frighten a shark. "Why, Gram, if you can't trust me, maybe you shouldn't have chosen me to be Mr. Castlemane's tour guide in the first place." She stood and crooked a finger at David. "If you'd like to accompany me, I have some people to see."

He nodded. But as Kate beckoned curtly to him and walked away, he caught the quartet of older women giving each other satisfied smiles, and he wondered just exactly what he had missed.

"You are not a gentleman," Kate said as he reached her side. "Why didn't you tell me who you were?"

"Your grandmother introduced us," he said, shrugging. "I didn't realize until too late that you hadn't caught my last name."

"And when you did realize…?"

"You were on such a roll," he said, trying to keep a straight face, "that it seemed a pity to interrupt."

Hot color rose beneath her satiny skin and a muscle jumped in her jaw; he could almost see her getting ready to explode. She studied him for a long moment—and then burst out laughing. "You're a piece of work," she said. "And that was *not* a compliment."

He grinned, surprised and pleased that she appreciated his humor, even more pleased by hers. "Little do you know," he said, "but it was."

She nodded. "So…do you really want me to introduce you around?"

He nodded. "I'd like that very much, if you don't mind."

She sighed, smiling ruefully. "Oh, I mind. But if I don't, I'll never hear the end of it from my grandmother."

He chuckled. "At least you're honest." She was absolutely delightful. It had been a long, long time since any woman had attempted to brush him off. And he was under no illusions. Kate Davenport might have given in to her grandmother, but she definitely was not happy about keeping company with him, even for one evening.

"Your land," she said, as she put one small hand in the crook of his elbow and began to lead him toward the buffet table, "is an approximately twelve hundred-acre parcel fronting the highway, bounded on one side by my family's ranch and on two others by Greenlaurel State Park, which includes the Llano Falls on Turkey Creek."

"I know," he said, covering her hand with his free one and bending his head so that he could hear her. "I've decided to—"

"Develop it," she said crisply, all traces of laughter gone. "I'd like you to reconsider that decision."

"Actually, I've decided to sell it," he clarified. "The potential buyer wants to develop it."

"Why do you want to sell it?" She stopped beside one of the white pillars that stretched from floor to ceiling here and there throughout the room. "It's your inheritance, isn't it? Doesn't the fact that your father valued it enough to want you to have it mean anything?"

Her pugnacious questions aroused a resentment he thought he'd left years in the past, and his pleasure in her company faded. "Frankly, no. My father only left it to me because I'm his sole heir. I can assure you that if he'd had anyone else to give it to, he'd have done so."

Kate looked taken aback. She took a deep, slow breath, then met his gaze fully. "David—Mr. Castlemane—"

"David," he said tersely.

"David," she repeated, her gaze direct and intense as she looked up at him. "Please accept my apology for my inexcusably rude behavior. We've clearly gotten off on the wrong foot and I'd like to start again."

He was fascinated. She didn't like him, he was sure of it, and yet she was swallowing all that anger and pretending to be polite and contrite, two things he doubted anyone who knew Kate Davenport would ever believe.

And that could only mean one thing: she wanted something from him. If there was a woman alive who didn't, he had yet to meet her. Most of them, of course, were interested in either his money, the prestige a marriage to him would bring them, or both.

No doubt about it, she was angling for something…something to do with his father's land. A small part of him registered the disappointment he'd been feeling since the moment Kate's face had changed upon hearing his name. She had liked him there for those all-too-brief moments after they'd first met. The attraction that had sizzled in the air between them had been genuine—far more real than the fake courtesy she was currently exhibiting. Suddenly, he felt tired. Sick and tired of all the games, all the manipulations and machinations. He couldn't remember the last time he'd gone out with a woman who simply liked him for himself.

And he honestly didn't expect that to change for the better. "Apology accepted," he said to Kate in a flat tone.

As she took him through the throng that crowded the elegantly decorated room, person after person spoke or waved at her. The younger women were mainly slick and glossy, with big Texas hair. A number of them were attired in barely there dresses that, while he appreciated the view they afforded, were in such poor taste that he actually winced a time or two. The older matrons flitted around making sure everything was humming along smoothly, haranguing the wait staff and keeping count of how many times their husbands checked out the girls in the skimpy dresses.

At the buffet table, a couple in clothing that looked more appropriate for a business meeting than the ball were holding up the line while the woman fussed at the chef who was carving paper-thin slices of perfectly done roast beef.

"But it doesn't look done," she said loudly. "The last thing I need is to get some disease from eating undercooked meat."

"Agnes, come on." Her partner nudged her along. "There are plenty of other things to try if you don't like the beef."

As the couple moved on, David followed Kate through the line. They found a small table and between bites, she kept the conversation light, regaling him with stories about various people she pointed out around them.

As soon as they finished, she popped to her feet. "Follow me," she said. "I'll introduce you to the members of the county commissioners. They're the ones who will decide whether or not to rezone your land."

She took his arm again and approached a portly older man with a receding hairline and a fringe of reddish curl. "Good evening, Mr. Barlow. How's Racy doing these days?"

"Fine, fine." The man's voice was a booming

foghorn of a bass. "Off his feed a bit, missing Melissa, but he'll come around."

Kate turned to David. "Racy is a nineteen-year-old gelding who is a little bent out of shape because his owner went off to college last fall." She turned back to the other man. "I brought someone I think you'll be interested in meeting. David Castlemane, Ronald Barlow. Mr. Barlow is the chairman of the Greenlaurel County Commissioners."

"Castlemane?" Barlow squinted at him appraisingly as he extended a beefy hand and met David's in a hefty squeeze. "You own that land out by Greenlaurel?"

"Good evening, sir. I do."

"Mr. Barlow," began Kate in a determined tone that warned David she wouldn't be ignored. "Before you make a decision about rezoning that land, I'd like to talk with you about the potential environmental damage developing that tract could do. It—"

"Aw, Kate, I don't want to talk business tonight." He waved an expansive hand toward the dance floor. "Why don't y'all get out there and cut the rug, enjoy yourselves?" He stabbed a finger in David's direction. "Nice to meet you, son. I knew your daddy slightly. He had a fondness for that piece of land."

"I wondered why he kept it," David confessed. "It's half the state away from his own outfit."

"Pretty place." Barlow's eyes twinkled. "You get Kate there to ride you out for a look. You'll see."

"It is lovely," Kate said as they strolled away. "Would you like to plan a trail ride tomorrow? I'd be happy to show you your land as well as a bit of the park if we can fit it in. Oh," she said suddenly, "I forgot you're a city boy. Do you ride?"

"Not in a while." Which wasn't a lie.

Too bad he hadn't kept track of his silver buckle from the high school bronc riding championships. David thought she sounded entirely too pleased by the idea that he might not be able to sit a horse. She made his lifestyle sound like an insult.

"Hey, Kate. How you been?" A redhead with memorable cleavage and a Kewpie doll's pert features waved them over.

"I've been fine, Lurlene. And you?" Kate's voice was perfectly civil, but David sensed she wasn't fond of the other woman.

"Just great, honey. Who's this handsome hunk of man you're leadin' around?"

"Lurlene Palmerston, David Castlemane."

"David Castlemane!" Lurlene made a show of surprise, although it was so poorly done David realized she'd known who he was before she flagged Kate down. "Of The Castlemane Group?"

"One and the same." He took the hand she offered. "A pleasure, Ms. Palmerston."

"Oh, pooh, you call me Lurlene, honey." She winked at him. "If Kate turns you loose, you come find me and I'll dance with you."

He thought he heard Kate mutter something beneath her breath, but then she said, "When I cut him loose, Lurlene, you'll be the first to know."

As they moved on, David touched her elbow lightly and she looked up at him. "If you sic that woman on me, I'll sell my father's land tomorrow."

That got a laugh out of her. "I'd have expected you to have someone like Lurlene hanging on your every word."

"Really? On what do you base that assumption?"

She hesitated. "Oh, you know. She's beautiful, stacked, and…"

"Brainless?" he suggested.

Kate smirked. "I never said that."

Brat. He decided to shake her up a little. "Overbuilt redheads don't turn me on. My tastes run more to petite brunettes with big brown eyes and terrible tempers."

He'd startled her, he could tell by the way her eyes flew to his and then bounced away again, but she was hard to rattle. All she said was, "If I run across any, I'll steer 'em your way."

Over the next hour she dragged him from group to group, introducing him to so many people he finally gave up trying to remember names. She was correct and pleasant, but the momentary warmth he'd seen earlier when she'd laughed was gone, and she acted as if she would be glad when the onerous duty of squiring him around was ended.

"You know, honey," said a tall, thin woman whose name completely eluded David, "if you were smart, you'd hang on to this fella. My Ella Ruth can tell you eligible bachelors don't just fall from trees. She's been looking for a couple of years now."

Kate just smiled at the woman, although he could see the muscle ticking madly in her jaw again. "I guess I'm just not smart, am I?"

It bothered him more than it should have. Why did he care if she wasn't interested? She was hardly his type. By her own admission, she abhorred social obligations, and besides, she appeared to be a lot more of a social liability than she was an asset. She liked to work *outdoors,* for God's sake. He liked women who were active in their communities, women who could stand beside him and make small talk other than a discussion of collecting sperm from a stud bull, or the mating rituals of the jaguarundi, each of which she'd already brought up once tonight.

Still, Kate maintained a steadfast wall of reserve which fascinated him. He couldn't remember the last time he had been interested in a woman who failed to reciprocate the feeling. Although, he re-

minded himself, she hadn't been completely disin-
terested at first, before she'd realized who he was.
The thought was a small salve to his chagrin. Yes,
she'd been looking right back at him.

When was the last time he'd experienced such
an all-consuming desire for one woman to the ex-
clusion of all others? Kate intrigued him with her
prickly, headstrong exterior, and the surprising
warmth he occasionally glimpsed beneath it. Physically he couldn't keep his eyes off her. She was
tiny but perfectly proportioned, and his fingers
itched to slide over all that creamy flesh exposed
by the copper dress. The fabric clung like a second
skin, showing off long, slim lines, firm muscle and
a tight little ass on which there was not an ounce
of extra fat.

She was standing a little in front of him and he
eyed the back of the dress. The designer who'd
come up with that low-cut back should be re-
warded. But as he noticed another man enjoying the
same view, he scowled. Ridiculous as it seemed, he
didn't like the thought of other men ogling her in
that dress. If there was any ogling to be done, he
wanted to be the only one doing it.

Just then she turned and caught him, too quick
for him to hide his attraction. Their eyes met and
something leaped between them, a spark of desire
that left him dry-mouthed and wanting nothing

more than to have the right to peel that dress right off her.

But she looked away again as if the attraction between them wasn't worth pursuing. And that pissed him off. She was pretending dislike, but he was convinced that behind her careful facade was an interest equal to his own.

And that pissed him off, too. She was just like all the other women who chased him, playing hard-to-get when in reality they were usually willing to act on any mutual attraction the moment he pressed the issue. Only it wasn't his money she was after.

It was his father's land.

Grimly, he smiled to himself as he realized he'd nearly swallowed her talk of environmental concern. How far would she let this charade of dislike go before she allowed him to persuade her into his bed? And how soon would she make her move, hoping to seduce him into deeding that land over to her?

As the band came back from a break and started into a soft, romantic slow tune, David decided he was sick and tired of all the introductions and meaningless small talk. If she wanted to seduce him, he was more than willing to speed up the process. It was her problem if she found out later he wasn't paying for what he'd gotten free. He took her hand and pulled her onto the dance floor with a muttered apology to the people they'd been talking to.

"What are you doing?" She tugged at her hand, but he didn't let go.

"Let's dance." He pulled her into his arms, folding her closely against him. The unfamiliar sensation of her lithe little figure pressed against him was so good that he nearly sighed out loud in pleasure.

"I don't want to dance with you." Her body was rigid and she tried to pull back, but he held her easily in place.

"Kate," he said into her ear, playing the game. "We could be so good together. Can't you feel it?"

"If I were wearing my boots, I'd stomp your toes so hard you'd limp for a month."

He laughed, hugging her closer. "You have any more sweet nothings to whisper in my ear?"

"Not unless you tell me you're not selling that land."

Ah. Here it came. "And if I did that…?"

"I'm not for sale, if that's what you're implying," she said, throwing back her head and looking him in the eye as she divined his insinuation. The action arched her spine and he used the chance to pull her closer.

"All right," he said, reminding himself to be patient. She must have sensed his doubts, because she was putting on a pretty good show. "I'm selling the land. You're not for sale. We've established both points. This is going nowhere fast. How about we call a truce tonight? No more land talk until tomorrow?''

"How about you let go of me and go find somebody else to annoy?"

"That's part of the truce. I want to dance with you."

"Why?"

"How should I know?" He was uncharacteristically blunt. He dropped his arms and took a step back so he could look at her. "You're annoying as hell but there isn't another woman in the room I'd rather be with."

Silence. He was already regretting his words. She was looking up at him, her eyes bewildered and…was that a flicker of hurt?

Immediately he regretted the harsh words. "Kate, will you dance with me?"

She hesitated, and now he was sure he'd hurt her feelings.

"Please?" he said.

"All right." She wouldn't meet his eyes, but when he opened his arms, she stepped into them. After an awkward moment or two, she relaxed against him, laying her head against his shoulder, her face turned in so that his lips nearly brushed her forehead when he lowered his own head.

The moment was surprising in its sweetness. He felt an unexpected tenderness for the tiny dynamo nestled against him, and his hands gently stroked up and down her back, bare but for the miniscule strings that crisscrossed from shoulder to waist, holding her dress in place. He fought a ridiculous urge to lay his cheek against the shining crown of her head, to place his lips right at the spot where the widow's peak dipped down squarely in the center of her hairline. The unfamiliar feeling made him wary. For the first time in his life he could see how a man could be hoodwinked by an appealing woman.

And as he held her in his arms and led her to the beat of the music, he wondered just what he'd gotten himself into by agreeing to come see the land he'd inherited. His father's solicitor had told him it wasn't necessary, but that his father had hoped he would. He guessed it was just one more futile attempt to please the old man that had made him accede.

Either that or the fact that his father had *told* him what to do his entire life. If he'd ever *asked* before, David couldn't remember the occasion.

Chapter 3

You're annoying as hell.

It shouldn't have hurt, but it had.

Kate let him lead her around the dance floor, feeling ridiculously close to tears. She didn't care what he thought, she assured herself. He was nothing but a city boy who didn't have a clue what developing his land would do to the environment.

The only reason she was still dancing with him was because she was feeling guilty for presuming to lecture him about his family. Clearly, she'd hit a nerve, and she was sincerely sorry for that. Also, it was easier than standing around looking pathetic, waiting to be asked to dance and making her grandmother worry that her only granddaughter was an unattractive wallflower. Dancing with David solved a lot of problems. It was as simple as that.

Right.

It would be easier if she couldn't stand the man. Unfortunately, she found him arousing, attractive, easygoing, surprisingly amusing and intelligent. And vulnerable, dammit. She was a sucker for vulnerable. She replayed again the defensiveness in his uncharacteristically sharp response when she'd tried to guilt him into honoring his late father's wishes. Clearly, the two hadn't been close. She wondered if they'd resolved whatever differences divided them before his father's death. It sure hadn't sounded as if they had, and she'd had to restrain herself from comforting him.

Somehow, she didn't think comfort was at the top of the list of things he wanted from her. The very thought made her shiver a little in instinctive reaction.

His arms were strong and secure around her, his chest was hard beneath her cheek. She was very aware of the warmth of his body against hers, the proximity of his mouth to the top of her head. She'd been kissed before, but she suspected that kissing David Castlemane—which of course she had no intention of doing—would elevate the experience to a whole new level.

She had no plans to find out. She'd made a fool of herself once over a man who'd been out of her league. David Castlemane made Nolan seem positively harmless by comparison. The man should wear a sign that read *Explosive When Heated*.

"Kate!" The voice was feminine and Kate raised her head from its too-comfortable spot on David's chest.

"Hey, Rosie. You look pretty tonight." It was true, although perhaps not in the conventional fashion. Her friend's dress was emerald-green, the perfect color to bring out the green of her thick-lashed eyes behind her gold-rimmed glasses. But the dress was too long, and Rosie clutched a serious handful of it bunched in one fist as she moved. The puffy sleeves fell down her upper arms, framing her bare shoulders and elegant neck in a striking way of which Kate knew her friend was entirely unaware. With her long silky hair falling down from the bun in which it had started, she reminded Kate of nothing so much as the heroines on the covers of the classic Gothic romances her grandmother loved to read, standing on a windswept cliff in a storm.

Rosemary Linden's grandmother and Kate's own were thick as thieves and the girls had known each other for years. Kate had a soft spot for Rosie, who was much shyer and more vulnerable than either of her confident, outgoing sisters. Earlier Kate had spotted Phoebe, the youngest Linden sister, in the middle of a crowd composed largely of adoring young men. Phoebe was the most obviously beautiful of the three green-eyed sisters, although Kate privately thought Rosie would give her a run for her money if she ever relaxed enough to smile and flirt.

Tonight, Rosie looked positively overwhelmed by the crush of people, and Kate tried to set her friend at ease. "Rosie, this is David Castlemane. He's the one who inherited the land between the park and the ranch. David, Rosemary Linden. You met her grandmother earlier."

"It's a pleasure, Ms. Linden." David smiled at Rosie, who blushed and looked at the ground.

"Just Rosie," she said, twisting her fingers together.

"Rosie's a botanist at the Greenlaurel Botanical Gardens," Kate told him.

Her friend nodded, looking at David. "I heard you're selling the land to someone who plans to develop it. Is that true?"

"I plan to sell the land," David said. "The future owner would have to address your question."

"But, Mr. Castlemane, there are some terribly vulnerable species of native flora in the park that could be badly affected by a housing development right next door." She made *housing development* sound like a fatal disease. "There's one large area of virgin Ashe juniper which is a preferred nesting habitat for the endangered golden-cheeked warbler. Do you realize how little natural habitat that bird has left?" She sucked in a quick breath. "You have a moral responsibility to protect those plants and animals who depend on that space."

David had the grace to look uncomfortable. "Ms. Linden—Rosie—if you'd like to buy the land for the same price I've been offered, I'll give you first option. But it wouldn't be economically sound for me to keep it when I never plan to use it, and I doubt you or anyone else is willing to match the standing offer."

Rosie shook her head, her whole demeanor woebegone. "You're right. I could never come up with that kind of money. Not many people could, given the price a developer is willing to pay." She sighed. "Everyone's interested in ecology and the environment until it gets in the way of *their* lives and *their* pocketbooks."

An uncomfortable silence followed her words. Rosie's face was pink, as if she was embarrassed by her own temerity, and David must wish he were anywhere else, Kate thought.

"Who's that with Tara?" she asked, indicating Rosie's elder sister. Rosie had made David squirm even more effectively than Kate had, and she decided it was time to take pity on him.

She studied the man and woman several tables away. Tara's willowy figure was graceful, her oval face perfectly made up. The woman never seemed to have a hair out of place, and the subtle way she undercut Rosie's confidence often aggravated Kate to the point of considering rearranging Tara's flawless features. Kate had taken up for Rosie often enough in the past that she knew Tara detested her for it. The feeling was definitely mutual.

"That's Tara's fiancé," Rosie said. "Want to meet him?" And before Kate could stop her, Rosie beckoned to her sister.

"Her fiancé? You mean Tara actually plans to wed a mere mortal?"

"Kate, be nice." Rosie's mild rebuke was so like her grandmother's had been an hour earlier that Kate knew David was laughing without even looking at him. She dug an elbow into his ribs as Tara Linden approached with a tall, dark-haired man.

"Katherine." Tara nodded graciously to Kate. "Aren't you just the cutest little thing tonight? You look so…clean and ladylike." With that small dig she switched her attention to David. "Hello, I'm Tara Linden."

"Rosie's sister. She's older than we are," said Kate. "As you can see." She smiled innocently as the taller woman's eyes narrowed. "This is David Castlemane. David, Tara's a corporate attorney. Beneath that glamorous exterior, she's as bullheaded and opinionated as I am."

Tara's face was a thundercloud by now, and David hastily extended his hand. "Nice to meet you." He switched his attention to the man with her. "David Castlemane."

"A pleasure," the man said. "Jake Ingram. You've got the magic touch with business ventures."

David grinned as the men exchanged handshakes. "It takes one to know one. It's good to meet you." His expression sobered. "How have your businesses fared since the World Bank Heist?"

"All right. We've just had a few minor inconveniences, thank God," said Jake. "Not like some people. You?"

"I was lucky, too." David shook his head. "But it's been less than two weeks. My biggest concern is how people's fear of investing is going to affect the economy in the long run."

"It worries me, too." Jake Ingram nodded at Kate as Tara performed the introduction. "Good evening. My brother Zack and I went to school with your older brothers, I believe."

"You have my sympathies." Kate smiled at Jake, wondering why in the world he was marrying

Tara Linden. Despite her obvious beauty and intelligence, the woman had a streak of self-centered meanness a mile wide. It was probably one of those deals where only other women recognized it, though. Too bad. There had to be a million women out there after him, and at least half of them deserved to find a guy who seemed as nice as he did more than Tara.

Jake Ingram was in the news constantly, his financial wizardry a legend across the country. And he was gorgeous in the bargain, almost as tall as David, though not quite, with dark hair and blue eyes. His eyes were darker than David's though, she thought. David's were lighter, and when he got intensely interested in something, they turned the color of a summer sky—

Cut it out, Kate!

"Where is Zack, anyway?" Tara asked. "We haven't seen him all evening."

Jake shrugged. "He said he was coming. I'm sure he's around here somewhere."

"Mr. Castlemane!" A sharp-featured, older woman steamed toward them through the crowd, towing a gray-haired man behind her. It was the same people she'd noticed giving the chef a hard time at the buffet table earlier. The pair who'd been notable for their inappropriate attire as well as the woman's boorish behavior, Kate recalled. The couple were dressed somewhat more casually than most of the ball's guests, she in a severe dark business suit and he in a sportcoat with khaki pants. They looked extremely out of place amid all the dazzling gowns and tuxes in the room. "We've been looking for you forever," the woman said, her tone almost accusatory.

David's eyebrows rose. "I didn't realize you planned to attend the ball." He turned to Kate and the others. "This is Agnes Payne and Oliver Grimble. I hired them to survey and prepare a comprehensive report on the land my father left me." He introduced the two land experts to the group.

"We met earlier," Rosie said.

"Yes." Agnes Payne barely glanced at Rosie, all of her attention was focused on Jake Ingram.

"Mr. Ingram." Oliver looked confused. "Didn't we just see you over there?" He looked at the far end of the ballroom.

Jake chuckled. "That probably was my brother Zack. People often get us confused."

"Are you twins?" his partner asked.

"No. Actually, I'm adopted. We're the same age and we just happen to resemble each other a great deal."

"Where do you live, Mr. Ingram?" Agnes spoke again, her eyes still on Jake.

His eyebrows rose. "My family lives right here in Greenlaurel."

"And how about you—"

"So tell us about yourselves," Kate interrupted. She sensed Jake's discomfort with the questions, but more, there was something very...*intense* about the way the woman had zeroed in on him. "How did you get into your work—what is it, exactly, that you do?"

"We're surveyors," Oliver said quickly.

"I'm sure you'd be bored to tears with the details," Agnes said dismissively.

"Actually," said Kate, "I'm a forestry student. And as you might know, Rosie is a botanist. We both will be very interested in the data you'll be collecting when you survey the Castlemane tract. Are you looking at it from an environmental perspective or merely a topographical one?"

"Oh, both, both, of course." The woman turned back to Jake. "You say you were adopted—were you an infant or an older child?"

There was an electric silence in the group. No one, thought Kate, could possibly be unaware of the rumors about genetically engineered children who'd been adopted, could they? The woman must be incredibly thick.

"I was quite a bit older," Jake said. "Why do you ask?"

"No special reason," Agnes said quickly. There was another awkward silence. "It's just that I was adopted at the age of twelve and I wondered how you adapted."

"You know," said Kate. "David and I will be taking a riding tour of his land tomorrow. Why don't you two come with us? I could answer any questions you have before you get started."

Both of the surveyors turned and looked at her. Oliver looked completely bewildered.

"Questions about the land," Kate prompted.

Agnes shot her a venomous look. "We'd be happy to," she said, and Kate got the impression the woman was gritting her teeth. What the heck was going on with these two?

"But, Agnes, I don't ride," said the man.

"Oh, don't be stupid," she said. "You ride well enough to go on a little tour. We won't be running the Derby, you know."

"All right." He sounded unhappy and unconvinced, but he subsided.

"Jake," said Tara, "I'd like to introduce you to my great-aunt. She's just over there." She nodded her head in a general dismissal to the whole group. "It was lovely talking with you all. Enjoy the ball." And she swept away, one arm tucked through Jake Ingram's.

"I, uh, I have to go, too," Rosie said.

"You *have* to?" Kate teased.

Rosie nodded, glancing at her watch. "It was nice meeting you, David." She turned to the other couple. "If I can help with your work, please just ask Kate to give me a call."

"Thank you." Oliver smiled at her, although in Kate's opinion it wasn't much of an effort. "We certainly will."

The awkward silence returned after Rosie scurried away.

"Well," said David, "how about I come by your hotel and pick you up on the way out to Kate's ranch tomorrow?"

"That sounds fine." Agnes's voice was hearty. "We'll see you then." She turned and walked away, leaving her partner to follow along.

"Let's say nine," David called after them.

"Nine." The woman nodded as she kept walking. "Nine it is."

David turned and looked at Kate, his eyebrows raised.

"That," she said, "was very weird. Where did you find those two?"

"Actually, I didn't find them." David looked as annoyed as she felt. "If I had, you can be damn sure I'd never have hired them. I asked my assistant to find me someone with expertise in evaluating land. Looks like she might have called the first number she came across." He grimaced. "I owe Jake Ingram an apology. What a pair of bores. They'd better be good at what they do or they'll be unemployed fast."

Kate smiled. "Remind me never to get on your bad side."

"I have a hard time picturing you being intimidated by my bad side," he said dryly. "Now, shall we dance again?"

"I'd love to." And she meant it. In his arms, she could forget that they were bound to be adversaries in the morning. She was just going to enjoy herself for the rest of the evening.

Tomorrow she could go back to being Prickly Kate.

Another hour passed. Inside the mansion, the soft lighting and genteel music made for a dreamy atmosphere of unreality. Outside, a storm had begun, complete with blinding flashes of lightning and claps of thunder that rattled the old house's windows.

They hadn't spoken more than a few words since the encounter with her friends and his soon-to-be-former employees, and that suited David just fine.

Kate Davenport was quite possibly the most enchanting woman he'd ever met. As another song ended, he reluctantly released her small, pliant body

from the close embrace in which they'd been dancing. Her feisty spirit, coupled with a natural sen-
suality of which she barely seemed aware, interested him. A lot, he thought, stifling the urge to
laugh as he recalled the way she'd needled that self-
important sister of Rosie Linden's.

It was too bad she had such an agenda over the
land deal he planned to conclude while he was here
in Greenlaurel. Kate seemed like the sort of person
who would have trouble separating business from
pleasure.

And the only thing he wanted from her was pleasure. Lots of it.

If only that damned land of his father's wasn't
standing in the way. Not for the first time, he wondered bitterly why the old man had chosen to keep
him in his will. David certainly hadn't expected it.
And if he didn't own the land, there would be no
reason to believe that Kate wanted to manipulate
him into changing his mind about selling it. That
was the only reason he could imagine for her softer
attitude.

A twinge of doubt attacked his surety. Between
Kate and her friend Rosie, they'd almost convinced
him that preserving the land for endangered species
was of primary import. He reminded himself not to
be gullible.

Once the land was sold and there was no friction

between them, he might have to start all over with
Kate, but he was more than willing if that's what
it would take. She might be annoyed that she hadn't
been able to sway him, but now that he knew she
wasn't indifferent to him, he was sure he could
overcome that. He realized he'd already decided to
pursue her, and what he pursued, he nearly always
caught. Kate wasn't going to be an exception.

Her grandmother waved at them, and he almost
flushed. If the older lady knew what he was thinking, she'd probably have him tarred and feathered
and tossed outside the town limits. But she was
beaming as they approached the table where she
held court with a group of other ladies, including
the three he'd met earlier.

"You two dance as if you were made for each
other," Irma said as they approached.

"Very subtle, Gram," Kate said. "Why don't
you just ask him to marry me?"

"I imagine if he wanted you, he'd ask you himself," said Irma, completely unfazed. "David, I'd
like you to meet—" But Irma broke off in midsen-
tence, her eyes widening as her mouth formed a
perfect circle of awe.

"Dear merciful heavens," he heard one of the
other ladies say in a hushed tone. "What on
earth…?"

"That Conrad boy should be declared a national treasure."

"That Conrad boy," whispered another, "is my grandson, girls. Show a little respect." There was a short silence. Then, "But he is a hunk, isn't he?"

The ladies giggled.

David turned to look in the direction they were staring, noting that Kate was staring, too.

A man had entered through the French doors at the back of the ballroom. Tall and lean, his dark hair was plastered to his head. The black tuxedo he wore was molded equally closely to a broad-shouldered, heavily-muscled body. Clearly, he'd been caught in the rainstorm.

He sauntered squarely through the middle of the dance floor as conversations died and silence descended over the room. The man seemed totally oblivious. The heels of his hand-tooled black—and soaking—dress boots rang on the polished wooden floor. He made small squishing sounds with each step and a sodden, muddy path trailed behind him. He swung the largely empty contents of a six-pack from one hand with complete nonchalance. As the entire crowd goggled, he disappeared through the arched front entrance and in a moment, the sound of the heavy front door slamming shut echoed throughout the room.

It was, apparently, the signal for conversation to begin again.

"Who was that?" he asked Kate.

"Mitch Conrad." She was grinning. "No one could ever say Mitch goes with the flow. Most of the time he swims upstream against whatever it is he's expected to do. A man," she said happily, "after my own heart."

He was surprised at just how much he disliked this Conrad guy the minute she uttered those words. "I don't think so," he said. "The two of you would spend all your time trying to outdo the other in outrageous behavior."

Her eyebrows rose. "I take exception to that. I've been positively restrained tonight."

"But the real you shines through," he muttered.

She laughed. "Now *that's* my kind of compliment."

Chapter 4

The following morning was clear and sunny, with a fresh feel in the air due to the moisture last night's ferocious storm had left behind. Kate strode from the house to the barn a few minutes before nine, lecturing herself.

She'd spent far too much time in the bathroom this morning, wondering if the simple braid she usually wore hanging down her back was *too* simple. If her jeans were too faded. If she should wear the new western shirt she'd bought at the rodeo last summer or one of her customary old T-shirts. In the end, she'd gone with her normal mode of dress, figuring he might as well get used to seeing her as she really was.

David Castlemane was not someone whom she needed to impress, she reminded herself. Except in the sense that she needed to impress upon him how vital it was that his father's land be preserved from any development that would upset nature's fragile balance in the park and its surrounding environs.

In the barn, she saddled her horse, Sprint, a handsome chestnut gelding with black socks, tail and mane. Then she deliberated on a mount for David. Two of her brothers had ridden out earlier, but there were still seven horses in their stalls. All but two were geldings, and both those were mares, too docile for what she wanted. The cutters weren't really necessary for the steady riding she planned today, and in the end, she chose Ghost, a paint gelding with the endurance of a marathoner and the spirit of a big-top ringmaster. Ghost was just enough of a character to require good horsemanship and a strong hand, but not so rowdy that David could accuse her of giving him a troublesome mount, she decided with satisfaction as Ghost snorted.

She gave the gelding a sharp rap on the barrel to convince him to let her buckle the saddle securely, and when she led him out, he cantered around the corral twice, kicking up his heels as if he had energy to burn. Of course, if David wasn't much of a rider, Ghost would give him a day he'd never forget....

Moving back into the barn, she saddled two more

horses for Agnes and Oliver. She wasn't particularly looking forward to spending a day with either of the pair. Agnes Payne had left a bad taste in Kate's mouth for some reason she couldn't pinpoint. One thing she knew, she'd definitely taken exception to the rude manner in which the woman had attempted to grill Jake Ingram, but there was something more, something she hadn't been able to define, but disliked instinctively. It was akin to the way she felt about Tara, and she *knew* her intuition was accurate where that witch was concerned. And that only made her wonder all the more about David's "land experts." She couldn't wait to see just how much they knew about surveying.

As she led out the last horse, she was distracted from her musings by the sound of a motor. Her timing was perfect. A dark blue SUV rattled over the hill and across the last cattle guard and she stood by the rail waiting until it came to a stop near the barn.

"Good morning." David emerged from the vehicle, a pair of Oakleys shielding his eyes from the bright sun. She was just about to chide him for not wearing a hat when he reached back into the truck and came out with a straw summer hat that looked brand-new.

"Good morning." She cleared her throat, which seemed to have some kind of obstruction clogging her vocal cords. "Welcome to the Triple Creek."

"I see you've already got a horse picked out for me." His tone was easy.

"And for your employees."

His smiled faded. "We won't be needing those."

"You fired them already?" She was a little shocked even though she heartily approved. David seemed so easygoing—she couldn't imagine him summarily firing someone. Then she recalled the steel in his voice last night when they'd discussed his new employees. He might appear easygoing, but beneath the surface, David was a force to reckon with.

"I didn't have to. They disappeared."

"What?"

"I went to their hotel, but they'd checked out. So I had my assistant call to set up a meeting and discovered the number had been disconnected and the address of their business is a vacant lot."

"You're kidding!" It sounded like something out of a suspense novel. "So...what do you think is going on?"

David shrugged. "I have absolutely no idea. They haven't done anything illegal—that I know of—and I stopped payment on the retainer I'd given them, so I didn't lose anything. But it sure is odd."

"*They* were odd," she said with feeling. "Remember how Agnes tried to grill Jake? She seemed awfully interested in him. Maybe you should let him know what happened."

David eyed her as if he weren't sure of her sanity. "And tell him what, exactly? The man would think I'm crazy."

She hesitated, trying to think of a way to share the information without sounding kooky and paranoid. "I hate to say it, but you're probably right."

"Probably?" He arched an eyebrow. "That's the closest you can get to admitting I'm right and you're wrong?"

"I wasn't *wrong*," she said stoutly. "Being cautious isn't a bad thing."

David was grinning. "The voice of experience? Funny, you don't seem to be the cautious type."

Kate stuck her tongue out at him. Turning to the corral, she whistled for the horses. "Just let me put these two away again and we can get started."

"I'll help." David caught the taller of the extra mounts by the bridle and led him through the gate back into the barn.

She watched him covertly as she unsaddled the smaller horse, Cuss. He knew what he was doing. In fact, he looked extremely capable and comfortable, as if the motions were familiar ones he'd performed many times before. Apparently, he'd been around horses a bit more than he'd wanted her to believe.

After the two extras were put away, she called Ghost and Sprint over and introduced David to his mount. He blew gently into Ghost's nostrils, laughing when the gelding snorted, and gently ran his hands over the pretty paint. His voice was a low croon that clearly enthralled Ghost, who stood with his ears pricked forward, his large eyes fixed on the man speaking to him. Listening to the deep, tender tones as he stroked the animal's neck, Kate realized that David had much the same effect on her that he did on the horse. She, too, felt mesmerized, caught by the soft verbal caresses, longing for more. If he ever spoke to her like that, she was in big trouble, she thought darkly.

David mounted Ghost while she was still putting water and a lunch in her saddlebags. She looked up to see him controlling the dancing gelding with easy, collected motions, confirming her suspicions that he was a better than average horseman.

"All right," she said. "You weren't being exactly truthful about your riding abilities, were you?"

He shrugged, but his blue eyes were alight with laughter, as if he knew what she'd been hoping for. "I haven't been on a horse in a couple of years, but I rode in my childhood."

She set her foot in the stirrup and boosted herself easily into Sprint's saddle. "Every day, no doubt." But she was smiling.

"Well," he said, "I used to compete in saddle-bronc."

Her mouth fell open. Staying on a bucking horse

for the requisite eight seconds, with or without a
saddle, wasn't something for the average horseman.
She just shook her head. "There goes my fantasy
of watching you get dumped in the dirt."

He laughed aloud. "Be nice, Kate. You're trying
to influence my decision on my father's land, remember?"

Abruptly, the moment didn't seem so funny anymore. "I remember," she said soberly. "Come on.
I'll show you your property."

Wheeling the gelding around, she headed for the
east pastures. "Follow me. Your outfit is just over
the ridge a couple of miles." She took him on a
direct route through Davenport land to where his
own began on the other side of the fences her father
had erected.

"These fences keep the cattle where we want
them," she said as they passed through a gate and
she stopped to close it behind them, "but it doesn't
impede much of anything else. Mule deer, prairie
dogs, coyotes, jackrabbits and other critters go over
or under it." She cast him a sidelong glance. "You
said you were raised up near Lubbock. On a
ranch?"

He nodded. "My father's."

"Where was your mother?"

He looked startled. "She was there, too."

She'd wondered, from the way he'd continually
referred only to his father, if his mother had been

out of the picture. "You don't say much about her."

He laughed, but it was a harsh sound rather than one of amusement. "You've known me less than twenty-four hours, Kate."

She nodded, conceding the fact, but continued to look at him with her eyebrows raised.

Finally, he shrugged and made a dismissive gesture. "There isn't much to say. She was my mother. She and I lived with my father on his ranch."

"How did your parents meet? Was she ranch-raised?"

"No, she was from Maryland. They met at a party when Dad went east to buy a bull."

It wasn't nearly enough information, given the tension that radiated from the stiff set of David's shoulders, but she could tell he wasn't happy with the topic.

"My parents met at a dance," she told him. "Dad came with a date, but when he saw my mother, he paid his best friend five bucks to take the date home."

His shoulders relaxed a fraction. "Some gentleman."

She chuckled. "He always said once he saw my mother, he couldn't even think about other women."

"I assume I'll meet your parents when I come to stay."

She shook her head. "Just Dad. My mother died when I was two."

David turned his head, and his blue eyes were warm with sympathy. "I'm sorry."

She smiled at him. "Thank you, but it's all right. I barely remember her."

"Did your father remarry?"

She shook her head. "Gram says a little piece of him died with her. Besides, what woman in her right mind would marry a man with four small children?"

"There is that." He glanced at her, his eyes twinkling. "And I bet you were a wild hare when you were little." He smirked. "Littler."

"Hey!" She shot him an evil glare. "I get enough short jokes from my brothers. I don't need you starting! Besides, I may be vertically challenged, but there's nothing you can do that I can't."

A slow, sensual grin spread across his face. "No?"

Hastily she said, "You know what I mean." Then she urged her mount forward so she couldn't see the expression that still lingered on his tanned features.

She took him across his land so that she could show him where the park began. At the present time there were no fences beyond her father's outfit—an ideal setting for the wildlife that populated the protected area.

They stopped for lunch beneath a stand of cottonwood trees that stretched up beside a small spring. David dismounted with a groan. "I'm going to be sorry for this tonight."

She couldn't prevent the grin. "A little tender?"

He massaged his butt, looking rueful. "A little." He indicated the shallow pool beside which they stood. "Too bad that's not a little deeper. I'd take a swim."

"That would feel good, wouldn't it?" She took off her hat and wiped the sweat from her forehead before replacing it, trying to ignore the image of David taking off his clothes that tried to enter her mind. "There's a bigger water hole at the far end of your property. I'll take you down there sometime while you're here and you can have your swim." She grinned. "I hope you've been swimming more recently than you've been riding."

But he didn't smile in return. "That's one of my workouts," he told her. "I swim three mornings a week before I go in to my office."

"Ah." Swimming and workouts. That explained the muscle she'd noticed beneath his tux last night. "And what, exactly, do you do once you get into your office?"

He shrugged. "Keep an eye on the stock market for any significant movement. I'm talking about finances," he clarified, "not livestock."

"I knew that," she said indignantly, and he chuckled.

"I meet with people I've hired to assess aspects of whatever I'm currently interested in acquiring, I check the bottom line on what I think it would cost me to rebuild whatever it is—"

"Such as?"

"Could be anything. Once I bought a failing ski resort, another time an alpaca farm. Land deals are frequent, as are manufacturing businesses of all sizes. One of the few things I steer clear of is trying to rescue a restaurant. Too risky."

"I pegged you for someone who enjoys risk-taking."

"There's a difference between taking a risk and stupidity," he pointed out, and it was her turn to laugh.

"True." Then she sobered, thinking of recent events. "Last night, you told Jake the fallout from the World Bank Heist hadn't really affected you very much. Do you expect it to?"

David shrugged, waiting a beat and clearly choosing his words with care. "I hope not. But my concern is exactly what President Stewart addressed in his speech last week, namely how fearful people become."

"People like my father." She shook her head. "All he seems to be able to talk about is whether or not the banks are prepared to foil another virtual break-in.''

"That's it." David spread his hands. "If they don't trust the market, they won't invest. If they don't invest, market shares and the Dow drop. When that happens, people become even more afraid to invest. I think that's exactly what whoever pulled off the bank deal wants. Yes, they took a lot of money, but even more than that, the possibility that they could do it again, any time, anywhere, frightens potential investors. Whoever did this understands finance and the markets. They *want* the world to be jittery and fearful.''

"I didn't watch the speech," she confessed. "Do you think it had any impact?''

"God, I hope so." He sighed as he went on to discuss the issue further.

It was surprisingly easy to talk to him, and when they made their way back to the barn just before the supper hour, Kate realized she'd enjoyed the day.

Perhaps too much so.

He went back to town to check out of his hotel before tossing his duffel bag in the back of his SUV and returning to the Davenport ranch. He hadn't packed that morning, thinking that Irma Davenport hadn't been serious about her invitation to stay, but she'd caught him just as he and Kate had left the barn and demanded to know where he'd thought he was going.

He'd stammered like a schoolboy while Kate stood by, laughing openly.

But she'd stopped laughing when he'd finally gathered his dignity and told Irma he'd be delighted to accept her invitation if it wouldn't put anyone out. From the corner of his eye, he'd seen Kate open her mouth. But apparently, so had her grandmother. Irma had turned one gimlet eye on her granddaughter and said, "Of course not. We're all looking forward to having you visit. Aren't we, Katherine?"

Kate had nodded with surprising meekness. "Yes, Gram."

Still, it had rankled that after the day they'd shared she didn't want him around any more than she had last night. By the time he arrived back at the farmhouse, his mood had gone about as far south as it could.

Grabbing his bag, David stepped out into the still-bright spring sunlight, squinting as he strode across the yard. He sighed in relief as he gained the shade of the big oaks surrounding the farmhouse.

It was a beautiful place. The house looked to be old, but clearly had undergone some extensive remodeling. He was fairly sure the matching wings on each side of the main structure were newer, but the whole effect was so well done most people never would have thought of it.

Mounting the two shallow steps to the porch, he banged on the front door with somewhat more force than necessary. If Kate didn't want him here, then she could just tell him so.

Light footsteps crossing the floor inside had every muscle in his body tensing. But when the door swung open, it was Irma who stood there. He should have known Kate wouldn't walk with such a light step. She probably stomped.

"David!" she trilled. "We're so delighted you've accepted our invitation."

He suppressed the urge to snort. "It was very kind of you," he said, following her into a small foyer that opened onto a living room on the left and a dining room on the right. Stairs led to a second story, while a hallway straight back led to a large, sunny kitchen.

"We'll take your suitcase up in a minute," Irma told him. "Let me fix you a glass of tea. It's a scorcher today. Doesn't bode well for the summer ahead, does it?"

"No, ma'am."

"I hope Katherine thought to give you time to rest in the shade during your ride today."

"She was a very good hostess." He followed her into the kitchen, looking around with interest. It was clearly the center of family life in the Davenport home, with flowered curtains and a wallpaper border near the ceiling in the same design. Copper pots hung from a cooking island—they weren't for show but looked well used. A big round oak table dominated a sizable space in front of a bay window that faced toward the barn, and an open door on the back wall showed glimpses of a gleaming mud-room. It was pretty, yet practical, with feminine touches that didn't seem fussy.

A lot like Kate, although he doubted she'd enjoy the comparison.

Irma set a tall glass of iced tea with a sprig of mint in front of him. "Katherine went back out to check a fence. She should be coming in soon."

"I feel guilty about monopolizing her time," he said. "Am I keeping her from work?"

"No," Irma assured him. "She told me this morning that she would just take you around with her while she did chores. And we've looked after your father's land for years, so that's not a problem."

"You...looked after my father's land?" He wasn't sure he understood.

Irma smiled. "I guess it's your land now. We have a maintenance contract. You know, keeping up fences, checking for poaching. Really there wasn't much to be done." Her smile was wistful. "I guess if you're selling it you won't need any of that anymore."

"No." Why did he feel like he was committing a crime? "I guess I won't."

"We'll continue until you decide what you're going to do." Irma briskly crossed the kitchen. "Here comes Katherine now."

He hadn't met Kate's father or brothers yet, but he was willing to bet the only person in the world who could get away with calling her Katherine was standing right in front of him. The thought made him grin into his iced tea glass.

But the smile faded. Why did all of these folks assume there was a decision to be made on what to do with his father's land? He'd decided months ago, after he'd learned of the old man's death, to sell the site.

The back door opened and Kate strode in. "Hey," she said by way of greeting him.

"Katherine." Her grandmother gave her a disapproving look. "David is our guest and should be treated as such."

"I am treating him like a guest," Kate said. "I didn't make him come out here and shovel shit with me at six this morning, did I?"

Irma's face went stony. "Please don't use foul language in front of me, Katherine."

Kate's posture, which had been rigid and aggressive a moment ago, suddenly softened. She crossed the kitchen and kissed Irma on the cheek. "I'm sorry, Gram.'' She looked at David. ''I apologize for my language.''

He could see the laughter buried deep in Kate's eyes, and he could barely restrain his own chuckle. She really was a brat, although he'd found the kiss she'd bestowed on her grandmother oddly touching. Sweet, if one dared use that word in connection with Kate.

''Where's your suitcase?'' She started for the front hall.

''I'll get it.'' She was too tiny to be dragging around his luggage. ''Just show me where it goes.''

''All right.'' She took the stairs at a gallop, leaving him to follow with his bag. At the top, she pointed at various doorways they passed. ''Two of my brothers share that one, this one is Evan's. He's the oldest. This is my dad's, and my grandmother's is along the hall. Mine's here, and the guest bedroom is right down here.'' She opened a door and stepped inside. ''You have your own bathroom. Lucky dog.''

''This is nice.'' He surveyed the Native American woven blankets, the clay pots, baskets and simple Mission-style furniture. ''Thanks. I'll be very comfortable here.'' *As comfortable as I'm likely to get knowing you're sleeping on the other side of that wall.*

''I'd better get going. I've got to get cleaned up and help Gram with dinner. Take your time. We eat around seven.'' Kate turned on her heel and he suddenly realized she was nervous. He guessed he couldn't blame her. Standing just a few feet away from a big soft bed with her beside him was making David jittery, too.

Chapter 5

That evening was his first meal under the roof of the Davenport family. It was a memorable experience. Kate's three strapping brothers and her father were hearty and welcoming. And loud.

Very loud. All four Davenport men were as big as he was, and built like lumberjacks. Kate must resemble her deceased mother, he thought, eyeing the width of her father's shoulders straining the seams of his work shirt as the man washed his hands at the kitchen sink. Then again, how on earth a woman as petite as her daughter could have given birth to these giants was a mystery. Maybe Kate was adopted.

But no, none of the Davenport siblings could get

away with disclaiming the others. The brothers shared a marked resemblance that went well beyond their dark hair and eyes, and it was repeated in Kate's much more delicate features. Her oldest brother, Evan, was more serious and focused than either of her younger brothers, but something in the way he angled his jaw when he and his father got into a disagreement about the amount of feed they'd used over the winter, reminded David strongly of his sister. And all three appeared to have inherited their father's booming voice and weren't shy about making their opinions known.

He watched, fascinated, as the youngest, Martin, tried to come to the table without changing his clothes.

"Martin," Kate said as she carried a steaming bowl of mashed potatoes into the dining room, "you smell like gasoline. Go change your clothes."

"Aw, Kate," the man protested, "I'm working on the tractor engine and I've got to go right back out after dinner. What's the use in changing?"

"You stink," Kate said. "As far as I'm concerned, that's the use. Now go."

Martin opened his mouth to argue, but Kate whipped down the dish towel she'd thrown over one shoulder and snapped it smartly at his backside. "Go. Now."

Her brother grunted and turned toward the stairs in the hall. "Bossy." He looked over her head—

not a difficult thing to do—and caught David's amusement. "Bossy," he repeated again. "Stay out of her way or she'll flatten you."

David had a sudden mental image of himself lying on his back with Kate's small, firm curves plastered atop him, and he nearly said, "I wish," before he realized how suicidal *that* would be. Martin was as tall as he himself and had shoulders the size of a small house. Not someone he wanted to antagonize.

"Scram." Unaware of David's thoughts, Kate narrowed her eyes at her brother and snapped the towel threateningly. Martin disappeared up the stairs. "You have five minutes," she called after him.

Martin made it back downstairs within the allotted time, and as soon as David tasted the marinated chicken Kate's grandmother had prepared, he knew why. But he had little time to savor it before Kate's father began to grill him about the market.

"So, David, Kate tells me you have a background in investments." Jackson Davenport's eyebrows lifted as he surveyed his dinner guest.

"I do." He met his host's keen, dark gaze and felt a strange sense of déjà vu. Kate had her father's eyes, no doubt.

"I do a little trading," Jackson said casually. "Don't know what to make of this World Bank problem. Shakes my faith a little, knowing my money could be gone with one stroke of some clown's computer key.''

"You're certainly not alone in feeling that way.'' David phrased his response carefully. He'd had much this same conversation over and over again since April first.

"And if this Achilles character could get into the World Bank, God only knows what else he could hack into,'' Evan added. "What if he decides to break into our missile systems and launch a few? That's all it would take for that nutcase in Rebelia to launch his own attack.''

"And we'd be at war just like *that*,'' said Kate's father, snapping his fingers to emphasis the point.

"Y'all just stop talking so negatively.'' Irma spoke from the foot of the table. "Didn't you listen to a word of the president's address the other night?''

"Actually, no,'' Kate murmured. "Martin, Dennis and I were in the barn half the night. We had three cows calving and one presented wrong, remember?''

Irma nodded. "Well, then, let me repeat it.'' She ticked points off on her fingers as she spoke. "President Stewart believes we have to fight our own fears and not let ourselves get all worked up about the bank theft. Achilles is human; he'll be caught. The president also said we should lead the international community in monitoring Rebelia without getting involved in a war. Essentially, the more we know about that awful DeBruzkya maniac, the better equipped we are to stop him. And the last thing he discussed was not letting these wild rumors about genetically altered children lead to anything as rash as a moratorium on all genetic research. It's amazing how crazy some people are getting about perfectly legitimate research.''

"Isn't that the truth," said Kate. "I overheard the most ridiculous conversation at the dance last night. Where are people getting these ideas?"

"Gossip is an amazing thing," David said. "And I think that some people enjoy the sensationalism and fear. But most are sensible. If we don't allow ourselves, as a nation, to fall victim to a 'fear the worst' mentality—" he directed his words back to Kate's father "—we should get through this bad patch."

"I hope so." Jackson shook his head. "I've been wishing I'd taken my broker's advice to diversify, but it's too late now."

David grinned. "It's never too late. But I wouldn't sell anything right now. When they catch Achilles and whoever else is behind the theft, the markets are going to rebound big-time."

"*If* they catch them," muttered Jackson. "I hope you're right. Because if they don't, there are going to be a lot of folks in a world of hurt."

* * *

On the second day they toured the eastern borders of his land. David asked intelligent questions about the flora and fauna, and Kate found herself falling into all-too-comfortable long silences, instead of arguing her case for his land every minute.

As they sat having lunch on a blanket by the larger spring she'd promised him, he said, "So how'd you get interested in forestry?"

She finished the last bite of her sandwich. "I've never been much for housework or cooking. Whenever Daddy and the boys would let me, I was outside working with them. But I'm not big on rounding up cattle for the rest of my life. There was an older man who took care of the park—he just retired a few years ago. Anyway, I enjoyed all the things he showed me, and taught me, and one day I realized that I'd like to work as a park ranger, too."

"What did your father have to say about all this?"

Kate shrugged. She plucked a blade of grass and thoughtfully began to chew it. "I think he would have been pleased if I'd wanted to ranch, but he's been very supportive."

"He doesn't think you should be pursuing something more ladylike?"

The question tickled her funnybone and she snickered. "Do I look like someone who'd succeed at a 'ladylike' occupation?"

To her surprise, a faint red flush colored his neck. "Sorry. That was my father talking. He had very definite ideas about what kinds of occupations were suitable for women." His mouth twisted. "He had definite ideas about damn near everything."

"Well," she said, trying to smooth over the sudden serious note, "I'm a loss at anything involving cooking or decorating. Cleaning...I'm good at that because it's necessary."

"If you're not good at things, it's because you don't care to be. I think you would succeed at darn near anything you put your mind to," David said.

Flustered by the compliment, she said, "That's one of the slickest ways I've ever heard someone call me bullheaded."

"I didn't mean it like that." David reached out and idly touched a strand of hair that had come loose from her practical braid. "You're smart, strong-willed and once you make a commitment, you follow it through."

A silence hung in the wake of his words. She didn't know what to say. What to do. There was an intensity in the depths of his sky-colored eyes that made her mouth dry and her stomach jittery. The way he'd spoken reminded her of the gentle way he talked to the horses.

"You don't know me well enough to be sure of that."

"I knew you the first night we met." His eyes

were very blue and very sure as they locked on hers, and she swallowed.

Then, before she could figure out how to react, he said, "You're very lucky."

"L-lucky?"

"That your family is so accepting of your career choice. My father had a blue fit when he found out I didn't want to take over his ranch." He looked thoughtful. "Of course, you're a girl. Your father might feel differently if one of his sons hadn't chosen ranching."

Kate shook her head. "No. For a while, Martin worked as a mechanic. He wanted to open his own garage. Dad just wanted him to feel good about whatever he was doing."

"Since he works on the ranch now, I take it he wasn't successful?"

"Oh, no," she said. "He actually had built up quite a good business. But he missed working outdoors, so two years ago he sold it and moved back out of town. And Evan got a teaching degree in music and taught in a high school for five years before the land called him back home again. Dennis is the only one who knew he wanted to work with Dad from the get-go."

There was another silence. Finally, David said quietly, "Like I said, you're lucky."

"Your father was unhappy with your choice of careers?"

A bitter laugh that contained no humor escaped him. "Unhappy with my choice of careers is an understatement. I was either going to be a rancher, or else."

"Or else what?"

"Or else he would cut me off completely."

"He didn't want you to go on to college?"

"Only if the degree was animal husbandry or agriculture—something 'useful.'" He grinned, but it was more a showing of teeth than a genuine expression of pleasure. "Fortunately I got a scholarship to study finance, so he had no leverage."

She heard the pain he didn't share. "That must have hurt."

"Are you kidding? Winning that scholarship was the thrill of my life at that point."

She wasn't going to let him get away with that. "Being rejected by your father couldn't have been fun."

David only shrugged. "I got along okay without him."

And he *had* gotten along okay without his father, David thought bleakly. He'd been erased from the Castlemane family—not that there'd been much of one to start with—as completely as if he'd never existed. He supposed he should be grateful to his father for passing along the stubbornness and grit that hadn't allowed him ever to cave in and contact the old bastard.

But he didn't want to talk about his father anymore. Didn't want to dwell on the lonely college years when he'd had no home to go to during school vacations, the recent years when he'd had no one who really cared with whom to celebrate his successes.

"Let's go for a swim," he said to Kate. "You promised me one yesterday."

She shook her head. "No bathing suit."

"So?" When she cast him a speaking glance, he laughed. "Well, if you don't want to go natural, we can wear our underwear. In this heat, we'd dry in no time."

"You go ahead." She leaned back on her elbows. "I'll just hang here and take a little siesta."

"Nope. Either we both get in or neither of us does."

She lay back, closed her eyes and tipped her hat over her face. "Then I guess nobody goes swimming."

He'd never been able to resist a dare, and her blatant defiance came awfully close to an out-and-out challenge. Grinning, he shucked off his clothes, leaving only his boxer shorts. They'd dry fast, as he'd said, and Kate wouldn't be as uncomfortable as she might be if he swam stark naked.

He could tell she was still awake by the rigidity

Inviting Trouble

of her body and the way her breasts rose and fell in quick, shallow breaths. She was nervous. Good. He liked knocking her off balance every once in a while. He couldn't remember if he'd ever met a more self-sufficient, self-assured woman in his entire life.

Taking two strides across the blanket, he dropped to one knee and swiftly lifted her, cradling her in both arms. She was so small it wasn't a great effort, and he walked to the edge of the pool while she was hollering and wriggling. There, he paused.

"Put me down!" She sounded furious, and just the slightest bit panicked. He had her arms trapped against her body, and he figured it was a good thing, because if her hands were free she probably would have slugged him by now.

"Nope." He grinned at her. "I want to swim, and I'm not swimming alone."

"The hell you aren't!"

"Hey," he said. "I'm a nice guy. I was planning to give you time to get out of some of those clothes, but if you're going to cuss and carry on…" And he waded a few steps into the water.

"David!" she screeched, working her arms free and clutching at his shoulders and neck. "Don't you dare drop me in with my boots on! I'll get in. Just let me take my clothes off."

"Promise?"

"I'm not a liar," she said in a testy tone.

Their faces were inches apart. An invisible arc of electric tension stretched taut between them and he noticed she wouldn't look him in the eye.

"Okay." He turned and headed back to the springy grass at the edge of the spring. But when he got there, he didn't set her down immediately. He desperately wanted to feel her body against his, to slowly savor every inch of her lithe, curving figure as he let her slide to the ground. But she was already nervous and he was afraid if she felt how aroused he'd already gotten just from holding her, she'd hop on her horse and bolt.

Carefully, he set her down, making sure she didn't touch his lower half. Then he turned quickly before she could notice the state of his shorts and waded deeper into the pool. Diving beneath the surface, he came up shaking his head. The pool was clear and cool, wonderfully refreshing after the dry heat of the Texas spring. Although, he thought wryly, it did little to calm his raging hormones. "It feels great," he reported. "Come on in."

"Just give me a minute." She was hopping around on one foot, pulling off her second boot. "Close your eyes."

"Do I have to?"

She shrugged, and began to unbutton her shirt. "I guess not." But he heard the tremor in her tone. Miss Katherine Davenport wasn't as brave as she'd like him to believe.

Letting himself fall backward into the water, he began a steady crawl across the pool, giving her time to finish undressing without an audience. After a few minutes, he stood in chest-deep water and glanced toward the bank. And nearly had a heart attack right there in the pool.

Kate still stood on the bank, balancing on one leg as she dipped a toe into the water. Her arms were crossed self-consciously over her breasts and she looked like she wanted to cover other parts of herself as well.

She had stripped down to her underwear, too. And God, what underwear. It was…it was red. *Red.* Of all the things he'd expected, that hadn't even been on the list. It wasn't particularly seductive, he noted, just a simple cotton style that covered everything, the briefs rising to just below her belly button, the bra a sensible one that didn't push her up or together like so many women seemed to favor these days. But still…*red.*

"Don't be shy. You're very adequately covered." He wondered if his voice sounded as garbled to her as it did to him. His tongue didn't seem to want to work right.

"I'm not shy. I've seen bathing suits a lot skimpier than this." She uncrossed her arms but she still didn't get in the water.

Technically speaking, she was correct. But he'd bet those bathing suits hadn't contained a slim, firm little body with high, full breasts a flat belly and slender, beautifully muscled arms and legs. God. He could feel himself getting harder despite the cool water.

Staying deep in the center of the pool, he beckoned to her. "Come on in."

She shook her head. "I'll just wade a little. I'm not that hot."

"Are you kidding? It's ninety degrees in the shade."

She put both hands on her hips, her whole stance bristling with annoyance. "I can't swim, okay?"

He was dumbfounded. The notion had never entered his head. He almost apologized, but with Kate, he already knew better. "Then that's all the more reason for you to get in here," he said instead. "I'll teach you."

Chapter 6

She had to be crazy.

Why else would she be floating on her back in a spring-fed pool with David Castlemane directly behind her head? She could feel him there, could feel just the lightest touch of his palms between her shoulder blades giving her a little reassurance as she worked on learning to float.

"Who taught you to swim?" she asked, righting herself.

"My father."

"You sound as if it's a good memory."

"It is." His voice was reflective, his smile reminiscent. Clearly, all his memories of his father weren't bad ones. "When I was growing up, I thought the world revolved around my dad. He took me out with him every minute I wasn't in school, taught me how to ride, how to rope, how to—''

"How to *rope?*" And he'd wanted her to believe he wasn't very accomplished on a horse.

"I was never really good at it." He grinned. "Bronc and bull riding were my specialties."

She shook her head, and a reluctant smile tugged at the corners of her mouth. "Just how good were you?"

"Got a silver buckle one year on the circuit before I started college."

Her eyes widened. "Holy cow. I bet your father was proud of you."

David nodded, and a little of the amusement left his face. "He was."

And something as stupid as a career choice had driven them apart. Sympathy welled within her.

"Why didn't you ever learn to swim?" he asked.

She turned her palms up in a questioning gesture, letting him change the subject. "None of us swim. There isn't that much opportunity on a ranch. And my dad can't swim, either, so there wasn't anyone to teach us." She laughed, stirring the water with her arms. "I could have sat by this pool all day and it wouldn't have occurred to me to get in it."

"Feels pretty good, though, doesn't it?"

She nodded. "What's next?"

"Payment."

She looked at him, not sure she'd heard him right. "What?"

His expression altered, his eyes growing heavy-lidded as the atmosphere between them changed. A moment ago, they'd been friendly, the attraction that seemed to grow by the day firmly under control. Now…now the air was laden with the scent of sensual intent. The world seemed to slow down, her focus to narrow until there was nothing else but the two of them standing waist-deep in the sweet, cool waters of the fresh spring.

"A kiss," he said in a low, rough voice. "Just one kiss."

"I don't think that's a good idea," she said, striving for a normal tone although her pulse had begun to race.

"Kate." He stepped closer, water swirling around him as he set his hands at her waist and drew her nearer. "I didn't say it was a good idea. In fact, I'm pretty sure it's a lousy one."

"Why?" Although she'd been the one to say so first, it irked her that he agreed.

"I…had a life plan before I came here," he said. "You're screwing it up."

"Well, excuse me." She tried to pull away from him, but he wouldn't let her go. "Why *did* you come here, anyway?"

He shrugged. "I never expected my father to

leave me anything. I guess I was curious about what was so important in this piece of land.''

"And now you know. It's a *very* important parcel—"

"Kate." He silenced her by simply touching a single finger to her lips. "I've been wanting to kiss you since the first time you walked into my arms on that dance floor. May I kiss you now?"

May I...? She was stunned by the courtly request, and completely charmed. And if she were honest, she'd been wanting the same thing. What could it hurt, as long as she knew what he was and that he was temporary? True, she never intended to get involved with a city guy again, but as long as she went into this with her eyes wide open, there was no harm in it. Besides, it was just a kiss. It would only be a bad idea if she gave it more importance.

Slowly, she nodded. "Yes," she said, and her voice sounded husky and strained, not like hers at all.

Already he was drawing closer, his dark head coming down to blot out the bright sky. Then his lips were on hers, lightly molding, pressing eagerly, as small thrills of heat that had nothing to do with the Texas temperatures shot through her.

His mouth grew firmer, the kiss changing from gentle exploration to a stronger need to know. His tongue lightly teased the line of her closed lips and he nipped tenderly at her full bottom lip. Kate sighed, unable to resist his skilled demands, sliding her arms around his neck as she opened her mouth to him.

The action brought her flush against him, and she felt his hands tighten at her waist for a moment before he wrapped her tightly in his arms, one going low around her back. He was fully aroused beneath the water and the thin boxers he wore, and she shuddered deep inside at the erotic feeling of him pressed hard against her belly.

His other hand came up so that he could spear his fingers into the wet mass of her hair, cradling her skull and tilting her face more fully up to his. As she responded to the kiss, his hand slipped down and around, cradling one breast in his big palm, flicking his thumb over the tender nipple beneath her cotton bra.

Oh, God, she wanted him. She'd never even known a man could make her feel like this, with her body throbbing and begging for his possession.

The kiss changed, becoming deeper, more aggressive as he sought the sweetness she offered. Kate's head was spinning; her senses overloaded. David's body was hard and muscular, stronger and tougher, she thought hazily, than she would have expected given the fact that he sat behind a desk most of the time. He was so much larger than she that she felt surrounded by him, her body quivering with desire incited by the leashed need that vibrated through him.

She tore her mouth from beneath his. "David, wait," she panted.

His hands stilled on her body. "How long?" he said hoarsely.

That startled a laugh out of her. "I don't know. This is going too fast for me."

Slowly, he lowered his forehead to rest against hers. "Holy hell," he said quietly. "That...got a little out of hand." But he didn't release her, and she was all too aware of his erection still pressed intimately against her.

She brought her hands down from his neck, spreading her palms flat against his chest and putting a little space between them. His skin was amazingly hot, slick from the water, bisected cleanly down the middle by a ribbon of curling black hair that disappeared beneath the waistband of the boxers. She cleared her throat. "That got more than a little out of hand."

The corners of his mouth lifted briefly but his eyes were a sharp, deep blue with intent as he looked down at her. "I want you."

Her eyes flared wide with surprise. Although *that* was obvious, she hadn't expected such a blunt approach.

"This—we—uh, it wouldn't be smart," she managed. Good, Kate, very articulate.

"Feels pretty smart to me." He slid both hands down her back, tugging her forward again and lodging her firmly against his hard shaft. She heard herself gasp; he actually groaned aloud. "Only one thing I can think of," he rasped, "that would feel better."

She wondered if he knew how seductive the words were, creating in her a longing to give herself to him completely. But she wasn't that kind of girl, she reminded herself sternly. She barely knew David Castlemane.

And besides, even when she thought she'd known a man the last time she'd taken such an irreversible step, her judgment had been totally lousy. The memory cooled her ardor a little.

She stiffened her arms, pushing him away as she took a step back, and his hands fell away. Her body felt hypersensitive, and she thought it was a wonder the cool water around her didn't steam where it met her overheated flesh.

"I can't," she said. "I'm sorry if you think I'm some kind of tease. It wasn't supposed to be like this."

It wasn't supposed to be like this.

No, indeed, David thought, it certainly wasn't. He'd come back to Texas out of some stupid kind of sentimentality, never intending to keep his father's land.

The last thing he'd expected, or wanted, was to

find a woman who scrambled his brain so badly he could barely think. She wasn't even his type. He tended to go for stacked and statuesque. Or at least he had until the night he'd walked into the Blue-bonnet Ball and gotten a good look at Katherine Davenport in a dress the color of a new penny, with eyes that shouted attitude and intelligence.

The ride back to the ranch was a long and silent one—a less than comfortable one for him since his body reacted every time he thought about what had just happened. His pants and the hard leather saddle had no mercy for his predicament. He eyed Kate's back in front of him and wondered what in the hell was going through her mind. He was pretty sure most of his brain cells had been fried to a crisp by the heat they'd generated when he'd kissed her in the pond.

God. What a kiss that had been. He'd rushed her. He knew he'd rushed her, maybe even scared her a little. But God, how could he have been expected to ignore the temptation of her taut little body in that siren-red lingerie?

His whole body tightened as he thought of the way she'd slid her arms up around his neck and their bodies had fit against each other, the way she'd opened her mouth and her tongue had come shyly out to meet his. She hadn't told him to stop, only to wait.

Had she only been hesitating, trying to work up

her nerve for seduction in hopes of influencing him?

The mere idea left a bad taste in his mouth. When had he become so cynical?

But his enjoyment of the memory was tarnished now, and by the time they arrived back at the stable he felt himself sliding into a dark mood. After unsaddling and caring for his horse, he left Kate standing in the barn with a curt, "See you at supper," and headed for his room, where he booted up his laptop and spent the next few hours catching up on work, deliberately keeping himself too busy to think.

But it wasn't easy to turn off the thoughts churning around in his brain. He knew she was attracted to him, saw it in the way she cast furtive glances at him when she thought he wasn't looking, the way her breathing sped up and her voice grew husky when he got too close. So despite her ultimate motive, there was, at some level, an attraction.

But dammit, he wanted more than that. He wanted honesty. Was she really holding out for his promise not to sell his land to developers? He needed to know.

She was quiet over dinner, and although he tried to catch her alone later, Kate managed to evade him after helping clear the dishes. It was a small and quiet group, since her grandmother apparently had a monthly Monday evening bridge group with whom she had dinner, and two of her three brothers had gone into town.

"Chasin' women," Jackson Davenport volunteered. "You should have gone with them."

"Oh, Daddy, David doesn't want to stand around in a bar talking to a bunch of buckle-bunnies," Kate said sharply.

"How do you know?" he asked, grinning for the first time since he'd returned to the house. He hadn't heard that term in years, and he hadn't heard anyone female use it…ever, maybe.

To his surprise, a deep red blush crawled from her neck to her hairline. "My mistake," she said in a frigid tone. Then, before anyone could speak again, she swept out of the room and they heard her footsteps ascending the stairs—all right, stomping up the stairs—to her room.

There was a slightly stunned silence in her wake. Evan and Jackson looked at David, eyebrows raised.

David spread his hands. "Don't ask me."

"You know," said Jackson thoughtfully, "her mother was a hardheaded little spitfire like that. The worse she talked to me, the better I knew she liked me." His eyes narrowed. "I don't like to be a nosey old so-and-so," he informed David, "but if there's something going on between you and my daughter, it had better not end with her getting a broken heart."

Evan coughed, and David saw that he was trying not to smile. "You sound like a protective father, Dad," he said. "Which is ridiculous. We all know Kate can handle herself."

David rose quickly, gathering his plate and utensils. "I'll, ah, start cleaning up." As he exited the dining room, he could hear Evan still chuckling.

The moment was light, but David's mood was darker than the early dawn sky when he woke in the morning. He could hear the Davenport men downstairs having breakfast and he knew they'd be getting an early start. It was branding season and they'd need every minute of daylight they had today.

Kate hadn't come out of her bedroom the rest of the evening and he hadn't heard her yet this morning. He lingered in his own room until the sounds of the men faded. The last thing he needed was an audience watching every move he made around her, he thought grumpily as he finally descended the steps.

Irma greeted him, but there was no Kate in the kitchen. "Kate's already in the barn," her grandmother informed him cheerfully before he had to ask. So after a quick breakfast, he headed for the barn.

She was filing down a hoof on one of the geldings when he walked in.

"Good morning," he said.

"'Morning."

"Kate, I want to talk to you—" But he'd barely begun when she was talking over his words.

"There's nothing to talk about." She never looked up at him once as she released the horse and stood, turning to hang up the file. "I agreed to show you around your land. If you have questions about that, I'll answer them. Otherwise, your tour is over."

"I don't think so." He stepped closer, and before she could avoid him again, he took her by the shoulders.

This time, when he set his mouth on hers, he demanded the response he'd sensed she could give him. The bridle she'd held hit the floor with a jingle as he pulled her closer and she clutched at his wrists with her small hands. Her mouth was warm and pliant, opening to him with little reserve, and when she sank against him, he caught her as triumph surged through him.

"David," she finally said when he lifted his head, "what are you doing?"

"If you have to ask, I must not be doing it right."

"Oh, you're doing it right." Her tone was breathless and shaken. "But...*why* are you doing it?"

He kissed her again, lingering over it. "Because I want to."

"Oh." She appeared to be taken aback.

"You're an attractive woman," he said, gauging her response. "Don't you know that?"

Her expression was unreadable. "I've been told that before."

He got the impression she wasn't recalling a particularly inspiring moment in her personal history. "It's supposed to be a compliment," he said.

She sighed, then slipped free of his arms. "It was," she told him. "But there are a lot of things more important than looks. Better saddle up. I want to get that fence fixed this morning."

And just like that, the conversation was over.

They rode out a few minutes later. David took the same lively gelding she'd given him last time. They rode side by side, but Kate seemed as far from him as the moon, distant and lovely, but unreachable. At least she was speaking to him again. He could almost believe her pique from the night before had been jealousy.

What she'd said a few minutes ago was right in many respects. There *were* lots of things more important than looks. But mutual attraction was certainly high on the list, and generally people who were drawn to each other looked through a filter that showed their partner in a desirable light.

He and Kate were attracted to each other, no question. And no matter what she said about going too fast, he wasn't backing off. He'd never met a woman with whom he'd shared such instant rapport. They'd silently recognized in each other something...some indefinable thing that was too compelling to walk away from without exploring it.

He sensed that the last thing she wanted right now was to get involved with someone. And God knew with his schedule he didn't need the complications of a steady woman who would demand his time and attention and throw fits when she didn't get it.

But...he wasn't sure either of them had a choice anymore. Whatever was between them was strong. Strong enough to pull him toward her despite his reservations, despite the knowledge that a part of his appeal for her was his land.

They rode silently for maybe twenty-five minutes before she pointed to a section of fence and rode that way. "Daddy said he thought there was a strand coming loose here. Looks like the post is all right. The wire just snapped."

She dismounted, so he did, too. As she withdrew wirecutters, a heavy-duty staple gun and thick gloves from her saddlebag, he cleared his throat. "So what things are more important than looks?"

Her hands froze in the act of uncoiling wire for a second, then she went right on with her task. "Compatibility, for one."

"In what way? No two people can be completely compatible, can they?"

"I'm talking big-picture things," she said, concentrating on the work.

"Such as?"

She threw him a distinctly sour look. "I'm tired of this subject."

"Tough," he said. "I'm not. Besides, you started it. So tell me what you mean by big-picture."

"Education," she tossed back. "Lifestyle. Finances, to name a few."

"Is that last one what happened to you?" he asked. "Some guy tried to get his hands on your family money?"

"Excuse me?" Her voice was frigid. She rolled her eyes. "Hardly." Then, belatedly, "What makes you think something happened to me, anyway?"

He snorted. "Almost every minute you're around me you're playing defense. Somewhere along the line you were seriously disillusioned. I'd like to know what happened."

To his everlasting shock, angry tears filled her eyes. Instantly, she turned her back to him, dashing them away with stiff motions.

"Kate." He put his hands on her upper arms and gently rubbed up and down without trying to turn her to face him again.

"Funny," she said, and her voice was tight as if she were desperately trying to contain any emotion, "but after all this time I still remember the humiliation more than any feeling I ever had for the guy.''

"What did he do?" He kept stroking his palms lightly up and down her arms.

"Nothing, really." She sighed, an enormous exhalation that shook her whole tiny frame and her slender shoulders sagged. "He was in town on business from Phoenix. Handsome, sophisticated, every woman's dream. I was nineteen and as stupid as they came."

She turned around and met his gaze squarely. "I let him seduce me. Turns out it was lust instead of love. I overheard him one day telling someone what a 'dumb little country hick' I was." She backed up a pace when he would have hugged her. "He was right."

"There's a big difference between stupid and naive," he said. "You were the latter."

"Whatever." She shrugged. "A lesson in life."

"No," he corrected. "A lesson in how shallow and callous that particular dope was."

She laughed, although her eyes still held the remnants of hurt remembered. "I like the sound of that."

He forced himself to smile, sensing that she needed a lighter note. "Glad I could oblige." But beneath the smile, he was clenching his teeth. Thinking about a young Kate's feelings being

crushed by some insensitive idiot made him wish
he knew the guy's name. It might be primitive but
he would derive intense satisfaction from planting
his fist right in the middle of the jerk's face.

Chapter 7

Over the next two weeks, Kate showed David every inch of his land, a good portion of hers, and as much of Greenlaurel State Park as she thought was necessary for him to understand why the Castlemane property was so crucial to the health of the local ecosystem. Although she'd tried several times to box him into a discussion of the land deal he was on the verge of making, David was equally adept at sidestepping.

As was she. He'd caught her in the barn twice more and kissed her senseless, but she'd been more careful after that. It wasn't, she thought, that she disliked kissing him. God knew she'd like to do a whole lot more than that, but the memory of her youthful stupidity was a strong one. And while she no longer believed he was shallow enough to hurt her in the same way, David had said from the beginning that he was leaving. No way was she going to be left behind, her heart breaking into little pieces for a man she couldn't have.

She also was growing edgier with each passing day. David had made it plain his time here was limited. The two-week deadline of his visit loomed in just over twenty-four hours, and she wanted to know—*needed* to know—whether he'd reconsidered his plans.

He'd be leaving tomorrow afternoon, and he'd told her today would be the last day he'd be riding with her. She was determined to bring up the subject of his land during the time they were alone.

He'd be leaving. She tried not to let herself think about what that meant to her on a personal level.

He'd let her know he was interested in her, had given her several of those drugging kisses that made her forget everything but him. It was just physical chemistry, she told herself.

She scowled as she cinched the buckles of Sprint's saddle. What gave him the right to get her all stirred up, thinking about things she hadn't thought about for years, wanting things she thought she'd forgotten? What gave him the right to start her thinking about him and then just…just leave?

It didn't matter, she reminded herself firmly. David might have lived on a ranch once, but his feet were planted in the city now. Definitely not her kind of man.

On this last morning, she decided to take him over his own land one more time. She figured they'd have lunch by the big spring-fed pool on the Castlemane land where he'd first proposed teaching her to swim. Where he'd kissed her for the first time.

Just because she was taking him back there didn't mean anything special. It was simply a nice spot for a picnic and a swim. They'd gone swimming several times at the public lake in the park where tourists congregated, and twice more in a large stock pond on her family's land, but this would be the first time they'd been back to the spring.

The soft grass in the shade of the cottonwoods made a lovely spot for a picnic, which she'd helped Gram put together this morning, and after a short rest, he could give her one last swimming lesson.

For the rest of her life, every time she swam in one of the ranch's ponds, she'd think of these two weeks she'd spent in the company of David Castlemane.

As they approached the spring, she said, "This is such a beautiful spot, isn't it? I thought you might like to come back here on your last day."

David nodded as he dismounted, saddle leather creaking. "Great choice."

But if you sign those papers tomorrow, all this will be gone, hemmed in by asphalt and siding and neatly landscaped lawns.

She didn't say it.

He helped her spread out a blanket, then carried the basket he'd strapped behind his saddle over and set it down. Kate yanked off her boots impatiently, looking up at his silhouette against the bright blue of the sky. "Time to eat! I hope you're hungry. Gram got a little carried away this morning."

"Basket's heavier than a…a bear."

She grinned. "Or something."

"I thought you helped put this together."

"I did. But every time I started to close the basket, Gram handed me one more thing she thought we might like."

David laughed. Walking back to his horse, he returned with a black zippered bag. "She waylaid me, too." He unzipped the bag to reveal a chilled interior containing a bottle of California wine, a corkscrew and two plastic wineglasses. Turning the bottle, he looked at the label and his eyebrows rose. "A good vintage."

"My grandmother knows wines," she told him. "She even saves the labels of ones she particularly likes and files them with notes on what the wine was like. Me, I couldn't even tell red from white if my eyes were closed.'' The moment she said it, she cursed herself. *Nothing like pointing out what a hick you are. Way to go, Kate.*

With a few deft twists, he uncorked the bottle and poured each of them some of the pale liquid.

She busied herself setting out roast chicken, imported strawberries, her grandmother's potato salad, the pickles they'd canned last fall, deviled eggs and corn bread she'd baked under duress from Gram last night. The frozen crème de menthe brownies would be thawed to perfection by the time the meal ended and there were slices of cherry pie, as well. The cherries, too, came from goods they'd canned.

David was grinning broadly, eyebrows climbing higher and higher as she set out dish after dish, but all he said was, ''Two desserts?''

''She was afraid you might not like chocolate.'' Her delivery was deadpan.

He burst out laughing. ''Way to go, Mrs. D.''

He ate heartily, even finding room for one of each dessert. Kate watched in awe. ''You and my brothers…where do you put all that food?''

David patted his flat stomach. ''Right here.'' He eyed her critically. ''You only had one chicken wing.''

''And strawberries, an egg and a piece of pie. I'm full.''

He eyed her openly as they packed the food and

the empty wine bottle away. "You could gain a pound or two without any problem."

"No," she said definitely. "I couldn't." She reclined on her elbows. "I'm going to have to take a little nap. Shouldn't have let you talk me into that last glass of wine."

"It was too tasty to go to waste." He lay down a decorous distance from her. "A nap sounds good to me. Let the food settle before we swim."

Kate let herself lie all the way down, tilting her hat over her eyes in a habitual gesture. She liked the easy atmosphere between them. Her father and brothers tended to want to watch over her, which in turn drove her to prove to them that she was as tough as they were. And of course, they needed someone to keep them in line around the house. If not for her cracking the whip, they'd be knee-deep in mud from that bunch traipsing in and out in boots.

Her relationships with the men in her family were loving, but not always particularly comfortable.

But David...David seemed to accept her.

Seemed to, she stressed to herself. *He's from the city. He likes you well enough in this setting but back in his own environment, you'd be about as welcome as a bee at an ice cream social.*

Sighing, she clasped her hands over her stomach and willed herself to catch five.

A moment later, a large, warm hand descended

over both of hers. Her whole body went rigid as David's fingers brushed her stomach. But he only lifted one of her hands. Lacing their fingers together, he carried their linked hands down to rest between them on the spongy turf.

She went still.

"Kate." Her name was a soft, low sound.

"What?"

"I can hear you thinking all the way over here. Tell me what's going on inside your head."

"If you can hear me thinking, then you should already know."

He chuckled. "You have an answer for everything, don't you?"

"I aim to please," she said with false modesty, and he chuckled again.

But then he was quiet.

She didn't have to answer him. It was her choice to keep her thoughts to herself.

But...he was lying there, just waiting....

It was no skin off her nose. Let him wait.

Only...she knew he expected her to say something.

She waited him out as long as she could, but finally she couldn't stand the silence any longer. "All right. You win."

"I didn't even know we were playing a game."

"Ha. You knew exactly what would happen if

you waited long enough. What do you want to hear?''

David rolled onto his side facing her and removed her hat, laying it aside. ''Tell me what you were thinking.'' His tone was serious, and he switched hands so that he could prop himself up and still cradle her hand in his.

It felt so perfect that she couldn't draw away. She took a deep breath, not wanting to mar the moment. ''Just now, I was thinking that it felt...right, or something...to lie here with you. I was thinking that the way you're holding my hand was lovely.''

David cleared his throat. ''I was thinking the same thing.'' He lifted her hand and carried it to his lips, pressing a gentle kiss to her fingers, and she felt the tingle of electricity his touch produced clear down to her toes.

For an endless moment, she simply let herself fall into the piercing depths of his gaze. The atmosphere grew thick and still, laden with words unspoken.

David lifted her hand and placed it against his cheek, her palm cradling his face, his much larger hand covering hers, holding it in place. His eyes closed as he slowly rubbed his stubbled cheek lightly back and forth against the softness of her skin. Then he turned his head and pressed a kiss into the center of her palm.

Kate felt a shiver scamper down her spine. ''David,'' she whispered, and in her own voice she could hear the soft invitation, the need.

He shifted again, leaning over her until there was no tree above her, no bright sky, nothing but his face coming closer and closer, his clear, blue eyes holding her gaze until she could no longer stand the contact and let her eyelids flutter shut.

Then his mouth was on hers. He held himself on one elbow, the other hand braced on the far side of her body as he lightly fed from her lips, drinking the response she was unable to prevent.

When his tongue brushed lightly along the seam of her lips, she raised her other arm and slipped both of them around his neck. As she opened her mouth and let her own tongue meet his, she tightened her arms, drawing him down to her.

David rolled onto his side, pulling her up as well so that they lay together, arms wrapped around each other. He slid one muscular thigh between hers and pressed upward, and she responded to the sweet pressure, arching wildly against him. His kisses were perfect, making her yearn for even more intimacy.

So what would be wrong with that? She was a grown woman who made her own decisions. She was fully aware this time that the heat they generated together didn't mean anything more to him than a pleasant interlude that would fade from his mind once he got back to the city.

He rolled her onto her back and came fully over her, his weight pressing her into the soft grass as he kissed her wildly, hungrily. David out of control was something she'd never witnessed. It was thrilling. His hands were rough and hasty, but everywhere he touched her he left a small flame burning and soon she was half incoherent with need, her hands clutching at him. "David...please..."

"Are you sure, Kate?" he whispered. He fastened his teeth in her lower lip and bit down gently, worrying the tender flesh before soothing the small sting with his tongue. "It has to be what you want."

"It's what I want." Her voice was barely audible. She set her hands at the buttons of his shirt and unfastened the first button, then the second, her fingers growing more sure as she moved downward. "It's what I want," she repeated, lifting her head to gaze into his eyes.

He smiled slowly, then his head came down and he kissed her again, exploring the inside of her mouth with thorough strokes of his tongue. He kissed a path along the line of her jaw and down the tender column of her neck, making her shiver. Then he drew back. His eyes blazed with blue fires of arousal as he brushed aside the fabric of her blouse. He unclipped the front clasp of her bra with one hand, and his chest rose and fell as the cups sprang apart to reveal the creamy slopes of her breasts.

As if in a trance, he slowly lifted a hand and pushed her lingerie aside to reveal the dark copper nipples that crowned her breasts. "You're beautiful," he said hoarsely. "My imagination couldn't begin to compare." He cupped the sweet weight of one breast, his thumb slowly stroking back and forth across the crest. She felt her body quiver as arrows of need shot straight to her core, and she moved her legs restlessly.

Then he bent his head and took one taut peak into his mouth, and she cried out, her back arching as he used his mouth and his tongue to whip her into an even more needy state.

She needed him. And she needed to touch him, as well. She slipped her hand down between their bodies, brushing over his belt buckle and beyond, until her palm discovered the hard length of him pressed against the front of his jeans. David growled deep in his throat, his mouth coming up to possess hers as she flattened her palm against him and rubbed along the length of his concealed flesh. He pulled her hand away, then swiftly unfastened her belt and jeans before rising to his knees to pull off her boots. His hands were hard and sure as he stripped away her pants, taking her panties with them.

Kate lay beneath him, clad only in her open shirt

and bra, as he ripped off his own shirt and unfastened his pants. His hands were shaking, and she raised herself up to slide a hand into the back of his jeans, guiding them down over his taut buttocks. She lingered there, palming his hot, hard butt as he shoved his remaining clothing around his knees.

In a moment, his pants were out of the way. He was still on his knees in front of her, and her half-sitting position put her nearly at eye level with the magnificent sight of his very masculine, very aroused flesh. Slowly she raised her hand. David was looking down at her, eyes blazing with hot blue fire, and when her fingers curled around the heated shaft, he hissed a curse between his teeth, throwing his head back. The action arched his back and thrust his hips at her, and she grew bolder, stroking the fascinating silky flesh, marveling at the way it leaped and pulsed beneath her hand as she languidly stroked and caressed him.

David made a deep, primal sound. His hand shot out and locked over her wrist, stopping her movements. "My turn now," he said as he pulled her hand from his body.

He pushed her back on the blanket, kneeling between her legs, but he didn't touch her there right away. Instead, he leaned forward, kissing her deeply, then slowly worked his mouth along her jaw and back to her earlobe. He touched the tender place there and she jerked, feeling a shocking rush of moist heat gather between her legs.

David smiled against her skin, dragging his mouth down, along her collarbone and in to the small hollow at the base of her throat. His hand settled firmly over one breast and she gasped as he rolled the already taut nipple between his thumb and forefinger, until streamers of hot sensation ran like an electric charge from there down to her womb.

Her hips arched beneath him, and she felt his heavy shaft brush against her thigh. David's mouth fastened over her other breast and he began to suckle her, pulling hard on the sensitive peak while he let his lower body drop against her so that she could feel every inch of him throbbing between them.

But he only stayed there for a moment before shifting his body to one side. She could feel a trail of moistness where his eager flesh had left its mark, and then his hand smoothed steadily down from her breast to her aching mound. She cried out and arched against him and his hand slipped easily between her legs, seeking out the soft, swollen flesh. He drew his finger along her, exerting the slightest pressure, repeating the process until she felt herself parting for him, felt one blunt finger carefully working its way into her. She was so wet he had no trouble, and she gasped as he slid his finger strongly

in as far as it would go. He withdrew it, and then
pushed it in again, and she thrashed her head on
the blanket, her hands roaming his broad shoulders
and chest, frantically trying to pull him closer.

David's body was screaming at him to hurry, but
he refused to rush. Kate was the most amazingly
responsive woman he'd ever seen, her body react-
ing to his every stroke, every move. Despite her
protests, he withdrew his finger from her, then
clasped her wrists and spread them wide, letting his
lower body pin hers. Her eyes stared up at him,
wide with sensual promise. "David," she whispered.

He leaned down and kissed her, realizing that he
could do this every day for the rest of his life and
not ever miss other women. Slowly he pulled backward on his knees until his stiff shaft fell into the
shadowed cleft between her thighs. Immediately,
she raised her legs, clasping them around his hips,
and the action pulled him hard against the steamy
portal to her body. He probed, using his hips to
work himself steadily into her, gritting his teeth.
God, she was tight. Her flesh squeezed around him,
and each time he pulled out a little, it felt as if she
were clinging to him, begging him not to leave. He
was so hard he hurt, aching with the need for release, and finally, unable to wait any longer, he
surged forward, embedding himself to the hilt in
her heated channel. Her legs tightened around his

waist and she rocked her hips. "Move," she commanded.

He laughed. And then he gave her what she wanted. Hot, hard thrusts. He worked a hand between them, finding the little bud that had swelled with desire, pressing firmly down on it and rotating his finger as she screamed. Her back arched and her heels dug into the blanket as she bucked beneath him.

His world narrowed. The incredible feel of her body beneath him, around him, her scent in his nostrils, her little whimpers in his ears. Her tight little cove clasping and releasing, clasping and releasing him—

And that was all it took. As soon as he felt her coming around him, the rush of his release roared through him, surging in hot, wet jets out through his rigid shaft into her soft, receptive depths. His hands burrowed beneath her and cupped her buttocks, holding her firmly against him as he came, maintaining his tight grip until his last spasm had passed, until the last little shock had shaken her, until their bodies were limp with the total relaxation of utter satisfaction.

Only then did he release her and drag himself backward to his knees. She lay there, legs spread and limp, her hair a wild tangle around her, and he felt his heart twist in his chest. She was so beautiful.

Slowly, he lowered himself to her side and pulled

her into his arms. She lay cuddled against him, and he felt as if he held the world in the curve of his right arm. Turning his head, he touched her temple with his lips. "This changes things."

And it did. He'd never felt this way before, and he knew it was ridiculously fast to be asking her to marry him, but that was exactly what he intended to do. His tongue practically ached with the need to tell her he loved her. How could he possibly love her? He'd only known her for two weeks. And yet...

And yet he'd known her all his life. Known *of* her, though he hadn't fully realized what he was waiting for until she'd walked into his arms during the singles' dance at the Bluebonnet Ball. He'd known it that night, when she'd tossed his wealth back in his face despite his efforts to believe she was just like all the others who'd tried to snare him over the years.

He suddenly realized she hadn't answered him. "Hey," he said, "are you still awake?"

Her lips curved. "Yeah. Do you realize you still have your boots on?"

He grinned. "I guess I'm a cowboy at heart."

She was silent for a moment. Then she said, "So, have you decided what you're going to do about your father's land yet?"

What? David didn't move. He couldn't. Even breathing was beyond him for a moment. He couldn't believe what he'd just heard. Finally, a growing anger bit through his shock.

God! He'd been about to blurt out feelings of...*feelings* to her, and she'd been lying there plotting how to talk him out of his land the whole time. He couldn't believe it!

Fury rose and suddenly he couldn't get away from her fast enough. He rolled away, heedless of how she landed when he yanked his arm from beneath her. "You jumped the gun," he said, rising to his feet and pulling up his pants in one motion. As he fastened them, he said, "Here's a tip. The next time you want something from a guy, wait until *after* he says yes to let him screw you."

"David!" Kate stood, too, wearing nothing but her wide-open shirt. She didn't bother to clutch it around her, simply stood there, displaying all her delectable attributes as she stared at him. Her hair was a wild tangle of black curls around her face, her eyes wide and shocked. "I wasn't—I didn't mean—"

"Get dressed." He swept up her discarded pants and tossed them at her. "The sex wasn't that great, anyway. And even if I had been rethinking my plans for the land, I don't respond to blackmail."

She was dressing now, and by the time he'd located his hat, she was stomping into her boots with vicious disregard for the nearby blanket. "You son of a bitch. The last thing on my mind today was blackmail.'' She shook her head and he could almost see the sparks rising from her, she was so mad. She pointed at the blanket. "I thought we were making love. I *know* I was making love. And even though I knew you weren't staying, I wanted to have a memory—" Her voice hitched and abruptly she stopped speaking. "Never mind." She whirled and went to her horse, mounting easily with the fluid motion he loved to watch. "You can find your own way back to the ranch. And when you get there I want you packed and gone. Immediately."

Reining Sprint sharply, she wheeled and left him standing there in the dust kicked up by the horse's hooves.

David simply stood there as she rode away, replaying the scene in his mind. Something was wrong. Her expression was seared across his brain. He'd seen Kate mad, seen her exuberant, seen her melancholy. He'd seen her satisfied, quietly happy, humiliated or brooding.

But he'd never seen her hurt so badly that she couldn't wipe the pain from her eyes.

God, what had he done?

He knew Kate. She didn't give up. But she wasn't underhanded and sneaky in the way she went about things. If she'd really wanted to change his mind, she'd still be on that blanket with him. Talking her head off about the gray fox, hackberry trees and that damned golden-cheeked warbler. *Talking.* Not using her body to get what she wanted.

His stomach felt hollow and his throat was tight. He crossed to the blanket and picked it up, shaking off the dust. As he began to refold it, he lifted it to his face and breathed deeply for a moment.

His own insecurities had gotten the best of him, and he might have just ruined his only hope of a happy future.

He'd hurt Kate so deeply that she'd probably never forgive him. In his heart, he knew she hadn't let him have her as an incentive for the land. She'd lain down on this blanket with him because she cared.

I thought we were making love. I know I was….

Full-blown panic grabbed him. As fast as he could, he reloaded his packs and slung the blanket across Ghost's rump. Swinging into the saddle, he headed back in the direction Kate had disappeared.

Would she forgive him? Could she? He'd been just plain mean with the crack about the sex, because he'd known it would hit her squarely in her most insecure spot.

He figured it was fitting that he ate her dust the whole way back to the barn.

Chapter 8

She lingered in the barn, knowing she could duck into the loft or an empty stall when he came back and he'd never see her. She couldn't go into the house—her grandmother had invited several of her closest friends among the Belles for lunch today and, judging by the cars in the driveway, the ladies were still here.

The last thing she needed was for all of them to see her red eyes.

Hoofbeats approached and she whirled and ran for the last stall. Oh God, she couldn't face him now.

She put a hand over her mouth to stifle the sob that wanted to erupt. If there was a stupider woman on the face of the earth, Kate didn't know where. Anybody with a grain of sense would have known better than to bring up that land business right after the most wonderful, incredible lovemaking of her entire life.

David had never been loved for himself in his whole life, she suspected. His father had wanted to make him into someone else. His mother hadn't loved him enough to stand up against her husband's dictatorial ways. The women he'd met since, if the way the ones at the ball had behaved were any sample, had their eyes on his money and reputation before they ever even met him.

And after what had just happened, she probably had more chance of flying to Mars than she did of ever getting David to speak to her again.

Kate's horse was put away when he entered the barn. She must have gone into the house already. He wondered who all the visitors were, and if there was any way he could sneak by them. The last thing he felt like doing was talking to anyone.

He wasn't giving up, he told himself fiercely as he hung up his saddle, rubbed down and watered Ghost. He wanted Kate Davenport more than he'd ever wanted anything in his whole life. She cared, he was sure. Or at least, she had until he'd crushed her heart beneath his heel without stopping to think—

She stepped out of a stall at the end of the barn.

Taken aback, he simply stared.

"Can I talk to you?" Her voice was hesitant, softer than normal.

"Sure." Anything, just so she didn't leave. He walked toward her slowly. "Kate—"

"David—"

They spoke at the same time.

"You first," he said.

She bowed her head. "I'm sorry."

"For what?" he blurted. "I'm the one who should apologize."

Her head came up. She eyed him cautiously, and he was encouraged. Slowly, she began to speak again. "I'm sorry I jumped on you about the land at a bad time." Her eyes filled with tears. "Instead of telling you I loved you, I had to ask that stupid question."

"Kate." He stepped forward, then stopped. He wanted to take her into his arms but her body looked stiff and untouchable. "I was...reeling. Couldn't you tell what you do to me?" Then her words sank in. "You love me?"

She looked at him then, and he could see the sadness and regret in her face. "Yes. But it's all right, David. When I lay down on that blanket with you, I knew you weren't—"

"Wasn't what? Madly in love with you? Crazy about you?" He did touch her then, grabbing her upper arms and pulling her to him to set his mouth hard on hers, kissing her thoroughly before lifting his head again. "God, woman, you're the best thing that ever happened to me."

He grabbed her and towed her toward the barn door, stopping just outside in the bright sunlight. "Katherine Davenport, marry me. I don't know how we'll work out all the details and you'll probably lead me a merry dance for the rest of my life, but I don't ever want to live without you."

"David!" She launched herself at his chest and he caught her easily, holding her to him. "I thought—I was afraid you thought I only wanted you for that land. I don't care about the land," she said. "Sell it to whoever you want. I'll still fight like hell to try to derail any zoning changes, but I'll never stop loving you just because of that."

"I've decided not to sell the land," he said. "But I draw the line at ranching." He grinned. "We'll keep enough acreage for a small farm, and the rest I'll deed to the State Park Service to be added to the Greenlaurel Park lands."

"David!" she said. "Are you sure?"

"I'm sure. I can run my business from anywhere. Why not here? I'll have to travel from time to time, but knowing you're here waiting for me will get me through."

"I'll travel with you if you want," she offered.

"Part of the land we're keeping is that spring,"

he told her, grinning, "for obvious sentimental reasons. We'll build so that we can see it from the house."

She laughed as she kissed his chin. "Good idea. And I'll either work with Daddy or as a ranger." A funny look crossed her face. "I've never seen a pregnant park ranger before."

"A..." He immediately loosened his grip and leaned back to search her face. "Could you—"

She counted in her head. "I don't think it's likely. But I'm not on anything..."

"And I certainly didn't use protection." David shook his head, mildly astonished at himself. "I didn't even think about it."

"All I was thinking about was you," she told him. She hesitated, then took a deep breath. "I would like to have children."

"Children would be great," he said in a husky voice. "And definitely in the plural. No lonely only like me."

"I hope at least one of our sons is just like you." She laid her head against his heart. "I love you, David Castlemane."

"And I love you." He folded her more closely against him. He'd come to Greenlaurel to let go of his past. Instead, he'd made peace with it, and found a future he never could have imagined mere weeks ago.

* * *

Inside the house, Irma Davenport let the lace panel of the curtain she'd been peering through drop and turned to her three friends. "He's kissing her again," she reported. "And unless I'm mistaken, he doesn't look like he'll be letting go anytime soon."

"Three for three," Marjorie said with deep satisfaction. "First Rosie—"

"And my Mitch. I still can't get over that one!" Ida Conrad interjected, patting her heart.

"Then my darling Noelle found Aiden again," Georgia Ann said in her distinctive drawl. "I truly wasn't sure we were goin' to pull that one off, y'all."

"But we did!" Marjorie crowed.

"You know," said Irma, tapping a finger against her lips reflectively. "We really *are* good at this matchmaking business. Maybe we should try a few more."

"Well, Irma," said Marjorie, "you've got those three strapping grandsons just cryin' out for the right woman to come along…"

"I propose a toast." Ida picked up a glass of the light wine they'd been enjoying and held it aloft. "To the Bluebonnet Belles! May we make many more successful matches."

"To the Bluebonnet Belles," echoed the others. Irma turned and peeked out the window again.

"Uh-oh, they're comin' toward the house. Put down your wine and act sober, y'all. And for heaven's sake, pretend to be surprised when they tell us their news!"

* * * * *

There are more secrets to reveal—
don't miss out!
Coming in June 2003 to
Silhouette Books.
Forget everything you think you know,
and see what secrets live inside the

ENEMY MIND

by USA TODAY *bestselling author*
Maggie Shayne
FAMILY SECRETS: *Five*
extraordinary siblings. One dangerous
past. Unlimited potential.

And now, for a sneak peek,
just turn the page...

Chapter 1

Jake Ingram sat at his desk, wondering if he really was as good as everyone seemed to think he was. He'd been tapped to help the government track down those responsible for the biggest heist on record—the robbery of the World Bank. He wished for a moment that bank robbers would stick to the old-fashioned methods: burst in with guns and demand cash from tellers, or break in by night and crack the vault. But no, these bank robbers were far more sophisticated. The money had literally vanished overnight, through a spiderweb of computer transfers so complex it would take a genius to figure out where it had finally ended up.

Unfortunately, the genius chosen to do just that was him.

He hoped to hell he could live up to his reputation, but even for Jake, this was a challenge. The wedding would have to be postponed…again. Tara was going to be heartbroken. It occurred to him, just briefly, that he probably should be, as well.

The afternoon mail sat unopened on his desk, and he turned to it, knowing full well he was procrastinating. He had two equally daunting tasks to face: plunging headlong into the investigation and breaking the news to Tara. Taking a quick peek at the mail seemed more appealing than either.

He flipped through envelopes filled with tragic-looking stock market analyses, even worse financial reports, updates on how the world was responding to the knowledge that its most sophisticated and secure bank's computers had been accessed by criminals and robbed of a staggering amount of money.

Everyone was panicking, pulling funds, selling stocks. If the World Bank wasn't safe, nothing was.

Suddenly, he stopped flipping through the mail. There was one small envelope addressed to him in a handwritten scrawl. No return address, no postage stamp. Odd. He buzzed his assistant, and the young man appeared almost instantly.

Jake held up the envelope. ''Where did this come from?''

The younger man eyed the envelope and straightened his glasses. ''Found it under the office door when I came in this morning." Then he held up a newspaper. "You made headlines again today. That's four days in a row now."

Seeing his name emblazoned across the front page, Jake sighed. "I told the feds to keep my involvement quiet, but apparently they either ignored that advice or sprung a leak. By now the entire world knows I'm on this case."

"You think that's a bad thing?"

"I don't think it's a good one."

Fred tilted his head. "You need anything else?"

"No, go on." When Fred left him alone again, Jake opened the envelope, and a scent wafted from it as he did. It was oddly familiar. Violets. It smelled like violets. For a moment his stomach clenched into a knot and his throat tightened as if with emotion, but he had no idea why. He quickly forced those feelings aside and continued examining the envelope.

It contained a single sheet of lined paper covered in the same spidery script that was on the envelope.

Dearest Jake,
Everything you believe about yourself, about your life, is a lie. There are things in the past, things you don't remember—things you've not been allowed to remember. But now the time has come when you must know the truth about your past. Who you are. Where you come

from. You could be in grave danger, Jake. It's
time to exhume the buried past. Try to remember, Jake, try! It's more important than you
know. I'll help you find the truth. I'll be in
touch soon.

The letter was signed with a single initial, the
letter *V*.

Jake sat there staring at the note for a long time,
willing more information to appear on the page, but
of course none did. He licked his lips. It wasn't for
real. It couldn't be for real. There were very few
people in Jake's life who knew about the secrets
that plagued him most, the secrets of his past.

But they were secret only to him. He remembered nothing about his life prior to his adoption
by the Ingram family at the age of twelve. Nor was
there anything sinister about it—his birth parents
had been killed in a car crash, and his young mind
had been unable to deal with the trauma of their
loss. So he'd blocked it out. It was an extreme reaction, but a plausible one. It happened sometimes,
the doctors told him.

His adopted parents and his adopted brother,
Zach, were the only people who knew about the
post-traumatic memory loss and the pain it caused
him. They were the only people who knew about
the odd dreams that sometimes haunted his sleep.

And they wouldn't have told anyone else. He trusted his family beyond question.

But *someone* knew he didn't remember his past. Somehow, someone else knew. And whoever it was was trying to use that information now—to what end, he couldn't imagine.

Or maybe he could, he thought as his gaze slid to the newspaper lying on his desk, proclaiming his involvement in the investigation of the biggest robbery in recorded history. Maybe he could.

* * * * *

Five extraordinary siblings.
One dangerous past.
Unlimited potential.

What if you discovered that your seemingly perfect life was all a lie?

Follow the adventures of five extraordinary siblings in these romantic stories about hidden identity, finding family and coming to terms with your roots.

Where love comes alive™

FAMILY SECRETS

Five extraordinary siblings.
One dangerous past.
Unlimited potential.

What if you discovered that your seemingly perfect life was all a lie?

Follow the adventures of five extraordinary
siblings in these romantic stories about
hidden identity, finding family and
coming to terms with your roots.

50¢ OFF!

Your purchase of any Silhouette® Family Secrets title

Coupon expires June 30, 2004.
Redeemable at participating retail outlets in Canada only.
Limit one coupon per purchase.

52604889

Visit Silhouette at www.eHarlequin.com
FS50350COUPCDN
© 2002 Harlequin Enterprises Ltd.

Silhouette®
Where love comes alive™

If you enjoyed what you just read,
then we've got an offer you can't resist!

Take 2 bestselling novels FREE!
Plus get a FREE surprise gift!